A ROOM MADE OF LEAVES

KATE GRENVILLE is one of Australia's most celebrated writers. Her international bestseller *The Secret River* was awarded local and overseas prizes, has been adapted for the stage and as an acclaimed television miniseries, and is now a much-loved classic. Grenville's other novels include *Sarah Thornhill, The Lieutenant, Dark Places* and the Orange Prize winner *The Idea of Perfection*. Her most recent books are two works of non-fiction, *One Life: My Mother's Story* and *The Case Against Fragrance*. She has also written three books about the writing process. In 2017 Grenville was awarded the Australia Council Award for Lifetime Achievement in Literature. She lives in Melbourne.

kategrenville.com.au

A ROOM MADE OF LEAVES

A NOVEL

KATE GRENVILLE

TEXT PUBLISHING MELBOURNE AUSTRALIA

textpublishing.com.au

The Text Publishing Company
Swann House
22 William Street
Melbourne Victoria 3000
Australia

Published by The Text Publishing Company, 2020
Reprinted 2020 (twice)

Book design by Imogen Stubbs
Jacket image by Lisla/Shutterstock
Endpapers: adapted from a cross-written letter by Elizabeth Macarthur, courtesy State Library of NSW; photo by Kate Grenville
Typeset by J&M Typesetting

Printed and bound in Australia by Griffin Press, an Accredited ISO AS/NZS 14001:2004 Environmental Management System printer

ISBN: 9781922330024 (hardback)
ISBN: 9781925923469 (ebook)

A catalogue record for this book is available from the National Library of Australia

Dedicated to all those
whose stories have been silenced

Do not believe too quickly!
—*Elizabeth Macarthur*

I acknowledge Aboriginal and Torres Strait Islander people as the First Peoples of the land on which this story takes place, and I pay my respects to elders past and present.

I am grateful for the assistance of the Darug Custodian Aboriginal Corporation and the Metropolitan Local Aboriginal Land Council, whose generosity in consulting with me about the story is deeply appreciated.

EDITOR'S NOTE

A truly incredible and strangely little-known story: How Elizabeth Macarthur's long-lost secret memoirs were discovered

Some time ago, during the renovation of a historic house in Sydney, a tin box, sealed with wax and wrapped in oiled canvas, was found wedged under a beam in the roof cavity. The house was Elizabeth Farm, where Elizabeth Macarthur, wife of the notorious early settler John Macarthur, lived until her death in 1850. The box—jammed with hard-to-read old papers, cross-written to save space—was somehow, unbelievably, mislaid until recently, when through a chain of events so unlikely as to seem invented it came into my hands. The contents turned out to be her long-hidden memoirs.

In these private papers, written near the end of her life, she steps out from behind the bland documents that were her public face. They're a series of hot outpourings, pellets of memory lit by passionate feeling. With sometimes shocking frankness, they invite us to see right into her heart.

Australian history, like most histories, is mainly about men. Only a few women emerge from the obscurity that was their usual destiny, and Elizabeth Macarthur is one of them. Still, she's remained an enigma until now. What she did was extraordinary, but who she was—what quirks of temperament drove her—has always been a frustrating blank.

She was born Elizabeth Veale in 1766, a farmer's daughter from the tiny village of Bridgerule in Devon. As a young girl she was taken into the local clergyman's family, where she grew up in a world like that of her near-contemporary, Jane Austen. In 1788 she married a soldier, and a year later the two of them, with their infant son, sailed to the newly established penal colony of New South Wales. The genteel young woman from the Bridgerule parsonage was dropped, like a rosebud into a cesspit, into a violent and brutal society on the remotest spot on the globe.

The first mystery is what possessed her to marry Ensign John Macarthur. He was no charmer. She herself describes him as 'too proud and haughty for our humble fortune or expectations'. He was no oil painting, either, having been badly scarred by childhood smallpox. And he wasn't rich or distinguished: he was the son of a Plymouth draper, with no resources other than his half-pay. In the world of Jane Austen such a marriage would have been pretty much impossible.

But John Macarthur had one thing going for him: a ruthless single-mindedness in pursuit of his own advancement. By a relentless mix of bullying, flattery and fibs, within ten years of arriving in New South Wales he was the wealthiest and most powerful man there.

An admiring historian calls Macarthur a 'firebrand', and I suppose that's one way to describe someone who shot his commanding officer in a duel and orchestrated the gunpoint deposing of a governor. For each of these events Macarthur was sent to London to face trial. He was there for four years the first time and eight years the second, leaving his wife in Australia to manage their affairs.

Australians of my generation had it dinned into them that 'our nation rides on the sheep's back'—meaning that wool was the basis of our economy—and that John Macarthur was 'the father of the wool industry'. Streets and swimming pools and parks all over Australia are named after him in gratitude.

But here's the thing: the Australian merino—the sheep we rode on the back of—was mostly developed during the years that John Macarthur was in England. It looks very much as though the Father of the Wool Industry must actually have been the Mother of the Wool Industry: his wife.

So who was Elizabeth Macarthur? How did she survive marriage to perhaps one of the most difficult men on the planet? How did she know how to run a gigantic farming enterprise, or breed fine-woolled sheep, or manage a work-force of brutalised convicts? The pluckiest Austen heroine might have been daunted.

Now we come to the problem. Her husband left a mountain of paper to tell us who he was, but when we go looking for Elizabeth there's almost nothing: a few unrevealing letters home to family and friends, a half-finished account of her voyage to New South Wales, and a lot of dull correspondence with her adult children. The dozens of letters she wrote to her husband while he was away for those two extended absences are where we might expect to find a trace of the person she was. Somehow or other, though, not a single one of those letters has ever come to light.

Circumstances plunged Elizabeth Macarthur into a life inconceivable to a woman of her class and time, and some-

3

thing in her personality let her seize those circumstances and make them her own. She's fascinated generations of searchers. How maddening, then, to have nothing that would let us know what sort of person she was—until now.

I've done nothing more than transcribe the papers in the box. Of course, I had to use my imagination where the faded old ink was impossible to read, and I spent considerable time arranging the fragments in what I judged to be the best order, but beyond that I've let Elizabeth Macarthur tell her own story. It's been a pleasure and a privilege to be the first to read her words and bring them to the world.

Kate Grenville,
transcriber & editor

THE
MEMOIRS OF
ELIZABETH
MACARTHUR

PART ONE

PART ONE

MY DEAR SON James has given me a task for my last years, or months, or whatever time I have left beyond the many years I have lived so far. It is to compile an account called *The History of the Macarthurs of Elizabeth Farm*. Meaning myself and my late husband, John Macarthur.

He was barely cold in his grave when they began lauding him as a hero, even the ones who loathed him in life. Surely it must be one of the choicest revenges of outliving an enemy: to look pious at his name, turn up your eyes, put your hands together like a parson, and mouth all the false words.

The History of the Macarthurs of Elizabeth Farm. It sends a chill through my marrow. Even *the*, that least regarded word in the language, strikes me as absurd. How can there be *the* history? Beyond one *the*, watertight and trim, lies another, just as watertight, just as trim.

But James has made the task hard to escape. He has trawled through all the desks and drawers and come out with every remnant of the past he could find, to jog my fading memory. I look at them with a feeling like disgust. At some time in the unimaginable future, a reader will pore over all these items, looking for the past to show itself. To that person, and to you, the reader of these words, I can only say: *Do not believe too quickly!*

9

What are they, these proofs of the past?

Firstly, from my husband to myself, thirty-nine letters.

I feel a clutch of apprehension, even now, with him twelve years laid in earth, when I see that all-too-familiar handwriting. I knew in an instant the mood of the letter, from the way he addressed me. *My dear Elizabeth. My dearest Elizabeth. My dearest dearest Elizabeth. My beloved Elizabeth. My dearest best beloved Elizabeth.* It was a dependable equation: the more elaborate the endearment, the more unpleasant the letter.

Secondly, from Elizabeth Macarthur to her husband, one letter, of a dozen lines, dashed off hastily not long before he died, containing nothing more revealing than cheerful news of family doings.

Thirdly, twelve letters to England to my friends and family— the copies, of course, which careful Mr Macarthur insisted I always make. They are blameless documents, pious reassuring lies from beginning to end, with a little boasting thrown in.

Fourthly, my account of the first part of our voyage from England to New South Wales in the year 1790. Written with publication in view, it reveals little of myself.

Fifthly, two miniatures on ivory of John Macarthur and Elizabeth Macarthur. A gentleman and his lady wife had to have their portraits done on ivory, and the entire lack of ivory in New South Wales, or anyone with the skills to paint on it, did not deter Mr Macarthur. His idea was for sketches to be made here by Mr Bullen and sent to someone Mr Macarthur had heard of in Mayfair, who would translate them into ivory. The portraits are therefore at best approximate, but the point was not to record a likeness. It was to have a pair of costly portraits to hang in the parlour, even if some visitors were not quite sure exactly who was depicted.

Mr Macarthur sat sideways to be drawn, everything about him

always slant, guarded, sly, evasive. There is his arrogant thrust-out chin, his pugnacious lower lip, the haughty set of his head. He would have thought of that as *aristocratic bearing*, never guessing that the portrait revealed all the worst aspects of his nature.

For myself, I was happy to look Mr Bullen in the eye and was content with what he drew. But Mr Macarthur found fault. I was too plain, my expression too forthright. The chin too square, the eyes a little skewiff, the mouth smiling too much, or in the next sketch not smiling enough. Poor Mr Bullen scratched and rubbed, and tried again, and then again, until the paper was worn into holes and he had to take another sheet. By the time Mr Macarthur was satisfied that the sketch was what he wished his wife to look like, I was pretty sure no one would recognise me in this dainty person, all curls and dimples.

Yet these are the Macarthurs who will travel into the future. People will say, how resolute and commanding he was! And oh, what a charming and lovely wife he had—look, you can see it in the picture!

My first impulse was to burn the lot. But now I have a better idea than a bonfire. I will create one more document, one that will show all these others to be the heroic work of fiction that they are. What I am writing here are the pungent true words I was never able to write.

Late on this spring afternoon, the sweet time of long shadows that I love best, I feel an excitement, a breathlessness, at the scandalous pleasure of what I am embarking on. Thank God I outlived him. I think of that with a skip of the heart. How shocked people would be, or make out to be, if they knew. But I walk out into the sweet dusk and tell myself: not dead yet. Not dead, and free, at last, to speak.

When baby sister Grace died I was five years old, too young to know the word. *Dead*. I barely understood what a sister was, still hoped this new creature in the house, this squalling red bully, was only temporary.

Mother was still puffy-eyed from burying her when Father took the same distemper and was gone. It had to be explained to me, they thought they were explaining. *With the angels. In a better place.*

– No, I screamed, seeing the box on the trestles in the parlour, but how can he breathe, get him out!

At the service I kept twisting around, waiting for Father to come in the door and sit down with us. Mother liked to tell the story, laughing in a bitter way, about me twisting and wriggling, running to the door, looking down the lane calling out for him. No one could quieten you, she'd say. Father! Father! you shouted till Mr Bond had to take you out. I could not bear it, the noise of you, and of course I wanted him to come up the lane too, every time you called Father! it was a knife in my heart.

Before that was the feeling that the day could last as long as I wished, and none of it needed to be spent indoors. There was the feeling of fields, and animals busy about their own lives, and the way those lives were bound intimately to mine. When my hands were big enough I learned to milk the cow. It is almost the only memory I have of Father, the smell of his tweed, his big warm self beside me, taking my hands in his and putting them on the teats, wrapping my fingers around their damp softness. I felt him chuckle with pleasure when I got the knack of the little movement that made the milk hiss against the inside of the pail.

Being the relict of Richard Veale of Lodgeworthy Farm did not become Mother. She was broken by widowhood, or perhaps she had never been more than a reed leaning on her husband. She shrivelled, took to her bed, went into glum silent abstractions by the fire, punctuated with sighs that made me tiptoe away, frightened of this adult despair.

I heard her one morning, speaking under the window, softly, but the words floated up.

— I cannot even look forward to a son to take his place, she said, the *his* meaning Father's.

Mr Kingdon rumbled in reply, too rumbly for me to make out the words.

— The best I can hope for might be a son-in-law, if she can manage it, she said, the *she* being me.

Mr Kingdon must have tried to offer some kind of irritating comfort, in which a reverend like him was well practised, because there was a sharp edge when she answered.

— Well, sir, I can pray, and I can live in hope and expectation. But for the time being it is just me and a wilful girl with no looks and no portion either.

I had been leaning up at the windowsill, listening in an idle way, not much concerned whether they saw me, but at that I sank down out of sight and crouched against the wall, making myself shrink to the smallest volume. *A wilful girl.* That word, *wilful*, gave me a picture of myself I did not quite recognise. I knew I was a child full of sparks. Knew I had a temper and a quick wit, a quick tongue, and got into enough trouble for them. That was the person I was. But now I knew that you called that *wilful*. And being wilful—I heard it in my mother's tone—was something that made you unattractive, unpleasant, unlikeable.

I was hot with a sudden shame for being wilful, as well as for having no looks and no portion, ashamed that no one would want me. Ashamed for my mother too, in speaking that way of her daughter. I could smell the dust in the curtains and feel the cold draft from the crack where the skirting did not quite meet the floor. That smell and the feel of a narrow draft still fill me with the same terrible knowledge that came to me, hearing her words: I was not an orphan, but might as well be, for all I had a parent to look out for me.

FLOCKING AND FOLLOWING

The farm was entailed and, with Father gone, my second cousin John Veale got it. He did not hustle us out, exactly, but he sent us a cart full of empty chests and boxes, all the rope we'd need to bind them with, and a few bags of sawdust for the crockery.

We were made welcome at Grandfather's place—Mother's childhood home—but he was an old man set in his ways. Our crockery was never fished out of the sawdust, the chests were committed to the barn without being opened, only a box of clothes for each of us, so it was Grandfather's sheets we slept in and Grandfather's dishes we ate off. Mother had a small dower, the one I later had, enough that she did not have to beg Grandfather for a pair of boots for me or a new bonnet for herself. But it was pin money. And from Grandfather originally, so that too was from his charitable hand.

I yearned for Lodgeworthy. Soon after we went to Grandfather's, Mother and I passed it and I ran to the gate, my hand on the latch I knew so well. Mother had to seize me by the wrist and pull me away. Had to explain that if I raised that latch and walked in as I had done a thousand times before, I would be something called a trespasser. That was like being a thief. The only way I could enter the place now was to be invited. I could have no rights there, only a guest's temporary privilege.

I stood at the gate, with Mother's hand tight around my wrist, shouting. I remember, wilful girl that I was, wrenching away from Mother, with her calling Elizabeth! Elizabeth! after me, and running up the front path and lifting my hand to knock at the door. But I had never approached that door as a blank indifferent panel of wood, never had to knock to make it open, and the strangeness of the look of it now, and the picture of John Veale's pale unfriendly wife opening it, made me draw back my hand.

Mother was waiting outside the gate. She would not look at me. We went on down the lane in silence, though not before I pulled the gate closed so hard that I heard something crack.

Yes, I was a difficult child, I see that now. Not that I meant to be difficult, but I had a sense of my own will. Did I not have the right to feel what I felt, be who I was?

Like all the households about us, ours was one of comfort but thrift. Grandfather believed in using God's great lantern, which cost nothing. Eating God's bounty: eggs from our own hens, cabbage from our own garden, a shave or two of the pig killed at Christmas.

Grandfather was a man perfectly weaned from the things of this world, conducted his life in the radiance of God's glory. There was a lot of church-going, a lot of talk of Providence, endless heartfelt thanks for what we were about to eat. Church twice on Sundays, the Bible read every evening, prayers around the table before bed.

Young though I was, I knew not to ask the question to which I knew there could be no answer: *If God is good, why is Father dead?* It was the first falsehood, to bow my head with everyone else, to say the Amen loud as if I meant it. I watched Mother from under my lashes to see whether she was being false too, but I never caught her out.

But Grandfather was a kindly soul and loved me. Let me wander over the fields and make shelters with branches and leaves and creep into them. Did not stop me when I went out in the rain and spent hours diverting and damming the runnel of water down the slope behind the house.

17

– A clean child is not a happy child, he said, when Mother scolded.

Grandfather had a reasonable spread of acres and grew a little of everything: barley, turnips, hay. But what he loved was the sheep. He walked among them, his boots authoritative, and they scattered, running all earnest and stiff-legged and then, when they had got a safe distance away, staring back at him over their shoulders.

– God has constituted them to flock and follow, Grandfather told me. They are creatures of fellowship. While we poor sinners believe we can do it all alone.

Mother thought sheep were silly creatures, but they were not, only behaved in ways unlike us. I came to love them, understood their ways, cared for them. They were amenable creatures when you worked with their natures and not against them, and never quite stupid. Grandfather showed me how you stayed behind them, taking your time. How, when they turned to stare at you, you stared them out. How you waited till they were facing the way you wanted them to go, then you held out the crook to make yourself bigger than you were.

How could you not warm to a creature that, when you came near her lamb, ran forward and stood stamping her feet? Poor thing, she had no other power to defend her young. I laughed in admiration at her courage.

– God tempers the wind to the shorn lamb, Grandfather said, watching the lamb stumble, fall, get up again. Remember that, Lisbet, when life hurls its blasts at you.

Grandfather taught me all I would have needed to become the wife of a farmer. How to churn butter, how to fix a sick chook. How to count sheep, not as straightforward as you might think.

– You can never trust yourself, counting a flock, he said in his calm instructional way. There's something about sheep makes the counting miss. When it comes to counting a flock, always make a knot. Or a notch. Keep it in twenties. That's what you call keeping a score, see.

He had a bit of twine that he got out of his pocket to show me, undoing the knots from the last count, and handed it to me.

– Now you'll be right, he said, and I heard the smile in his voice, the tenderness.

Grandfather was what was called an *improving* farmer, which as a child I took to mean his reproving ways with a wilful child, and his rock-like sense of what was right and what was wrong, and how all that was right lay in the hands of Our Lord. Now I know that, in spite of his age, he was one of the new type of farmer, and that the word meant an attention to the breeding of stock. There was high excitement—even guarded Grandfather was excited—when he bought a ram from a Mr Bakewell. Until I saw it I thought it might be a sheep made of cake, or perhaps a sheep pie, something good to eat in any case, and was disappointed that it turned out to be wool and horn like any other sheep. It arrived on a cart with a man called Hale, who took it by the halter and led it like a prince through our gate while I petted the dog he had brought with him.

– Take care there, lass, Mr Hale called out. If you stand still he'll want to piss on your leg.

I thought this a fine bit of humour, but Grandfather was stern, I could see he had judged Mr Hale as a common fellow.

Grandfather was holding the ram's head up by the horns and Mr Hale, all hat from my point of view, was bending over the creature, parting its fleece with big rough hands to show, under the grey matted surface, the creamy wool.

– How'd you like a dozen like this fellow, he said, to get his end in among your pretty ladies?

– Mind, Grandfather said. Mind your language, Mr Hale, if you please, do you not see the young lady here?

Which was a surprise on two counts: that whatever it was Mr Hale had meant by those words, they must carry a weight of sin, and that a girl of nine was a *young lady* who had to be shielded from whatever those words meant.

Mr Hale looked over at me, perhaps as surprised as I was that the ragamuffin in her mud-rimmed skirt was a *young lady*. Then he and Grandfather were murmuring on about crimp and grease while I swung on the gate, back and forth, back and forth, scraping the mud off my boots on the bottom beam till there was a neat row of lumps, though there was no point to it, as my boots would be heavy with mud again as soon as I got down. The watery spring sun, the bleating of lambs from the field, and Grandfather murmuring on and on with Mr Hale, the ram with its unblinking eye waiting to be let go: that memory is as clear after seventy years as if it were yesterday.

With Mr Hale gone, Grandfather and I stood among the flock, the sheep all rustling and bleating around us while he explained why he had got the ram, spent fifteen guineas on it, which to my ear sounded like a vast sum, and the ram looked to my eye much like any other sheep. But this ram had *a wonderful heft on him*, Grandfather said, and *a grand fleece*, and was a *fine lusty creature*. When he put this ram over the ewes, the lambs they would drop would carry that heftiness, that grand fleece and that lustiness in their own blood. Then it was a matter of doing something called *in-and-in*, which meant choosing the best lambs every spring and joining them back to the same lusty ram and to each other, making sure to get a new ram now and then to stop the blood getting too thin.

Once I understood, I was entranced. It was like trying to look into the future, to see what would happen ten years later if you went one way, or whether it would turn out to have been better to have gone the other.

Which, as I write this now, seems to me not so different from the life of humans, as well as fine lusty sheep.

Bridie, daughter of the Reverend Kingdon, had been my friend from our earliest years. Lodgeworthy was at the bottom of the hill beside the river and the vicarage was at the top of that same hill, beside the church. She and I spent most days together and, after Mother and I went to Grandfather's, I stayed with her many nights too, because from the vicarage it was a fair step back to Grandfather's house. It was simpler for me to stay with the Kingdons for a few nights on the trot, rather than go back and forth. Bridie and I shared the high bed in her room, Mrs Kingdon came to tuck us in and blow out the lamp, and it was as good as having a sister.

Mr Kingdon was an Oxford man for whom learning was as important as food and drink. His sons were all sent away to school and although he did not consider school essential for a girl, he devoted much care to teaching Bridie, and he found that she paid more attention to her lessons when she had a companion. I was a quick study, quicker than Bridie if the truth be told, and he took pleasure in my quickness. Reading, writing, elementary arithmetic, the kings and queens of England, the principal rivers of the world in alphabetical order. Latin, but only enough to learn the Kingdon motto under the Kingdon coat of arms: *Regis donum gratum bonum.*

Mr Kingdon was pleased with my progress, but when he took me aside into his study one afternoon, and showed me a list of words and asked me to read them one by one, I felt I should go carefully. How did I know? What did I know?

I could not have told you then, cannot tell you now, only that I decided not to display quite how well I could read. The first words he showed me were easy, easy, easy. Bridie would read those words as well as I did. Then they became harder. I read on, but more slowly. From Mr Kingdon I felt some complicated thing: curiosity, pleasure, satisfaction, but something else too. So that when I got to the word *colonel*, a strange word now that I write it here, I baulked.

 — I cannot read it, I said, although I knew the word as perfectly as the easy ones before it.

I felt a kind of relaxation in Mr Kingdon, as if he were relieved. I was disappointed, he should not have accepted so easily. I nearly said, *Oh, now I see it is colonel!* But even as a child I already knew, without anyone having told me, that it would be best for me not to be too clever.

BUYING A RAM

Then John Leach came to buy a ram from Grandfather and, if the rain had not started to pelt, he'd have bought the ram and gone. But it did, so Grandfather brought him into the house to eat dinner with us and wait out the storm. Turned out, John Leach knew Mother's cousin over in Taunton, had met Father once at Holsworthy, and even a child of eleven could see Mother perk up at his attention to her.

That child did not warm to him, did not like the way he set out to charm her mother, was sullen and sulky at his cajolings, his jocular enquiries after her pup and her needlework, and what did it matter—this big red-faced person was come to buy a ram, and would put it in his cart and go off—that a girl behaved scarcely this side of discourtesy?

Until John Leach began to visit without wanting to buy a ram.

So John Leach, widower, wanting I suppose someone to keep house and be in the bed with him, got his eye on Grace Veale, widow. I remember no discussion about my place in the arrangement, perhaps mercifully no sugared explanation for the fact that I was not invited to be part of the new marriage.

Mother told me that she and Mr Leach would go to his place at Stoke Climsland, but I would stay on with Grandfather.

– What a wonderful opening for you, pet, she cried. What a lucky girl you are! To keep on with your lessons!

I knew this was no more than a pretext for leaving me behind. Mr Leach and I were like two dogs bristling. I wanted to keep my mother to myself, of course. And Mr Leach had no desire to share his life with a girl too big for her boots from all the learning the parson was giving her, a girl he considered indulged and indolent, with too many vicarage airs and graces, who would not take kindly to being told to get out at dawn and milk the cows.

It was true, I had no wish to live with Mr Leach and have him watch every mouthful of his food as I ate, have him tell my mother that I needed to get my nose out of that book and do a hand's turn. But a great emptiness opened up in me when I realised my mother had made a choice, and the choice did not include me. That wilful girl was not wanted.

I held a bouquet at the wedding and stood alongside Grandfather and the other guests, all of us throwing rice at my mother. A handful struck her on the cheek—from my own hand, as it happened—and she flinched and for a moment looked at me square-on, as I seldom remember her doing. I knew then what I had always guessed: my mother did not much like me. She might believe she loved me, because what mother did not love her daughter? But there it was in that unguarded look: she did not like me.

And that afternoon John Leach and Grace Leach rattled off in his gig, a spoke split on one wheel, I noticed. I remember it now, that split stave, and the way I was thinking hard about it as I smiled and waved. It was so as not to be too aware that I was bidding farewell to my mother. Stoke Climsland was not terribly far, not as far as Bath or Plymouth, but from that day on she might as well have been at the end of the earth.

Soon she was mother to another daughter besides myself. Isabella Leach. Isabella was the final bit of dovetailing, wedging the new shape into place once and for all.

But I had Grandfather, who loved me, and stood smiling as I tackled my first sheep with the shears, clipping away as he had shown me, until the creature was in two separate parts: bald bony shrunken animal in one place, a heap of fleece in another.

In some way, without it exactly being announced, it came about that I was to live at the Kingdons'.

— Your grandfather is old, Mr Kingdon said.

It was the nearest anyone came to explaining. *But Grandfather has always been old*, I wanted to say, but one did not answer back to Mr Kingdon, his holy face in stern iron folds.

— We welcome you, Elizabeth, Mrs Kingdon said. We are glad to have you as family with us.

At the Kingdons' it was not done to walk about in the mud and shit of the farmyard in your old pinny, learning how to get hold of a ram without it butting you. Living there was different from visiting. A young lady of the vicarage did not get her hands dirty, but looked on while others dirtied theirs. Her life was not the sheep and the chooks, but drawn-thread work, French seams, run and fell.

Things shifted, too, between myself and Bridie. Being Bridie's almost-sister at the vicarage was my life now, and I had better make sure that she and I did not fall out, because what would happen then to a girl without looks, without money, and as good as without a family? Where would a girl go who had been abandoned, as it felt, first by her father, then by her mother, and at last by her grandfather?

I had to be careful, and I became timid of a mis-step. In fact my new situation seemed nothing but the possibility of mis-steps. I put a guard on my tongue, not to speak out boldly with something that might make them turn to me with the thought, *oh, perhaps she will not do after all.*

26

Wariness became a habit, and brought with it a new irreso-luteness. The brave girl Grandfather had smiled on cowered from thunder now, and was thrown into confusion by unimportant decisions. I became someone not totally removed from herself, but not quite herself either. Someone more obliging, more agreeable. Someone who had folded herself up small and put herself carefully away, where no one could see her.

GOD'S ARRANGEMENTS

I was twelve when I moved to the Kingdons', Bridie a few months older. Mrs Kingdon took us both aside and told us that we would soon be experiencing what she called our *time of the month*. Her embarrassment made her sound cross as she tried to find a better word than *blood*. Told us how to manage the rags.

It silenced us, cheeky girls that we were. Not to be believed, that stuff would come out—blood!—from between our legs, and have to be staunched under our skirts with these cloths, which then must be smuggled out to where Mary would take them, without John or Amos seeing, and wash them, and return them to our chest of drawers ready for the next month.

— Every month? Bridie said, her voice a squeak of horror. Every single month?

— Yes, dear, Mrs Kingdon said. If the month passes without it, you are with child.

She sighed.

— God has arranged His creation in ways we do not always understand, she said. But it is a joy to have a child and, without this business, there are no children.

Bridie and I went away to the orchard without looking at each other. At last she came out with what I was thinking.

— It makes me sick, just the idea, she said. It will not happen to me.

I could hear she believed it and was comforted. I was not, and with a spurt of nastiness wanted to tip her comfort out.

— In that case you will never have children, I said.

We both knew poor Mrs Devereaux in the village, married but childless, and the pall of misery that hung over her, and the way she was spoken of, as if she were blind or misbegotten.

– Yes, Bridie said. Why would that be so bad?

But when she glanced at me I saw her fear and desperation. It was what I was feeling too, faced with the choices that were no choices.

In the bed later I knew Bridie was awake, thinking as I was that we had left behind the safety of childhood and were launched on the chartless seas of being women.

– I will never marry, she said into the darkness. Are you awake, Lisbet? I will never marry.

She laughed, that wild laugh no one in the drawing room ever heard, I was the only one who knew it. When I heard her drawing-room titter, I admired her for such a fine bit of theatre, when I knew her to be someone else entirely. But feared for her too, and for myself, because how could a person sustain a lie her whole life?

– So you will be an old maid, I said.

There was a long silence.

– Yes, an old maid, she said. A spinster. A nun. A witch. The Witch of Bridgerule.

Outside an owl spoke secretively.

– I think you are braver than I, I said.

But I had not finished the words when her voice, rough with feeling, rode over them.

– Could there be another way?

The owl hooted sadly, sadly, and the tree brushed at the window. We had only a few more years, was what I felt us both thinking, then each of us would be either a wife or a poor sad spinster.

– There's widow, I said. Better than wife or old maid, if it could be arranged. Painlessly, of course.

She laughed again, one coarse yelp.

– Yes, she said, and black is so becoming.

I saw it like a cheerful engraving in a frame: the widows of Bridgerule, busy in their black, happily beached on the far side of wifedom. But there was my mother, not freed but shrunken by her widowhood. She'd confessed to me once that she hated the widow's weeds, hated the way wives looked at her with pity or, worse, distrust, and clutched their husbands' arms.

– We could have a school, Bridie said. Miss Veale and Miss Kingdon. Their little school on the hill, their girls loving them and all around saying, Whatever did we do before the school on the hill? We could, Lisbet. People do.

– Yes, I said. We could.

But we both knew we were exchanging comfort, not possibility.

I remember her now, dead these thirty years, the truest, deepest friend I ever knew. Remember too the things we shared in the dark warmth of that bed. The things we did there, one to another. Bridie to me, me to Bridie, and both of us together. We never spoke of them. Had no words for them. Had no shame of them, either. They were what two humans did together. They were what came naturally, a satisfaction as natural and sinless as eating to answer hunger, or drinking to quench thirst.

WE SAW IT EVERYWHERE

Now that we were women we saw it everywhere. The dog's little shiny thing sliding in and out, and how frantic he got when the bitch was in heat, as if only death would stop him getting to her. The ram pawing and sniffing at the ewe. She indifferent and her sisters with their heads down, cropping away as if to say, oh, we are much too busy. The ram lunging and clutching at the ewe. Over in a moment, the ewe still plucking at grass.

Of the two of us, Bridie was the bold one. What I only thought, she said.

– Frankly, Lisbet, she said in that dry way of hers, I could take it or leave it, if that's what it's like.

In Bridgerule we saw no Troilus and Cressida, no Romeo and Juliet. We could see that men, when they could, took their pleasure with a woman, more or less any woman. And that women, when they could, took a man, no matter what he was like, if he could offer them a future. Only in the pages of books did we see any swooning and sighing. In the books the lovers wed on the last page, and what came after was a gauzy silence. We pored over the books, but they gave no guidance to girls trying to make sense of what was in store for them.

Bridie could come out with bold words—at least when she was alone with me—but that was because she had a mother and a father to look out for her, brothers who would protect her, and could look forward to a substantial dowry from Mr Kingdon when the time came. She and I might laugh together, but my laughing was hollow. I was not beautiful. I had no family, no portion. I was not connected to anyone of importance. My sole asset in the world was my maidenhead. I had just that one thing. I was beginning to understand that I must drive the best bargain I could for it, because once it was gone I had nothing more.

As we grew into young women, young men paid calls. Officers from the barracks at Holsworthy, masters from the school Bridie's brothers attended, sundry curates. The men leapt to their feet when we entered the room. When we were leaving it they leapt to open the door as if we were incapable of turning a doorknob. If we walked in the fields they jumped over the stile so they could grasp our hand and put an arm around our waist to assist us. But without the voluminous skirts and petticoats, the shawls that slipped off our shoulders, the need for modesty that locked every natural movement, we would have had no need of assistance. So much elaborate courtesy and so many gallant platitudes did not obscure the puzzle that between our legs was something so precious we had to be made prisoners.

Precious, or dangerous? That was not quite clear.

We were never alone with any of these men, one woman with one man. Always it was shallow public talk in the company of others. The rambles Bridie and I had shared as children, over the fields and along the lanes, were discouraged, unless—as if by chance— one of Bridie's brothers would be rambling in exactly the same direction.

– Bridget, you are a woman now, Mrs Kingdon said in mild exasperation after we had slipped away one morning. And Elizabeth, you too. I have to say it plain—there are men who will take advantage of a maid.

– Take advantage, Bridie said. Mother, what exactly?

Mrs Kingdon hesitated. I saw that her hesitation was not any shyness about explaining, because her concern was greater than her shyness. The problem was not modesty but the words, or the lack of them.

— You have seen the rams, she said at last. And the way the farmers keep them separate from the ewes. They let only the chosen ram in with them. But the ram is not so particular. Will join with any ewe if given the chance.

She took Bridie's hand, and mine in the other.

— You girls are precious. Your future happiness hangs on keeping yourselves safe. Do you understand, dear girls?

Not quite, if the truth be known.

— So are boy children culled, the way the boy lambs are, Bridie said out of the dark that night. I don't think so, otherwise would I have six brothers?

— No, I said. But in a way yes. The fellow with the most money has his choice of woman.

— And what will his choice be, she said, then answered her own question. A rich woman, or a good-looking one. Not us on either score.

I heard a noise from her, was it a laugh or a sob?

— They look at us, Bridie said. Up and down, and most especially at our...charms.

— And what of us, I said, do we look at their charms?

For there was the way men stood, an elbow on the mantelpiece, in their tight pale trousers, with the relevant part of themselves framed between the dark wings of their jacket.

— I watch a man's face, Bridie said. Looking for...I know not what. Attention to something other than my charms? Perhaps an interest in myself?

— An interest in yourself! I repeated.

I felt the bed tremble with her laughing, then tremble more

with mine too. A man interested in yourself! It was amusing enough to set the bed shaking so hard it might be heard below us in the room where Mr and Mrs Kingdon lay in connubial intimacy, and that thought was enough to stop us.

A father—one less remote than Mr Kingdon—might have done better. A father might have been able to find the blunt words for it. *They will flatter you*, a father might have said. *They will sigh over your loveliness.* A father would say, *Do not even for one moment believe them. Do not, on any account, allow that penetration of your person that is the true goal of all those blandishments. Laugh*, such a father would say. *Do it kindly, by all means, but laugh him to scorn.*

I met Mr Macarthur on the day I stood godmother to the Kingdons'
newborn, a sweet babe they named after myself. That was good
Mrs Kingdon's idea, to draw me a further degree into the safety of
her family, give me a little more substance to bolster my prospects.
Bridie and I were twenty-two. Mrs Kingdon could see what we
could not: that the years were beginning to race by.

Captain Moriarty walked over from the Holsworthy Barracks
with his friend Ensign Macarthur to join us for the baptismal
celebrations. Captain Moriarty was a fair smiling man with a
distant family connection to the Kingdons, and it was clear that
he was there that day for Bridie. Like me, she was no beauty, but
Mr Kingdon would make a useful father-in-law. He struck me
as pleased with his magnanimity in offering the gift of himself
to plain Miss Kingdon.

I saw how close his chair was to Bridie's, how he hitched it
closer on the pretext of clearing the edge of the rug. Watching
Captain Moriarty looking at her, the way the men came and sized
up Grandfather's rams, I had to accept that Bridie and I would not
be together for much longer.

Mr Macarthur was there to give his friend a chance with
Bridie, and it was up to all of us to give them some air. Mrs
Kingdon poured tea and managed what she did so well: the dance
of conversation.

– Miss Veale is making a little study of our grasses, our
pastures, she said and smiled at me, but then glanced uncertainly at
Mr Kingdon. I could see she was wondering whether the study of
pastures—less ladylike than other studies—might give the wrong
impression of Bridie's friend, and therefore of Bridie herself.

So I smiled at this Captain Moriarty and this Mr Macarthur, not because I liked the look of either of them, but because I wanted to reassure kindly Mrs Kingdon.

– Yes, I said. But of course it is only our local domestic Devon grasses, sheep's fescue and the like.

Then I was concerned that might seem a mild rebuke to Mrs Kingdon, as if I were backing away from her pride in me, and the dance was in danger of becoming a stumble. But my scruples and doubts, and Mrs Kingdon's scruples and doubts, were swept away by Captain Moriarty, who, it transpired, knew more about grasses than anyone else in the room.

Legs astride as if addressing a public meeting, he held up a finger.

– Ah yes, Miss Veale, very interesting, he said. *Festuca ovina*, sheep's fescue. And I wonder if you are familiar with the somewhat rarer viper's fescue?

Well, naturally I had never heard of viper's fescue, and said so. Whereupon Captain Moriarty gave us the benefit of his considerable knowledge on the subject, and Mr Kingdon and Mrs Kingdon and Mr Macarthur and Bridie and I all nodded, and by the time Captain Moriarty had finished enumerating the points on his fingers, Miss Veale's little study of the local grasses was a speck on the conversational horizon.

There was a small pointless pleasure in exchanging a glance with Bridie. *What a windbag!* But then she smoothed back her hair, the lock that sprang out from her temple like a cheeky rejoinder, replaced the teacup in the saucer without a sound, and in placing it on the side table turned herself a fraction further towards Captain Moriarty.

The glance was a consolation, but I knew a great loneliness in that moment, and from that day something awkward fell between myself and Bridie. We had shared that glance, but we could not say aloud what we both knew: Captain Moriarty might be a tedious know-all, but Bridie would say yes if he asked. No more than any other woman could she afford to wait for Troilus or Romeo.

So, while Bridie and Captain Moriarty sat in the parlour, or took a turn about the garden, Miss Veale and Mr Macarthur were there too, engaging in lively conversation with each other, behind the screen of which our friends could make their way towards an understanding.

Mr Macarthur was an ugly cold sort of fellow. There was nothing smiling or pleasant about him. A sullen bottom lip gave him the look of a petulant child, and he was badly marked by the smallpox. His eyes looked not quite right, as if they'd been put in carelessly, too far apart and one higher than the other. He was haughty too, glancing around with his curled lip as if finding Mr Kingdon's parlour wanting.

But he was hardly in a position to be superior. He was the cheapest rank of officer, ensign, in the cheapest regiment, old Fish's that had been hardly raised before it was disbanded, the war finishing too soon and leaving him stranded. Everyone in the room could do the sum: four hundred pounds tied up in his commission and nothing to show for it. *An ensign on half-pay*. The phrase was a byword for failure.

There was no question of him setting out to charm me in the same way Captain Moriarty was laying himself out to charm Bridie. An ensign on half-pay was in no position to lay claim to a woman with no portion. Added to that was his youth: he was only twenty-two, my own age. Or perhaps twenty-one. He was a little cagey about his age, as about many things.

– Oh yes, he announced, I am considering the Bar, for all the world as if the Bar was beating a path to his door.

He was of course a gentleman. At least had the manners and

education of a gentleman, rode with the hounds when he had the chance, he said, and could quote Horace and knew a little Greek, which reassured Mr Kingdon that he was a person worthy to take tea with his family.

But it came out that his father was in trade. Was—to put it bluntly—a draper. The way Mr Macarthur put it, his father was in a big way, his business no hole-in-the-corner affair of a half-yard of ribbon. He supplied the army and navy with the cloth for their uniforms, and it was not to be thought that Mr Macarthur senior stood behind a counter with a tape measure around his neck. Still, it was undeniable that Mr Macarthur junior's commission had been paid for out of the profits from shirts and underlinen. It was clear how much these facts pained the son, a man whose every fibre was held together by pride.

Which was why we heard such a very great deal about what it meant to be a Macarthur. By Mr Macarthur's account, his grandfather had been the Laird of Strathclyde in Argyllshire, and so had his grandfather's father before him, and so on into the mists of time where, it was implied, the original Arthur from which the line descended was none other than King Arthur himself.

But the grandfather, along with his seven sons, one of whom was Mr Macarthur's father, had chosen the wrong side in the battles of those times, and had been supporters of the King Across the Water. Not, Mr Macarthur was quick to reassure us, that he was a Papist, but for reasons of politics and the greater glory of Scotland. After the defeat at Culloden they had been stripped of their lands and titles, and Mr Macarthur's father, after vicissitudes, had come to rest in Plymouth. There he married Mr Macarthur's mother and produced his sons. Mr Macarthur was the younger of the two, and that chafed at him. Not that he had ambitions to be a draper, but he was bitter that the brother had the family business in Plymouth for no other reason than that he had been born first, while Mr Macarthur was rusticating at Holsworthy waiting for a future.

— My dear fellow, Mr Kingdon said at last with rich sympathy. What a shocking story. Your father must feel it deeply.

— He does, Mr Macarthur agreed. It is a wound that will never heal, a daily affront.

There was feeling in the words. Mr Macarthur spoke of his own wound too, his own daily affront that he, descended from the Laird of Strathclyde, and perhaps from King Arthur, should be explaining himself in a modest vicarage in Devon. He was too proud to want to prove himself a gentleman but, in the cold reality of his present situation, was obliged to do so.

Captain Moriarty was propriety itself, bland as soap always, but Mr Macarthur blazed inside with something restless, something dark and acidic. There was a banked fire in him, and there was a quality about that banked fire that I found intriguing. Let me be frank: I was drawn to it.

He could be stony and silent, sitting there while Captain Moriarty made the running with Bridie. But in the garden, with Bridie and her captain within sight but out of earshot, he might set himself to amuse. He was a fine cruel mimic, could take off precisely the habit Captain Moriarty had of speechifying at solemn length. Mr Macarthur's lean features could take on precisely his friend's admiring astonishment at what a very great deal he knew.

It was nasty, and a nasty streak in myself responded to it. I found that there was a mimic within me too, who could perfectly take off dour Mr Kingdon and his rumbling pieties. I was not proud of mocking the benefactor who had been so good to me, but could not resist unleashing the sparkling and playful self who could amuse this aloof Mr Macarthur.

More than amuse. Through glances and hints too slight to be marked except by an eager girl, Mr Macarthur let me understand that I was the source of some interest, and I rose to his interest. It was not flirtation. If Bridie had said, Lisbet, you are flirting with him! I would have denied it, perhaps joked that what I was doing with Mr Macarthur was nothing more than rehearsal for when another more eligible suitor might make his way to the Bridgerule vicarage. That would not have been untrue, but it was not the whole story.

I did not see it then, but I can see it now: I was not watching him, but myself. Aspects of myself that had never revealed themselves were becoming visible to me, and the discovery was exhilarating.

The boldest moment came—my memory is as clear as if someone had made an engraving of it—the afternoon before Midsummer Night. Mr Macarthur and Captain Moriarty had paid us a visit and we sat in the parlour arranging to meet the following afternoon to stroll down to the village, where the people would have their bonfire and dancing. We, of course, being gentlemen and ladies, would not dance by the light of the bonfire, would not grow rowdy as the village folk would, red in the face and shining with the freedom of Midsummer Night, when all rules were suspended. But we would marvel at the way the fire blazed and crackled, how wildly the sparks flew when Axtens the blacksmith threw on another great piece of wood, how everything familiar was made strange by the night. And mark how, in pairs, figures made obscure by the firelight slipped away together.

Our visitors were leaving, there was a bustle of departure: Mr Moriarty and Bridie on the gravel outside, Mrs Kingdon going down the steps to join them, Mr Kingdon upstairs fetching a book he had promised to lend Mr Macarthur, and myself just outside the front doorway. Mr Macarthur had lingered in the drawing room and when I looked back there he was, framed by the two doorways so that the hallway was a tube of empty air along which we looked at each other. The air between us, that narrow line of sight, joined us in a kind of intimacy. At one end of that tube was the young woman who wondered how it would be to feel a man between her legs, and at the other a young man whose gaze was full of a pressing urgency of attention.

We had but seconds, and he knew how to use them. He put his hand on his heart with a delicate movement, a caress of himself, fingers spread on his coat, and tilted his head questioningly, submissively, yearningly. How much a person can say by nothing more than a tilt of the head!

That picture—lasting a second, no longer—entirely disarmed canny Elizabeth Veale. As I would not for an instant have believed words, I believed that hand on heart and the whimsical appeal of that tilted head.

Then Mr Kingdon came down the stairs, Mrs Kingdon looked back towards me, Mr Macarthur put his hat on, and Miss Veale sailed out ahead of him down the steps and out into an afternoon that, all at once, seemed so lovely as to make my heart race.

TREMULOUS AND STRANGE

Midsummer Night, myself and Mr Macarthur. Mud thick around our boots as we walked down towards the field where the bonfire illuminated the trees in strange upside-down ways. Bridie and Captain Moriarty were ahead of us, not glancing back, and Mr and Mrs Kingdon were taking the longer way by the road. And there was Mr Macarthur's strong hand, steadying me around my waist as I got over the stile, and his cheek close to mine.

– A particularly tricky stile, he said. I have heard of folk taking this stile much too lightly, Miss Veale, and regretting it—here, take my hand, I beg you!

Of course the stile was no better or worse than any other. Bridie and I had got over it without the slightest difficulty a hundred times. But I put my hand in his, and what with the darkness, and the unaccustomed and needless assistance, I somehow lost my balance, so that I briefly leaned, almost fell, against him. He did not let go of my hand, but led me along beside the hedge: not the quickest way towards the bonfire, in fact hardly a way to the bonfire at all, but I followed.

The darkness was full of rich complicated smells of vegetation under dew and shivers of breeze: underhand, low-to-the-ground, so different from day's frank gusts. The night was like a creature that lay hidden until, when humans slept, it lived its private life, shifting and breathing in subtle currents of cool air now from this side, now that, whispering among the leaves and drawing me into its secrets.

It was curiosity, as much as anything, that made me let events take their course. Curiosity—and, of course, his flattery. Oh, his flattery. And my vanity, in believing.

– Sweet, he murmured. Sweet mouth!

I heard the catch in his voice, felt his fingers trembling as he touched my cheek, traced the shape of my lips.

– Oh, oh, he sighed into my ear, his breath hot. Ah my dear, so beguiling, my dear.

It was new, undreamt of, that I had reduced a man to this inarticulate yearning. Almost begging. It filled me with a sense of how powerful I must be, after all. I felt myself to be as big as the night, free, a thing with no boundaries. The sky was infinite, the stars blazed like the exhilaration that filled me, their shifting pulses and shimmer a promise of time, space, eternity, all the things a woman never had. I was at last free to find my own size, and I was gigantic.

– Sweet, sweet mouth, he whispered.

Not the words, but the tremble in the fingers: that was what made me lie back against the hedge. The stars, the crackle of the bonfire on the far side of the next field, its flickering hectic light through the hedge: all was tremulous and strange. But this was Midsummer Night and all was strange, all was allowed, everything was new and I was, you might say, drunk with delight in the power I was discovering myself to have. This, then, was what it was all about, the care they wrapped us in, the fear they made us feel, the never-quite-spoken thing that made it necessary for us to be so relentlessly protected. Not our fear of their power, but their fear of ours!

Now I could feel his whole body trembling as it pressed me

down. There was a scuffling at the fabric between us, a wrenching-away, finally bare skin in the night air. Yes, I knew I was being assailed. Knew this was what I had been warned of. Had seen enough of those rams and dogs to know what was happening. I cannot claim that I did not know. But as surely as anything I had ever believed, I felt this to be my act, my decision, fully my own choice. How could there be any mistake? I was a colossus, a god. The feeble voices of warning faded, leaving nothing but a glory of certainty, a bliss that could not be wrong.

Just for such a very short time. Then he shifted away from me and stood up. There was a mighty shout from somewhere over there and the bleat of a puzzled woken sheep—and the event unspooled so that I saw what a lie it was. There was no more trembling, there were no more moans, no more sweet nothings about being beguiled. Only the anxiety I could hear in his voice, anxiety and coldness too.

– Get up, get up, Miss Veale, he said in a rasping whisper. Miss Veale!

I was no colossus after all. I was just Miss Veale, to be pulled to her feet with a cool steady hand under my arm, and to be led, like one of those sheep, beside the hedge to the stile. No tomfoolery at the stile this time, only his hand gripping mine with no motive but the need to get me over.

– Best go round the side, he said, as brisk as a gentleman ordering his carriage. Quickly now!

So we went scuttling along like rats in the shadow of the hedge and came out near the bonfire as if we'd always been there, and as separate as if we were strangers.

Well, I thought, waking up early next morning, Bridie innocently asleep beside me. *Now I know.* I kept saying the words in my mind,

45

there was a grim satisfaction in them. *Now I know.* As if knowing was a way of getting back a trace of that huge powerful person I'd been for those short mad minutes behind the hedge. *Now I know.*

I see now, sixty years too late, that he had not expected me to yield. The seduction of Elizabeth Veale was one of those unattainable ambitions that no one would expect to achieve. I am familiar now with the satisfaction it gave him to fling himself at the impossible. It was the chase, not the prey, that he loved. Coming out from behind the hedge, his coldness was in part disappointment. The fox had delivered itself up to the hunter. Where was the triumph in that?

CAUGHT OUT

I'd heard things, the way you do, and I'm ashamed to say I tried them all. Hot baths, jumping down from high places, skipping till you got a stitch in your side. Rosemary, I'd heard, and there was plenty in the garden, and I was determined, cold with the need of it, my will forcing it down, but with the direst need in the world no one can swallow enough rosemary to effect what I longed to effect.

I ran full pelt up the muddy lane from the village, so fast I slipped, hands flat down in the mud. Got up, went on running past what I could bear, but forced myself on, got to the top and wanted another hill. At the top of that bent muddy lane, where the church is—I can see it clearly in the eye of memory—the lane flattens, a straight level run all the way from the vicarage to Holsworthy. Now, if that dull lane, down which Mr Macarthur had strolled so many times, had only been a hill like the one I'd just run up, he might not have bothered. As it was, I stood looking along that lane in a hot sweaty pother, the stitch in my side a glorious hopeful pain. Surely no babe could stick to me after that!

There was no shame. There was simply a job to be done. Joan of Arc could not have had a steelier resolve.

I could not find a way to tell Bridie. She was sad, though putting on a brave appearance: Captain Moriarty had not, after all, made her a proposal. He and Mr Macarthur still paid calls, but he had clearly drawn back from any consideration of Bridie as his wife. To reveal my own situation would engulf hers and make it seem by comparison trivial, which it was not. Besides, how could I explain that something as childish as curiosity, and another thing as unworthy as vanity, had lured me to this pass?

But among women, in the intimacy of a household, that particular secret has nowhere to hide for long.

Bridie and I sat side by side on the wall between the house and the church, looking out into the August night. I had a fan. Not that it was such a hot night, but Bridie knew, and I knew she knew, and I had the impulse to hide. Not out of remorse at the wickedness of what I had allowed to happen. Only humiliation, that I'd been such a fool. To have been warned all my life, to have been taught a truth about the world, and then to think I knew better.

I had not been forced, or only by my own folly and arrogance, that let me think I was in control of what was happening—and my sad ignorance of the ways of men and their flattery. Oh, the thrill of having a man reduced, or seem to be, the mighty man brought low!

Behind the fan my cheeks burned. It was rage that burned there, the rage of not having been able to take a single step beyond the permitted without being punished. Not one step! Not once!

Now, telling over this old story for you, I can see it plain, as I could not then. I ask you not to judge too harshly. I would like to take that young woman by the hand and say, You were not a fool.

Or not only a fool. To stay always within the bounds laid down is to remain a child.

A flame had burned in me, to be bigger than those bounds. That should be no crime.

Bridie spoke all the words, around and around, gentle with me but distant, like a person safe on a ship calling out kindly to someone fallen overboard, beyond rescue. Then there was nothing more to say.

In that calm night, all her soft words said, her hand warm in mine, I recoiled from her pity. I had gone behind the hedge with eyes open. That night, with the world tilted irrevocably from one place to another, I decided: let no one pity me. As pride was the key to Mr Macarthur's character, refusal to be pitied would be mine.

Now I lay awake beside her, knowing that this was the last night of our old lives. The dawn streaming towards me was the last dawn of my secret, the morning ahead the first morning of my future. What future? To be married to that moody stranger, both of our lives poisoned by regret? Or some other fate, one so far beyond my experience in genteel Bridgerule as to be unimaginable? What exactly would a girl do who had no family and no money, only a belly containing a bastard child?

I lay watching the light quicken into the day when the unspoken would be spoken and a waterfall of consequences would drown me. I listened to the noises of the waking household. Soon I would have to take my place in it, and endure all that would have to be endured.

PAPERING-OVER

Mr Macarthur was a fastidious sort of man and loathed the smell of lanoline and sheep shit. He especially loathed the silly noise that is the only utterance a poor sheep has at its disposal. Picked his way across Grandfather's yard with his lip more than usually curled.

Thanks to the kindness of Mr Kingdon, my sin would soon be papered over, the words spoken, the ring lumpy on my finger. Mr Macarthur stood beside me, scraping at the mud on his boot. I knocked and called, again and again. But Grandfather had never had any truck with the papering-over of sins. Smoke rose out of the chimney, but he did not appear.

A SLIVER OF HOME

Mrs Kingdon had been a mother to me, had opened her home and her heart to me, and I had made a mockery of all her care. Yet she forgave me my betrayal. That thoroughly good woman spoke to my mother, who made over her small dower to me: not enough to live on, but my own. Then she found a girl from the village who was persuaded to become my maid.

– You will have need of someone with you, Mrs Kingdon said. When the dear babe arrives.

The dear babe! I blessed Mrs Kingdon then for her kindness, and I bless her memory now.

Anne was not yet fifteen, a tall skinny freckled ginger girl, timid and ignorant, but to take a sliver of Bridgerule with me, even a girl I barely knew, would be some comfort. She seemed to imagine it would be an adventure.

Mr Kingdon had not been able to look at me since the news had been broken to him, but in emulation of the merciful God whose vicar he was, he did not turn out the sinner under his roof. He pulled some string or other among his acquaintances that had the happy effect of securing Mr Macarthur a position with the 68th Regiment of Foot, soon to be sent to Gibraltar on garrison duty. Which served two purposes: to ensure that Ensign Macarthur would return to full pay and be in a position to support—no matter how frugally—a wife and child, and to get Mr and Mrs Macarthur far away from Bridgerule.

HAPPY EVENT

I was grateful for the pretence that it was a happy event, smiled till my jaw ached. Mr Macarthur did not pretend. Was severe and unsmiling, and made a deal of fuss about what would be written on the marriage paper. He must be John Macarthur, *Esquire*. Mr Kingdon flinched, blinked, was not sure, but Mr Macarthur would not yield and Mr Kingdon, poor fellow, only wanted the thing done with and the two of us gone out of his life. So there it is, and will last as long as the book in which it was inscribed: John Macarthur, *Esquire*.

The woman of metal, Elizabeth Veale, kept her chin high and her eyes fixed on Mr Kingdon as he read the words. I was calm, admired myself from a great distance for my calmness. But as the moment approached when I must say those two small words, my mouth became so dry that my tongue cleaved to the roof of my mouth, my throat closed, my lips grew numb.

No, I would not be mortified! Would not have people say, oh, she could not get the words out! So I sucked at my cheeks, forced my tongue around that glued-together mouth, dropped my chin, tried to think of a lemon, while Mr Kingdon steadily read through the vows.

I had rehearsed how I would say it. *I do!* Loud and sure, with not a scintilla of doubt. The start of a lifetime's fiction: *this is what I wanted*. Thinking of a lemon came to my rescue, but it was a croak, squeezed thin, that sealed my destiny.

Mr Macarthur's hands shook so much he had the greatest difficulty getting the ring on my finger. I could hear the breath coming hard through his nose, saw those trembling hands, and my own tremulousness left me. We were in this together, this stranger and I, as we had said, in sickness and in health, for richer or for poorer, and his weakness gave me strength. He was that foreign creature, a man, who spoke the foreign language of power and assurance, but we came from the same country, where a person had to appear to be someone other than who they were. The question that would shape our marriage was: would we be able to speak to each other in that secret language we shared? Would he trust me, would I trust him, enough to show each other willingly what I could see, without him wishing me to see it, in the trembling of his hands?

That night, in the cold room at the barracks in Holsworthy, I tried, the lamp blown out and two strangers in the bed, a narrow enough one, but still there was a space between us. A horse whinnied from the stables, someone shouted, a word repeated, it sounded like *Elephant! Elephant! Elephant!* But who in the world would be out in the yard of Holsworthy Barracks at night shouting *Elephant?*

Across the space, Mr Macarthur lay still as a stone. He could not have died, not in the few minutes since he had snuffed the candle, rustled out of his clothes, and slid in on the other side of the bed. Could not be dead, but was as still as if dead.

– I have never understood before, when they say *my heart was in my mouth,* I said.

I felt I must be shouting, the words seemed so loud in that cube of darkness, but I could only go on.

– Today I saw what they meant—so much was my heart in my mouth that there was no room for the spit!

I remembered how his breath had come so hard, getting the ring on, and told myself, *Begin as you mean to go on, or at least as you hope to.* I fumbled through the bedclothes and found his hand, pressed the fingers.

– And you, I said with my best effort at a light tone, was your heart in your mouth too, Mr Macarthur?

53

He did not speak, did not press my hand in return, and I felt the cold shaft of a mistake that would now have to be retreated from. But at last there was a movement in the bed, as if he were turning towards me.

– Yes, he said. I have never.

He stopped, coughed to clear something blocking the words, laughed in a choked way.

– You see, I cannot get the words out to say what strange waters I feel myself in.

I would have felt warmer if he had got an *ourselves* into that sentence, but like me he had spent his life up to this day being *myself*. The idea that we, each of us separately, were now a thing called *ourselves* was, I supposed, equally new and alarming for both of us. Was I ready to be *ourselves*? I was happy enough to take his hand, to make a joke about spit, but how much, truly, did I wish or intend to be *ourselves* with this stranger?

We were a married couple, had got to that state because of doing what only married couples were permitted. Having done it when not permitted, it would be perverse not to repeat it now. But this time he offered no sighs and sweet words. And for me there was no glorious swelling of power. There was only the act itself, workman-like, short and sharp.

Turned away afterwards from the body next to me, I wept. Bitter silent tears for the too-small pocketful of coins that I had squandered. For the road behind us that I'd travelled in fear and sadness, leaving everything I knew, everyone who knew me. Left in the deepest shame, made all the worse by false smiles, false joy, the falseness of the good wishes, the only sincerity the word on everyone's lips: *goodbye, goodbye*, meaning *and may we never see you again*.

PART TWO

PART TWO

We had got away from Bridgerule in the nick of time, for within a few weeks of the wedding anyone could see that I was with child.

And miserably so. I had heard women speak of morning sickness, had seen Mrs Kingdon go through a time of waxy sallowness when she was carrying the Elizabeth who was my god-daughter. There were many mornings when, leaning over the basin, cold with nausea, I wept with regret and remorse. At those times I believed in hell as I'd never believed in heaven. But I struggled through many afternoons as well, and at night I lay unable to sleep, hungry yet sickened by food. Did this mean the child was sick too, dying as I felt I must be? That would be a nasty trick for life to inflict on me, after all that rosemary choked down.

The four or five months I had to get through before the child would be born seemed an eternity stretching in front of me. The birth itself I could not begin to imagine. Mrs Kingdon had never got as far as explaining anything of what to expect in childbed. I suppose she felt that when the time came would be soon enough, and we had not asked, being in no hurry to find out. Of course we knew it would hurt, but how exactly? Like a broken leg? We knew women died, but how precisely? Quickly, or by inches? And by what miracle could an entire baby squeeze out from that small place?

Anne was the eldest of eleven, she told me, which was good to hear as it meant she must know what I did not: how to care for a baby. Her father was a labourer who had been employed from time to time by my father. She could not read, nor write beyond an uncertain version of her own name, and was an awkward clumsy girl, and frankly I dismissed her as a person of not much account.

I hoped she was discreet. She had her own place in the servants' quarters, but still there was not much she did not know about the way Mr and Mrs Macarthur got on with each other. Or how they had come to be Mr and Mrs Macarthur. All Bridgerule knew that, I was sure. So I held my head up and was perhaps cooler with Anne than necessary, perhaps playing the lady more than came naturally.

Until the day she appeared with her hair singed on one side and a glossy red ear.

– Why Anne, I said, whatever have you done?

– There was a moth flew in my ear, madam, she said. Driving me dilly with moving around in there, so I held a candle up, thinking, you know, it would be drawn to the light?

She looked at me sideways, biting her lip, afraid I would scold I suppose, but at the picture of this solemn girl holding a candle up to her ear I laughed for the first time in many weeks.

– Oh you clever silly girl, I said.

Gave her some salve to put on the ear and blessed Mrs Kingdon, who had chosen so well as to find a girl whose unpromising exterior concealed a certain eccentric practicality.

I was not far from Bridgerule and Bridie, but as the new Mr and Mrs Macarthur had spun away from the church in the borrowed gig, I knew that a shutter was coming down between me and that world. Bridie and I exchanged notes now and then. On both sides, though, was the reserve that came from knowing they might be read by everyone in the vicarage parlour. Oh, how much I missed our whispered conversations in the high bed we had shared! On paper our friendship was reduced to description of life at a barracks on my side, and mild news of our mutual acquaintances on hers.

There was the wife of a Captain Spencer whose quarters at the Holsworthy Barracks were large enough for two or three ladies to take tea together, and these few women became my society. Mrs Spencer was a pretty little woman, but bony and trembling like a whippet, as if her husband—so corpulent that he had to walk back on his heels to accommodate his belly—had sucked the flesh out of her. Her friend Mrs Borthwick, wife to Captain Borthwick, was an assured, well-put-together older woman, with a habit of tweaking her mouth up at the corners, a conscious appearance of cheer that overlaid I knew not what real feelings.

They were tea-party acquaintances, not true friends. A barracks was not a village. Nothing went deep, nothing had a past or a future. Still, they were good to me, ignorant girl that I was. Dry toast for the morning sickness, they said. Dry toast, and tea with plenty of sugar. I nibbled the toast, drank the tea. The sickness did not abate, not by any fraction, but I was comforted that there were people in the world who cared enough to try to help me.

SOMETHING SOFT

Which Mr Macarthur did not. I overheard him boasting to others about his clever wife, who wrote such a fine letter, and had read Sir Thomas Browne and Livy—in translation, naturally. But he never spoke warmly to me and never gave anything of himself. There was no more of the hand on the heart, no more of the mimicry that he had courted me with. All that was gone. It had been useful, but was not useful any longer.

Oh, he was courteous, never shouted and certainly never struck me. In that I knew I should count my blessings. But he was a husband of mechanical courtesies. He listened when I addressed him, but without interest, as if I were some stranger he did not need to get to know. Spoke in reply, but carelessly, with indifference. He did not dislike me or blame me for the situation we were in. Only, he was blind to me as a person.

Would I have preferred the raised voice, the raised hand? Of course not. But I had not known that a person could be so lonely, sharing a few square yards of space with another soul.

I longed for something soft from him, even something harsh if that was the only way for us to draw close to each other. From the beginning I had promised myself never to plead with him. I would not make myself pitiable. Poor pale, skinny, unhappy woman, indeed I was pitiable. But what can be gained by begging if what you need is not given freely?

Still, one morning the words came out of my mouth.

– Mr Macarthur, I said, can you never give me any soft word?

I heard the anger, and the note of pleading that I despised.

He turned from the fireplace, startled, and looked straight at me, and I thought, I should have spoken my feelings earlier. He can hear me, he will respond.

– My beloved wife, he said. An affection like mine must have displayed itself in so many unequivocal substantive acts that professions of it would be absurd!

He was smiling into the air, admiring what he was constructing.

– That I am grateful and delighted with your conduct it is needless for me to say, he said, rattling it off as if he had rehearsed. The consciousness you must feel of how impossible it is that such exemplary goodness can have failed to produce that effect, must convince you I am so, more certainly than any assurance that can be given.

My spirit curdled at these elaborations, that gave his wife what she had asked for, while at the same time withholding it. *I ask for bread and you give me a stone.* I knew now what that meant. It was not just that you could not eat what you had been given. It was that the thing you were given resembled what you needed, could be thought to stand in for it, and that was crueller in its teasing than a plain refusal.

I was too proud to ask, ever again, for a soft word from him.

ANIMAL SPIRITS

Mr Macarthur was an importunate husband with an excess of animal spirits that meant every night the tickle of him fingering me, and then all that followed. And in the morning too, because Mr Macarthur liked a waking embrace. And, for that matter, an embrace in the middle of the day if circumstances allowed.

For me the act was no more pleasant than it might have been for those ewes in the field. It was not the act itself. From the nights Bridie and I had shared, I knew what a gasping delight that could be. What sapped it of any pleasure with Mr Macarthur was not to do with the way our various bodily parts came together. The block to delight was the feeling that I, Elizabeth Veale as I still thought of myself, was no more significant to my husband than the choice of ewe was to the ram. It was nothing to do with Elizabeth Veale that set the bed creaking. It was some hunger in him, that had to be sated again and again. I was nothing more than the means for that fleeting satisfaction.

But those affections were his conjugal right, and Mr Macarthur never failed to exercise any right he was entitled to. As a wife, with nowhere to go beyond wifedom, I was no more than a tenant in my body. If the landlord came to the door, I was obliged to let him in.

Other women became invalids, and the relentless morning sickness made it no lie. But days on a sofa are dull indeed, and I could not bear to spend my life watching the stripe of sunlight from the window creep across the floor, waiting for night. In any case, Mr Macarthur was not much discouraged by my faint-voiced murmurings about a headache.

– Let me rub camphor into your temples, he would say. A guaranteed cure.

He would get up and by the light of the lamp would sit on the side of the bed, rubbing the dreadful stuff into my forehead in a perfunctory way before turning his attention to parts further south.

There were occasions, now and then, when the business was very much worse than other nights, pain and humiliation beyond bearing. I cried out against it, there could be no mistaking the word *no!* But at such moments Mr Macarthur became as deaf as any mad dog. In the morning I could not look at him, a husband who had inflicted such a thing on his wife.

THE USE OF NUMBERS

Mrs Spencer seemed over-tightened, as if about to snap, and one day among the teacups she did indeed snap.

— Men are such beasts, she blurted, and put her cup into the saucer so hard I thought it would crack.

Her features were creased up into a grimace that for a second made her dainty head into a screaming skull. No one said anything, there was only a tiny movement of the corner of Mrs Borthwick's mouth. As the silence extended itself, I imagined that each of us was privately viewing the way in which our particular man was a beast in the darkness of the marriage bed.

Then Mrs Spencer put her hand around the teapot and declared it warm enough for another cup, rang for more milk, and the afternoon resumed. She handed me my fresh cup of tea: dainty, smiling, and had I imagined the words she had said, or misconstrued what she meant by them?

As Mrs Borthwick and I walked back to our quarters, neither of us mentioned Mrs Spencer's outburst. We had never talked of the parts of our lives that went on behind closed doors. But now Mrs Borthwick spoke of her husband George in such a way as to let me understand that she found no pleasure in the conjugal bed. Pacing beside me as sedately as a nun, she went further. There was a gentleman, it seemed. A gentleman not her husband. With whom she was able to take a considerable degree of pleasure.

— Yes, my dear Mrs Macarthur, she said. I hope you are not too shocked.

Gave me a quick sideways look.

— Naturally I am obliged to see dear George. Every month seems prudent.

Prudent? I wondered, then in a spurt of understanding saw what she meant. I looked sideways at her but she was so impassively handsome and poised that I thought I must be wrong.

– Oh yes, she said. I find, my dear, that it helps to have some rhyme or what-have-you to say over, just in your mind. I have one or two things that work particularly well.

She sang out suddenly in a fine strong contralto: *Girls and boys, come out to play, the moon doth shine as bright as day.*

– I can recommend it, Mrs Macarthur, she said, for those particular times. Counting is also a great comfort. With dear George I have never needed to go beyond forty-five.

A bird lived somewhere outside our windows and many was the dawn that I lay still, listening to it sing, a short snatch of tune, over and over. *Dah dah, di di di, da da!* A lovely song. But there was no variation. I pictured the bird perched among the dark leaves, its feathers ruffling in the breaths of pre-dawn wind, trapped in that one sad utterance. *Dah dah, di di di, da da!* It might have had everything to say of what it was like to be alive in the hour before the sun rose and life began again. But it had only that one phrase. I imagined the bird weeping in frustration, opening its beak to let out all it knew, and hearing again that parody of what it had in its heart.

AMBITION

Mr Macarthur was a man on the make. Ambition propelled every-thing he did. For myself, nowhere would be home and Gibraltar was no worse than anywhere else, so I was prepared for a life in that place. But the prospect of marching around the ramparts of Gibraltar was failure to my husband. Only a dunce would meekly go where the regiment sent him. Unless a war broke out, there was no hope of advancement in the 68th, for there were already too many junior officers in the regiment, whose only hope of promotion was for a sickly season among their superiors. He chafed against the narrowness of his prospects and was full of plans to burst out of them.

He would sell his commission—it would be worth four hundred pounds! Sell it and set up at the Bar! He had read all the books, knew the law as well as any lawyer. He would set himself up, and word would get about, and in no time men would be clamouring for John Macarthur to represent them!

He paced up and down the room, laying it all out before me. The embers fell against each other, a flare of light across his features, the pockmarks standing out very rough in that brightness, and his eyes avid with the conviction of his glorious future.

– John Macarthur of Lincoln's Inn, he said, does that not have a ring to it?

– Why yes, I said. A splendid ring.

Unworldly country woman though I was, I doubted if it could be so easy, but did not want to dash cold water on his certainty. Let the world do that, rather than his wife. And perhaps it was possible after all. I allowed myself to think for the space of a minute how much more agreeable Lincoln's Inn would be than Gibraltar.

But within a week no more was said about Lincoln's Inn. Now it was that he would speak to a gentleman his father knew, who would find him a post at the Office of Ordnance in Portsmouth—oh, it would be a plum position, it would be the best thing in the world!

– But the Bar, Mr Macarthur?

I did not intend to needle him, it was that my life was locked in with his.

– Oh, do not keep me to every syllable I have ever uttered, he said. Your understanding is superior, wife, but your knowledge of the world does not equip you to instruct me.

– Mr Macarthur, by no means am I instructing you, I said. Only, since our destinies are joined, to learn what mine might be!

– I thank you for reminding me, he said. Indeed, it is our *joined destinies*—he put a little mocking weight on the words—that I am straining every fibre to ameliorate!

Stared me down, watching me try to pick apart what had just happened: something had been simple, and had in the space of half a minute's exchange become snarled beyond untangling.

Grandiose schemes were as necessary to Mr Macarthur as food and drink. Each scheme remade the world in the light of his conviction. He was remade, too, into a more glorious version of himself, so the two John Macarthurs ran side by side like a pair of well-matched carriage horses: similar but not the same, close but never quite touching.

He would speak to his brother, who had been school chums with Evan Nepean, who was now an important government official. He would speak to a cousin of a close friend of Sir Joseph Banks, who would give him a position of secretary to someone in the House of Lords. He would write to a fellow he had met through Captain Moriarty, to write to this fellow's brother-in-law, who was now high up at the Palace.

The Palace! I let out a sound that could only be described as a snort, that I had to change into a cough smothered in my handkerchief, but Mr Macarthur noticed nothing.

The first need, though, was to sell his commission, and it seemed that the obtuse, narrow-minded, hidebound men who made those decisions would not agree to that. Their view was that they had not given Ensign Macarthur a post on active service and full pay in order for him to fund his leaving of that service.

So it was still Holsworthy Barracks, a hotbed of intrigue and animosity and shifting allegiances between the officers: too many men with not enough to do except resent how their lives were slipping away. Backbiting, rumour, insults and ill will everywhere.

Through the other servants Anne often heard of the gossip before I did, and I learned that if I feigned disbelief she would be piqued to tell me more. At the start she was fearful and wide-eyed at what she heard, but after a few weeks she had seen enough dramas ebb and flow to enjoy them as if they were a play, put on by the officers for the entertainment of their servants.

I pretended more indifference than I felt, for I knew most of her stories were likely to be true. Knew, too, that Mr Macarthur had a finger in every one of those nasty little pies. He was frequently the one to compose some outraged letter full of legal Latin on behalf of an aggrieved fellow officer. What he liked best of all were the times when he could come up with some ingenious interpretation to turn an unassailable argument on its head. Oh, how he loved a loophole!

He took a special pleasure in what he called the long game. A quick victory was no victory at all. It took a special kind of clever-ness—exactly his own kind of cleverness, as a matter of fact—to set up some movement seemingly harmless, then another equally innocent, and set them to grinding together so that the victim was eaten alive without quite knowing what had happened.

I heard Mr Macarthur boast one night that he had never yet failed in ruining a man who had become obnoxious to him. The laugh he gave, having delivered himself of this, was a bray of triumph.

The well-placed invention was his best weapon, all the more effective for the fact that it always had a fleck or two of the truth that gave a texture of plausibility to the whole. I felt for his enemies, helpless before his slanders. The victim might at last get wind of what was being said about him, but by then the story would have streamed out into the world. Protest as he might, that first story would always be the one believed.

Mr Macarthur could never be caught out. Mrs Borthwick one day was interested in the date of our marriage, and exactly when the baby was due. That pair of dates put side by side might have made for an awkwardness, but he had a gentleman's answer, so smooth as to erase doubt.

– Oh, we were eager, he said, and chuckled indulgently. It was accepted that we had an informal understanding—we stood godparents to a friend's child, you know. And, well, our fondness for each other got the better of us. Did it not, my dear?

– Indeed, I said, and tried to smile. Indeed it did, sir.

There was that fleck of truth. Yes, I was godmother to Elizabeth Kingdon. The fiction—that he was therefore her god-father—followed seamlessly, a reasonable enough assumption. Who would ever bother to check? Even if some searcher of the future went looking for proof, he or she would find no piece of paper to confirm or deny it. Only this one, where I am writing the truth for you to know.

DUELS

Always, every week it seemed, there was the grand drama of a duel. If any of the officers' pistols had hit their marks, His Majesty's forces would have been sadly depleted. But strangely, no one, to my knowledge, ever came to actual grief in any of the duels.

Mrs Borthwick, whose George had evidently fought a duel or two, explained that the job of the seconds was to see to it that no one was killed. Together, watching each other, they loaded both pistols in exactly the same way, so that they misfired or fired wide. Their duty was to see fairness prevail, not to oversee death. It was enough, in the dawn of the duelling day, for a satisfying report to fill the ground and startle the birds out of the trees, and for a satisfying cloud of smoke to drift away across the grass. The noise and the smoke and the smell, and the important bustling about of everyone, the seconds with their measuring tape, the surgeon with his bag—all that satisfied pride and assuaged insult. No wound was necessary, certainly no corpse.

Like the other officers, Mr Macarthur was never without outrage at some grievance or insult, and blazed up at the smallest infringement of what he saw as his entitlement. There was a complicated set of boundaries that put a gentleman apart from others, and Mr Macarthur patrolled them with an eye and ear for the slightest deviation.

He stormed into our quarters one afternoon, his neck flushed in angry blotches, the muscle in his jaw shifting under the skin like a hidden creature bulging and flattening.

— I will demand satisfaction, he cried, and went to the shelf where his duelling pistols lay in their wine-coloured velvet.

71

I knew now that a duel did not necessarily mean death. Still, I hated the look of the pistols, feared the idea of a hot ball of lead hurtling itself towards the helpless flesh of a human being.

– But Mr Macarthur, what is at stake here? What did he do, exactly? Surely there will be no need for pistols!

It transpired that Mr Macarthur had agreed to act as second for Lieutenant Selby in his duel against Lieutenant Bannerman. But when everyone had arrived at the ground, it was discovered that Lieutenant Bannerman's second was a person called Baker, and Baker was not a gentleman.

– I told Bannerman, I will not be insulted, Mr Macarthur said. What was the fool thinking, to pair me with such a fellow as this Baker?

– But sir, can that possibly be worth dying for?

Dying! That roused my husband.

– My dear, he said, you insult me to imagine I would be the one dying. That is the least likely outcome in the world!

– I am sure you are a good shot, sir, I answered, enraged by his smugness. But this Bannerman may be a better one! Do you wish to leave me a widow?

– Oh, my dear wife, he said. Never fear! It so happens that my pistols have certain idiosyncrasies, and can only be safely loaded by someone familiar with them. Namely, myself.

His eyes shone with satisfaction.

– My dear, he crowed, it would become you to have more faith in your husband!

I was filled with weariness. Mr Macarthur would always have some trick up his sleeve—with his trusting opponents on the duelling ground, with his wife—to make sure he came out on top.

– Oh, then, so much for the man of honour, I said.

I wanted to hurt him, thought that might hit home. But he

did not seem to hear me, and left the room with the case of pistols in his hand.

I came to see that the particular grievance was of no importance. His status as a gentleman—yes, that was important to him. Of that he was so unsure that he needed to test it continually, to the death if necessary. I had heard a whisper that, before his entry into Fish's regiment, he had been apprenticed to a corset maker. The barracks were full of nasty rumours and I did not quite believe this one. Still, it stuck in my mind. If true, it would explain that desperate need.

But his anxiety ran deeper than snobbery. He went seeking insult because it was only in opposition to another that he could have faith in who he was. He needed to pin his conviction of his value on that flimsy idea of *honour* because he knew of nowhere else to pin it.

And I? Where did I pin my sense of worth? I could not say, yet I recognised an obstinate nub of something in myself that gave me the right to be the person I was. In the eyes of the world I had so little, and yet in that conviction of my own worth I had more than my husband, for all his cunning.

A SAD CASE

He had been sent away to school at seven, he told me. I had heard enough from Bridie's brothers to guess how the strong held sway in those institutions, made the lives of the weak a misery. A boy would quickly learn how to become one of the bullies.

He was at school when his mother died. No one had told him she was ill. His father continued to write the weekly letter, to which he replied with reports of cricket and how his Greek was coming along. She died, and he was not told, not until he went home for the holidays. His father said it was best that way. What was the point in disturbing him? Could he have cured his mother if he'd been there? Brought her back from the dead if he'd gone to the funeral?

I had thought myself a sad case. But I had been permitted to grieve for my father, and I knew my grandfather loved me. My friendship with Bridie had been true and deep, and the Kingdons had opened their lives to me. My husband had had no one, and that must be why some central part of him, some steady sense of who he was, had years ago gone like a mouse to hide away in its hole. But he could never admit the pain. He had to transmute suffering into a blade, to punish the world that made him suffer.

THE BLACK GLOOM

There were the mad enthusiasms, the wild schemes. But from those fevers he could plunge in a half-hour into a melancholy so deep he could not be persuaded to get out of bed. His face became frightening: staring and gaunt, wooden as a mask. There was no reaching him. Everything was hopeless, he whispered. He was worthless. His life a barren waste. You might try to jolly him out of the black gloom, but it was as if you were too far away to be heard.

How many wives learn, as I did, how to test the air in a room? To check the tilt of her husband's head, the set of his feet, his grip on a spoon, his fist beside the plate? To feel in an instant whether it was an hour of sunshine or shadow? The weather in those rooms was as changeable as Devon in May.

A FLAT SHINING BEETLE

Mrs Borthwick—poised, humorous, shrewd, handsome as a fine horse—might be a model of how a woman could manage her life to her satisfaction, but I saw no way to go from where I was now to such a place. Still, I was too proud to admit, other than in my private thoughts, what a disaster I had got myself into. I cultivated a glassy surface that deflected the smallest approach to a sympathetic enquiry. The pain of being unloved was pushed off to a distance where it could not touch. I became like those flat shining beetles that live in the heart of a rotten log, a creature of no dimension, able to disappear into the narrowest of cracks.

The pains came on me as we were making our way to Chatham Barracks, from whence we would sail to Gibraltar. We did not get anywhere close to Chatham, though, before it was obvious that the child was on its way, and we fetched up in some disarray at a poor inn on the wrong side of Bath.

I had begun to weep when the pains started, because with the first sharp pang I was obliged to believe what I had until then not truly believed, that there was no going back. Started weeping and did not stop. All the years of squashing down the tears, of being cheerful and obliging, saying only what was unexceptional, and the strange months of being married to a husband I could not reach— all that pressed-down sorrow came up like a bolus into my throat.

Anne knew a little more than I did of childbirth, but she was only a girl, and as the pains began to come fast and strong, I saw she was as frightened as I was. There was no midwife to be had for a woman only that day arrived in the city, so the companion of my childbed was the innkeeper's wife.

There was nothing gentle about her. Had no patience, she made clear, for a woman who had not taken care to plan what was upon her. But she knew what she was about, and was with me as I traversed a terrible landscape of pain and fear and chaos. Time was suspended, time did not pass, time could only be measured by the respites between the brutal grasping of some merciless fist in my body. The respite—six breaths between, then three, then one— were the times when I was given back myself, to feel air coming in and out of my chest, feel the water Anne offered me cool in my mouth, know that the world went on, time was passing in the usual way. But each reprieve was only to tease. The grip returned, distant at first and then roaring over me and through me and around me, sucking air and time away and flinging me into an eternity of the unbearable. Then the pains joined together end to end and there was no reprieve, only a flailing about in a black gnashing place that did not care a fig about me, wanted only to gripe and grip me until no person was left, no human, just a screaming animal.

The voice of the innkeeper's wife was the rope that kept me bound to life, with me in the hard place I was grinding my way through, but she was not in the pain with me. That was a place a person had to travel through alone. I met there a cold indifferent truth: that every person—even a loved person, and I was not loved— was alone. On the whole globe, there was no one but myself, and I was shaken and torn down to the merest speck of being.

The child the woman put into my arms was nothing like the plump pink babes I had seen, sweet tidy parcels being handed around a room full of smiling people. He was a dreadful little monkey, with legs like twigs and purple hands and a big round belly. He seemed to be on the point of expiring, his mouth opening and closing but only the smallest whimper emerging.

The innkeeper's wife took him away and I lay washed up on the bed as flat and limp as some dead thing fished out of the sea. It was I suppose the worst of all the hours of my life. That squalid inn, that sickly child, and Anne pushing water at me, crumbling bread in milk that I did not want. Poor girl, she meant kindly but she was no use to me, her face the face of a stranger. I knew that this was the world I was in now, a vile dirty place where I was alone, alone, alone. I wept again, storming and sobbing, it seemed the flood would never stop. Woe is me, oh poor me, woe is me.

The woman came back with the baby washed and wrapped, tucked him beside me and sat with her beefy arms crossed over her chest and her small shrewd eyes watching me with no great warmth. I saw that she knew what had happened to my life, knew the whole sad commonplace story without being told.

– Mrs Macarthur, she said at last over my sobs, and I thought she might lean towards me and take my hand, perhaps come out with a few cheering platitudes.

I felt myself get ready to cry harder, because I was sure my plight was beyond the reach of any platitudes. But her rock-like face did not soften and she did not offer any comfort.

– Only a fool could not see what you have got yourself into, Mrs Macarthur, she said.

She spoke in a mild way, like a person explaining to another how you might get from Bridgerule to the Red Post Inn. Paused for a good look at me, hair wet with tears bedraggled all over my cheeks. The horrible clinging hair was part of the misery that I wanted to drown in. I let it cling rather than push it away.

– How it strikes you, yes, that's as plain as a pikestaff, she said. And I will not say what another might, *But at least you have your sweet boy*, because he is a sad little scrap. Could as well die as live, to be frank.

I wondered if she was the Devil come to taunt me.

– You are a stranger to me so I can speak plain, she said. I will say this, as one who has laid out many a corpse. Here in this pickle is where you are and there is no one on this earth can help you out of it.

I braced myself for some pious thing about *God's mysterious ways*.

– And no one not on this earth either, to my mind, she said. She knew what I was thinking. No matter a body wear out their knees trying.

When she laughed it was a startling thing. Her face broke into its separate features, nose, big coarse cheeks, mouth.

– As for you, lass, you have a parcel of years to go, she said. Spend them wallowing with sorrow if you please, as you are now, waiting for a better thing that will never come. There is no one in this wide world to stop you, if that is the choice you make.

She stood, rolled down her sleeves, buttoned them as if finished with me.

– There is just this, though, lass, that I can tell you, she said. Which is, life is long. It has more corners than you can count. A woman can do many things, but she has to bide her time.

When she was gone, taking Anne with her, I wept harder at her hard words, and the way she had not tried to comfort me. I lay with my misery, the greedy tears pouring out of my eyes, dripping from my chin. Nothing changed, no one came. Only the quiet room, the child silent against me, and myself listening to my own gulps and gasps.

I could have gone on crying for ever, might have died in the extravagance of so much despair, but after a time there were simply no more tears. One last great dry sob turned into a hiccough. Then it was over.

The child stirred feebly, let out a faint mew, turned his head towards me, jerked his tiny fist. We were in this, both of us, together. Here was this sad ugly scrap of life, that could do nothing but let out that thin cry, twitch that fist no bigger than a walnut, turn his head blindly: and something in me went out to him. I picked him up, his vague eyes seemed to meet mine, his mouth made a movement, and I understood that, if he were to live, it could only be because I made it so. Poor feeble unlovely creature as he was, I could do no other than love him.

By the time that stranger my husband came back to the room, smelling of cigar and rum, I was sitting up against the pillows with the child in my arms. Anne had brought water and a cloth and a clean nightdress, had gently washed my face and tied back my hair.

– My dear, he said, and for once the endearment seemed to have feeling.

But he could not meet my eye. Was in some way afraid of me, I understood. I had come through pain and fear, had like every woman in childbed been within a hand's brush of death. I had proved myself stronger than life had ever asked him to be. Had come back knowing something that would never be known to him. It was secret knowledge, secret because it could not be told, only lived through.

He looked at the child, pushed back the wrapper to see his face.

– Well, he said, and it was easy to hear that, like me, he had expected a chubby rosy cherub, not this wizened creature. Put a finger to the child's pale cheek as if to check he was alive. The baby's head turned, the blue-veined eyelids flickered.

– My son, he said, uncertain, but doing his best to match the little thing in front of him with the proud words. Glanced at me for an instant, as if at a bright light.

– Edward, perhaps, he said. Edward Macarthur, that has a fine ring, do you not agree?

He was finding his way back to his familiar world, where he could take circumstances by the bridle and lead them where he wished.

Before the birth I had given some consideration to names. If a girl, she would be Jane, in honour of good Mrs Kingdon, and if a boy I wanted Richard for my father, or perhaps John for my grandfather.

— I thought Richard, I said. For my father. So perhaps Edward Richard.

I spoke gently, kindly. I had been sunk in terror and returned safe. I had met myself and hoped not to lose myself again. I could be magnanimous towards this man who had not been given those privileges.

I had long ago folded myself up small and put myself away. That had served me well enough. But then I had unfolded too wildly, too recklessly, in the wrong place and at the wrong time and with the wrong person. But between a person folded up small and a person too quick to believe herself safe in unfolding, there was the speck that was what was left when you took everything else away. She was here with me now, would always be with me. She would not turn to the wall and waste her life groaning at her fate. She would carry that precious speck of self on into the future.

I hoped that Edward would begin to flourish once we were installed in the barracks at Chatham, but he remained a sickly child, undersized, gaunt, whimpering in my arms. Anne and I came to know each other in the long nights and days of taking turn and turn about trying to comfort him. We tried sitting him up and lying him down, nursing him and burping him, swaddling him tight and leaving him unwrapped. In the end Anne made a kind of hammock for him from a shawl, tying him tight against me, and her clever contrivance gave us all some respite.

Dear Anne, she did not despair as I did, was not ready to give up on the child. Came upon me more than once, limp in the armchair with Edward crying on my lap while I sat and leaked endless tired tears. Led me to the bed, pulled the covers up gently as if she were the mother and I the child, and took Edward away until, waking from a dense sleep, I was ready again to put my shoulder to the wheel of this business of being a mother.

He lived a week, a month, two months, and I thanked the God I did not believe in that this child was not, as I had dearly wanted a year earlier, dead.

He was not yet three months old when Mr Macarthur came upon me nursing him in the big armchair by the fire. Edward and I were joined as if the one creature, my body relaxed against the cushions and his warm weight folded tightly in against me, his starfish fingers caressing the source of bliss and his little feet twining together in ecstasy.

When Mr Macarthur filled the doorway I did not have time to rearrange the tableau. A mother can hardly feel guilt for nursing her own infant, yet it was with a sense of being caught out that I had the impulse to cover myself. Edward on the instant felt the change in my mood, the smooth rhythm of his sucking faltered, he spluttered, choked, let out his thin bird-call of distress.

I saw Mr Macarthur's expression change as he stared at something he had never seen before: his wife lost in the delight of a loving embrace. What was that naked look? Shock, surprise: they were part of it. But something else too: loss, longing, loneliness, grief.

– A thousand pardons, Mrs Macarthur, he said, and the moment hardened into the courteous apology of a gentleman disturbing his lady wife. Forgive my intrusion, if you please.

Then he was turning and quietly closing the door.

Seeing that grief, no matter how quickly hidden, I understood that Mr Macarthur was a bully, a boaster, a charmer—a tweaker of every human string—not because he was simply made in a bad mould. Like me, he knew himself to be alone in the great spinning universe, a speck of nothing girded around by all the robust cleverness he took comfort behind. But where I had met that speck and greeted it as a companion, he only knew himself prey, as we all were, to doubt. Uncertain of his welcome, as we all were. He was, in short, a fellow soul, but too fearful to recognise another, or to trust her.

THE MATHEMATICS OF IT

Edward was half a year old when my husband came to me with the familiar light in his eyes that meant he had a scheme in mind.

– Dearest, he said, and I was immediately wary. Dearest, you have been patient beyond what any husband could ask for.

I smiled, thinking only, *what is it now?*

– When we decided to bind our two fates together, he said, I made a promise that I would cherish and keep you. I now have the happiness, dearest, to be able to tell you news that will fill your heart with gladness and gratitude—

– For God's sake, I cried. Out with it, sir!

– That I have this morning applied to join a new regiment, which has offered me promotion. Lieutenant Macarthur of the New South Wales Corps! Does that not have a splendid ring, my dear wife? We are to relieve the marines already out there, and will sail in December.

I thought he was joking, but my laughter was quickly snuffed out by the familiar tightening of the muscles around his mouth. He had expected joy, and joy was not what he saw.

– New South Wales! I exclaimed. The New South Wales Corps!

I was backing and filling like a ship in trouble, waiting for a wind to show me where to go. I knew nothing of New South Wales except that it was on the far underbelly of the globe, the latest *oubliette* devised by His Majesty as a repository for prisoners of the worst description.

– Ah, and why New South Wales, Mr Macarthur?

His words tumbled over themselves in their eagerness to lay out the glorious prospect that was the New South Wales Corps. Promotion was only the start of it.

– It will offer all manner of opportunities, he said. The commander of the Corps is Nicholas Nepean, his brother was a school chum of my dear brother's. Moreover, the governor there has it in his power to grant away land, large tracts of it, and will be persuaded to do so by a man putting his case well.

– But the place is a prison, I exclaimed. Of less than two years' establishment—it cannot be more than a clearing in the wilderness!

Oh, he had an answer to that, a sheaf of papers with the latest reports of the colony.

– Look, my dear, he said. See here—*rapid progress in building*! Crops flourishing *in a manner nearly incredible*!

He was almost gabbling, it was another of his manias. Would pass, if I was patient, like a squall of rain. *Do not argue*, I told myself. But I was so aghast at the idea of New South Wales that I could not be cunning.

– Mr Macarthur, these are nothing but marks on paper, I said. The people who are in that misbegotten place want to put it about that it is a success. These reports were written by men with their own fish to fry!

– Nonsense, he said. These are the best and latest reports, he said. Are you suggesting the governor of New South Wales is lying?

As so often, he had drawn me into a knot which any answer would only tighten. Seeking wildly for a way out, I changed direction.

– A place of the worst felons, I said. No matter how splendid the crops. Do you see yourself as prison guard to the dregs of Newgate?

Ah, that hit home. I felt him recoil and followed up my advantage.

– And what of your wife and child, sir? Do you wish your son to grow—if indeed he lives—in the company of thieves and murderers?

86

– Nonsense, he said again.

I saw I had over-reached myself. Doubt had left him.

– Have no fear, he said. Those accounts are glowing, but are already out of date. By the time our corps arrives, everything will be comfortable for our reception. Do not be blinded, my dear wife, by common and vulgar prejudices!

– Prejudiced I may be, sir, I said. But I will not do it!

Hollow desperate words. He knew as well as I did that *I will not do it* was hot air. He did not need to ask, *then what will you do?*

In any case, his thoughts were not about what his wife would or would not do. His eyes were flicking back and forth along the rug watching some other thing altogether.

– There is the matter of a small debt, he said at last. Incurred before my removal into the sixty-eighth. No gentleman could be expected to live on one-and-six a day.

– A small debt, I said.

His tone was casual and so was mine. But I went very still, waiting. *A small debt.* Twenty pounds? Fifty? Twenty pounds was half an ensign's yearly pay. Fifty pounds would swallow even a lieutenant's pay. I started to do the sum in my head, how much would need to be put away each week, for how long, to pay twenty pounds out over how many years.

– A couple of hundred, he said. A couple of hundred or so.

A couple of hundred. They were words I knew, and yet it was as if they were in a foreign language. Twenty pounds was something I could imagine, coins on a table spilling out on the wood. *A couple of hundred* was some other kind of thing altogether. There was no way to put a junior officer's pay and a couple of hundred pounds together in the same thought.

He licked his lips, his eyes went sideways.

– Perhaps five hundred.

I thought, *he must be teasing*. But he was not teasing. His head was down, I saw his stubby eyelashes come down over his eyes. I had never seen Mr Macarthur abashed, but he was very close to abashed now.

Our conversation had all at once floated away from anything I had the power to alter. There was no point to any calculation I might worry away at. My husband's debt was too big ever to be paid back by a soldier in peacetime, no matter how you might divide it into weekly scrimpings.

I had always assumed his commission had been bought by his father, but now I realised the money must have been borrowed. That, plus the supplementing of his one-and-six a day, could add up to a round five hundred. No wonder his boots were of the best leather, and he had been able to bring gifts of bonbons to Mrs Kingdon! Above all, no wonder he had been in such a frenzy to secure a better post than Gibraltar!

And now he was clearing his throat, going to the window and looking out as if there was something of interest there. Watching him staring out with his shoulder between himself and me, I saw he was expecting cries, rage, tears, was putting the barrier of that shoulder up between us. But what would be the point of tears or rage? Rage was indulgence. So were tears. As Mr Kingdon's finger had traced the twisting course of a river across the landscape of the map, relentlessly, down to the ocean, I was following the words *five hundred pounds* to where they led.

– Yes, I see, I said.

There was a kind of relief. It was not up to me to find the words to talk him out of the idea of New South Wales. Nothing I could do or say would change the monstrous fact. *Five hundred pounds*. He was right. New South Wales was the only way forward. Promotion and prospects were essential, and a new regiment the only path to them.

His shame had passed, and so had his need to present me with that bulwark of shoulder. He had spun away from the window now, was pacing as eagerly as if to walk all the way to New South Wales.

– Think of it mathematically, my dearest wife, he said. In Gibraltar there is zero chance of doing well. In the unknown of New South Wales, there is some chance—certainly greater than zero—of doing well. And a chance—somewhere between zero and infinity—of doing magnificently!

– Yes, Mr Macarthur, I said. A number has got us into this, so how remarkably fortunate it is that numbers will get us out of it.

He stopped his pacing long enough to look at me.

– My dear, he said. I understand. You are thinking of your dear mother.

– Not my dear mother! Myself, Mr Macarthur! Myself and the child!

But he could only hear the fine words he was preparing.

– Do but consider, my dearest Elizabeth, that if you must be distanced from familiar places—and as a soldier's wife how can you not be?—then it is much the same, whether you are two hundred or two thousand miles away.

I watched another flourish come to him.

– The same Providence will protect you in New South Wales, and the sun that shines on your mother and grandfather will also afford you the benefit of his cheering rays.

Hearing this flummery, I knew that he was as frightened as I was. A man certain of his ground does not need to construct a sentence like a Turk's head knot.

– Yes dear, I said. But you are not as sure as you say.

He blinked, prodded out of a sunny daydream. Blinked, and there it was, the fear, the look of a creature cornered.

89

– Ah, he said. Well.

For a moment there was peace, the peace of surrender. It was shameful of me, but I liked him better when I knew him to be as afraid as I was.

Then I misjudged and took his hand. He flinched, drew it back. For me, being together, fellow souls joined in fear, was some comfort. For him, that was weakness. In taking his hand I was telling him what I had seen, and that was something he could not allow.

I put it to Anne that she could go back to Bridgerule if she wished. She would find some future there, I supposed, a young man to marry, or someone else in need of a maid. I tried to keep out of my tone the bleakness I surprised in myself at the prospect of parting from her.

Her eyes shifted over her possibilities. I watched her making a calculation that would shape the rest of her life.

– Take what time you need, Anne, I said. It is no small decision.

– No madam, she said. I have made up my mind, I will come with you.

– Oh! I exclaimed, the relief plain to be heard.

But I could not take advantage of her ignorance.

– Are you sure, I said. It is half a year on a ship, and then heaven knows what. Rough, it will be rough, and hungry. There will be hardships we cannot imagine.

She gave me a smile, as if knowing I thought her too foolish to have considered any of that.

– Thank you, madam, she said. For not gilding the lily. But there is nothing for me in Bridgerule. I would rather take my chances.

I saw that she had seen this coming—if not New South Wales, then Gibraltar. Had weighed up the choices she had, and did not need to have me doubt on her behalf. She was more clear-eyed than I had ever been, in calculating where her best interests might lie. New South Wales might turn out to be a bad choice, but she was not rushing blindly into her future.

I was doubly glad that she was coming with us, because I feared more trouble was rumbling down on me. I had been told that a woman could not fall while she was nursing, but I was almost sure that I was with child again. If I was right, this child would be born on the last part of the voyage, through the fury and ice of the Southern Ocean. Relative to a convict transport on that sea, a dirty inn at Bath might seem like paradise.

I took her hands, surprised myself with tears in my eyes and an impulse to embrace her.

– Ah, Mr Macarthur said when I shared the news of the second child. You will be the first officer's wife to bear a child on that new continent!

– An honour I would as soon forgo, I said.

He heard the tartness in my tone and looked at me in surprise.

– It is what lies ahead of us, I said. There is not a great deal of choice in any aspect of the matter. I will set myself to it. But, Mr Macarthur, you cannot ask me to be delighted.

In the nights my heart was heavy at the unimaginable journey ahead of us, my companion this man lying beside me, his hand twitching in sleep as though flicking a crop against a horse's flank.

I wrote to Mother at Stoke Climsland. *Do but consider, my dear mother, that if we are to be apart, then it is much the same, whether we are two hundred or two thousand miles distance. The same Providence will protect me, there as in New South Wales. The sun that shines on me will also afford you the benefit of his cheering rays.*

We had got no further in our voyage to New South Wales than Plymouth, where we put in to load supplies, when Anne came to me with the news that Mr Macarthur had issued a challenge to Mr Gilbert, the master of our vessel.

– Oh, my dear, I said, they are pulling your leg!

She said nothing, but gave me a straight look. I realised I would be wise not to scoff, put aside my reluctance and made myself listen. She had heard it from the ship's cook, who had heard it from Mr Gilbert's servant: a duel, the following day, behind the Old Gun Wharf.

Mr Gilbert was a vulgar sort of fellow, and it was true that we had hardly left the Thames behind when a disagreement occurred between him and Mr Macarthur—as always, some matter of my husband's honour—that meant neither would speak to the other. But Mr Gilbert was God in the narrow world of the *Neptune*, and our destinies for the next half-year were entirely in his hands. Only a madman would pick a fight with someone who held such power. Whatever insult had been perceived, I assured myself that Mr Macarthur would find some way to smooth it over.

But the next evening, Anne came to me in our cabin to say that she had just heard from the sergeant that, an hour earlier, Mr Macarthur and Captain Gilbert had met. Mr Gilbert's ball had gone wide of its mark, but Mr Macarthur's had ripped through the sleeve of Captain Gilbert's coat, missing the man himself by half an inch.

With Edward in my arms, his face creased up in distress as if he understood what his father had done, I followed Anne up onto the deck. Mr Macarthur was below me on the quay, the centre of a cluster of men. I could not hear the words he was saying, but I knew the look of Mr Macarthur in triumph. He tossed his head as if in scorn, stepped back in order to pounce forward on some new sally, held up fingers and ticked them off as he enumerated insults or triumphs. From this distance he seemed to be performing a dance, retreating and advancing, turning to this side, to that, bowing, throwing out a hand in a regal gesture.

Something in me slowed down, as if my blood had thickened. From a great distance I watched Elizabeth Macarthur watching her husband. My life had slipped away from me since that night behind the hedge, had become something too close to be seen clearly. Now, standing at the rail, I seemed to remove myself from where I was, and in an endless still moment I saw the truth.

My husband was rash, impulsive, changeable, self-deceiving, cold, unreachable, self-regarding. I had learned all that, and thought it was the sum of him. Now I knew I was wrong. There was worse. My husband was someone whose judgment was dangerously unbalanced. There was a wound so deep in his sense of himself that all his cleverness, all his understanding of human nature, could be swept aside in some blind butting frenzy of lunatic compulsion.

My life, and the life of this helpless babe in my arms, was tethered to the hollow vessel of my husband's honour, and that was more important in his eyes than the humans who depended on him for their survival. Other people were to him no more than objects to be handled—with care, yes, with charm, with flattery, with smiles if smiles offered the best way to achieve what he needed. But other people were no more important than a shoe or a spoon. You could not hurt the feelings of a shoe. You did not have to wonder whether a spoon would suffer from the consequences of your actions.

I felt Anne watching me, felt her pity. I could not meet her eye. She knew me and my situation too well. But what I had seen and now had to find a way to confront was too sharp a pain to share.

– Let us give thanks to the Almighty disposer of events that nothing worse has taken place, I said. And hope that satisfaction has been had.

– Indeed, madam, Anne said, and we shared a glance at last.

When Mr Macarthur came to the cabin later he was like a tightened fiddle-string. He vibrated with glee and self-congratulation. He had winged Gilbert! And Gilbert, that poltroon, had missed entirely! Gilbert was to be stood down, it was said, and another fellow would be sent in his place!

There was nothing to be gained by arguing with him, any more than you might profit from arguing with a barking dog. Still, I argued.

– Yes, I said, and this new fellow will have been told that there is a passenger aboard with the temperament to challenge the captain of his ship to a duel. That is no triumph, Mr Macarthur!

He gave me a glance as if to say, *how could you understand*. There was a smirk, too, and a movement of the shoulder halfway to a shrug.

– Would it not have been the wiser course, sir, not to make an enemy of a person with such power over us?

I heard my voice gone shrill with fury, was shouting, did not care who heard.

– No matter what tricks you can perform with your damned pistols?

The smirk did not shift.

– Well, wife, he said weightily, as if with some pronouncement in mind. What a fine thing.

But even as he said the words he seemed to lose interest in them. He brushed at a speck on his sleeve, smoothed his hair above an ear, held out his hand to inspect the nails. Then, as if I had not spoken, as if he had not begun a thought, he left the cabin.

EAVESDROPPING

Far from bringing Mr Macarthur to his senses, the duel on the wharf spurred him on. Within a week of the ship finally sailing, he alienated the new captain, a Mr Trail, by complaining on behalf of the soldiers about their ration. Fumed and sputtered. Suddenly nothing was more important than the welfare of the men.

– Let someone else take up their cause, I said. Nothing good will come of you interfering.

– I consider it my duty, he said, smug as a parson. These poor fellows are being cheated, actually going hungry!

He tried to pull his superior into the fight, but Captain Nepean was too canny to be drawn. He was a cold fish, very conscious of his position: commander of the New South Wales Corps until an officer of higher rank could be persuaded to take on the task. Beyond that he was one of the Nepeans of Saltash, his brother Evan an influential person high in the government. Evan Nepean had gone to school with Mr Macarthur's brother James, and it was thanks to that connection that Mr Macarthur had been offered his new post. Captain Nepean must have known that Mr Macarthur's position in the regiment was solely due to his brother's influence. Would have known, too, about the five hundred pounds. He bowed courteously to me with my swollen belly when he saw me taking the air on the after-deck, but was always on his way somewhere else and never paused.

Nepean's refusal to support him further inflamed my husband.

– But sir, I said, trying to jolly him out of his rage. Captain Nepean knows on which side his bread is buttered, and so should you!

Now Mr Macarthur became convinced that Captain Trail and Nepean were plotting against him. This officer and gentleman was moved to creep up the passageway so that he could apply his ear to the door of the captain's cabin. What did he hear? Something to heap fuel on his rage—or perhaps nothing. By now he was taken over by a conviction that nothing could shake, a pale outrage at the perfidy of Captain Trail, Nepean, the bosun, anyone.

Nepean and the captain had comfortable quarters in the upper deck, which outraged Mr Macarthur, for we were relegated to a half-cabin below, with the convict women on the other side of a light partition. He smarted under the indignity—it offended not his compassion but his pride, that he should be reduced almost to sharing a cabin with felons.

Oh, I remember that vile cabin. The convict women swore and groaned, shouted, screamed, farted. There was an unceasing clatter and rumble, the confused din of too many women shut in too tight a space. Now and then one of them sang in a loud cracking voice. *Love divine, all loves excelling.* I never saw the women, but came to feel that I knew the one who sang, because the others shouted at her to *close your damn cake-hole, Mary Anne, for the love of God!*

Mr Macarthur maintained that every one of these women was a harlot who deserved nothing better, but I did not believe him. By now I had learned enough about the narrowness of a woman's choices to guess that they were not all harlots, only less lucky than I had been.

Their situation was far worse than mine, but I shared some of their sufferings. There was one—or perhaps more than one—who groaned and puked, and I knew that on the other side of that thin wall was a woman racked with the same morning sickness that was racking me, and must be awake with the same sweaty fear for the future of herself and her unborn child.

But I had privileges unimaginable for those women: a degree of privacy, the assistance of a girl who uncomplainingly endured the hardships alongside me, and the power to go up onto the deck and take the air whenever I pleased.

Until, that is, Mr Macarthur's eavesdropping on the captain and Nepean was detected, at which point the passageway was nailed shut. Actually nailed. Mr Macarthur braved the other passageway—which I had never used, for it was the hospital for the convicts—but he forbade me to risk contagion. Confined in that smelly cabin with my sick child, sick myself, without the respite of an hour up on deck, I was better off than the women I could hear, but not by so very much.

We were nailed into the cabin for twenty days, and Mr Macarthur spent them scheming. Not how to free us, but how to bring Nepean before a court martial as soon as we got to New South Wales.

– Mr Macarthur, I pleaded, for God's sake forget Nepean, forget Trail—think of us, and find a way to patch up the quarrel!

But each time he came down again from the deck it was to record on a growing pile of paper some new proof of Nepean's perfidy so it could be given in evidence later.

There was no actual escape, but I found some form of it within my own being. My self withdrew into a smaller and smaller space until it was too distant to be touched. I would have accepted death with indifference. In that merciful blur, time was suspended. At a great distance I heard Edward's feeble cries and attended to them. They were nothing more than a sound, of no more importance to me than the creaking of the ship's timbers or the groans from beyond the wall. The creature that was me had crept away and left nothing more than the shell of a woman curled up on the bunk.

Then my husband came to me and Anne and told us to pack all our belongings, for we were to exchange our place in the *Neptune* for one on the *Scarborough*. I had no idea that it was possible to decamp from one ship into another in the middle of the Atlantic—husband, wife large with child, infant, maidservant, baggage—but he assured me it was, as soon as there was calm weather. He was as triumphant about it as if it were exactly what he had always wanted.

How was he able to get his way? Or was it that Trail and Nepean wanted him gone? I was too sick to care, only knew it as deliverance.

On the *Scarborough* Edward and I shared a cabin with the wife of Lieutenant Abbott. She made room for me and Edward with grace, although our gain was her loss.

She pitied me, I saw it in her eyes. Everyone on the ship knew that it had pleased Mr Macarthur to act so provokingly as to make our lives on the *Neptune* a living hell. That, having created the problem, he had then gone about solving it in the way that gave the greatest inconvenience to the greatest number. It was not my imagination that, on the *Scarborough*, the captain, the officers, even the seamen, treated Mr Macarthur warily, as one might deal with an unpredictable dog.

We reached the Cape safely, but my husband contracted some virulent African fever there, and during our passage through the Southern Ocean he lay in the cramped dirty cabin they called the hospital. I nursed him, in so far as I could, and was in that cabin with him for weeks, for Mrs Abbott feared contagion and could not risk herself and her own child. Nor would I risk Anne, who had put her fate in my hands. Good woman that she was, Mrs Abbott took over the care of Edward, and made sure Anne brought me what I needed and left it in the passageway. Other than that, it was myself and my groaning husband alone in that cabin. When a dangerous dog falls ill, who will come to help?

But I exerted myself in every way I had ever heard of to keep him alive, fighting the fever with cold cloths that became hot as soon as they touched his skin, tipping such remedies as were available into his mouth, until I was dizzy with exhaustion and felt the child inside my great belly shifting as if to complain.

I could not let him die. Bad though it was to be Mr Macarthur's wife, it would be worse to be his widow. There would be nothing for me in New South Wales, that place of prisoners and soldiers. There would be no genteel families whose children would need a governess. No one would need a seamstress. Possibly someone might think the widow would do as a wife, but it was unlikely. Mrs John Macarthur, pale, thin, with a sickly runt of a boy and a baby at the breast, would not be any man's first choice.

I would have to take a passage on the next ship back to England, along with Anne if she would return with me, and if my small dower could stretch that far. And then? I felt a choking panic at the picture of myself standing on the dock at Plymouth with my bags and boxes, Edward beside me and the new child in my arms. My mother would feel obliged to give us refuge for a time. I would embrace the half-sister I had met only at my wedding, and we would all say how glad we were. But they were strangers to me, and I to them. There would be no home to be made there.

With Bridie I might pass a few hours. We had exchanged letters just before we sailed, from which I gathered she was still at the vicarage and still unmarried, though putting the best face on it with cheery news about the doings of her brothers, as if marriage was nowhere in her thoughts. She and her mother would welcome me and Edward with the courtesy due a visitor. I would try to explain what would be unimaginable to them, the voyage to New South Wales and the voyage back again. When the visit was over, they would embrace me and speak vague phrases about another visit, and Edward and the baby and I would step out into the lane.

And Grandfather? He might forgive me, because forgiveness was what our Lord taught. But I would never again have the same place in his heart that I once had. I would always love him, would always for his sake pretend a faith I did not have. He would perhaps always love me, though with the grief of recognising I was a lost sheep.

But how would it be, sitting in his kitchen at the scrubbed table, his boots beside the hob, and Edward sulky and fearful at this bristly bearded stranger who could not warm to the child who was the living proof of my sin? Good old man, he would take me aside and with those eyes sharply blue in his sunburnt face he would ask me in what status I stood with my redeemer, and I would tell him he need have no apprehension for my religion. But those eyes missed nothing. He would know that I spoke a cunning form of words in which a lie can pretend to be the truth.

My most earnest and sleepless work did its job, and it seemed that Mr Macarthur would live. But those weeks exacted their price. At the point where he began to recover, I felt the pains of labour begin, many weeks before their proper time.

That daughter could not have lived. Yet she did live for an hour, this tiny bony creature, her blueish lips puckering at the air she was not yet ready to breathe, her veined eyelids flickering at the light she was not yet ready to see.

I knew she could not live, could not have lived even if I were safe at Bridgerule with the doctor beside me. Still I held her close and hoped. In that extremity I persuaded myself that a merciful Providence might hear me, and prayed. I held her frail body and willed the warmth and strength out of my own into hers, nothing existing in the world except the places where her skin touched mine, where life might flow between us.

Anne was clever enough not to try to clean her, or wrap her. Drew a shawl over the two of us together and sat quietly with us.

I called her Jane, in honour of good Mrs Kingdon. Whispered her name into her tiny ear, *Stay with me, Jane*, thinking that if she had a name she could not go. Perhaps I only said the words in my mind, but was sure she heard. *Stay with me, stay, stay.* But there was not enough skin, not enough shawl. No skin, no shawl, would have been enough.

When I could no longer pretend she still breathed, a great cold numbness crept in where hope had been. By the time the parson came I wanted no man near me. I was perhaps a little wild with him. I remember him going sideways through the doorway ducking his head, a spider in his dark clothes, the Bible big and black in his hand the last part of him to disappear.

The hereafter. I bowed my head with everyone else as Captain Marshall read the service over the canvas bundle, but I knew there was no hereafter. Only the here, the now, and then silence.

Still, each year on the day of her birth and death I think of Jane. Not with grief, not with regret or longing or rage, but in stillness, honouring the fact that there was, for a short time, such a person in the world.

No one would remember her, only myself and Anne. Now you, too, know of her. It eases my heart to record her existence. To tell you her name, and tell you that she was loved.

Mr Macarthur walked off the ship at Sydney unsteady, the pock-marks a nasty pink on the chalk of his cheeks. But walked.

FORM OF WORDS

I composed a glorious romance about all this for my mother. I would not lie, not outright. I set myself a more interesting path: to make sure that my lies occupied the same space as the truth. I am reading over the copy now, decades later, with admiration for my young self. I did not refer to the horrors of the nailed-up cabin. The dangerous Captain Trail became merely amusing: *a perfect sea-monster*. To reassure her of my husband's power to arrange things for my advantage, I let her believe that it was I who had requested an exchange of ship. *This exchange proved in every respect satisfactory to me*, I wrote, as if the event was no more significant than taking a turn in the garden.

It gave me a mocking angry satisfaction to fool everyone so well. But I well remember the bleakness of folding up that letter and sending it off. To be clever in quite that way is to live within a great solitude.

At the end of this letter full of sunny embellishments, there was a message to Grandfather. Since the day he had been told of my fallen condition I had not seen him. I had written to him several times, but received no answer. Now, aware of how unlikely it was that I would ever see him again, I longed to beg his forgiveness. He might refuse to reply to any words from his lost sheep, but I hoped he might soften enough to hear them. *Tell my Grandfather, with my love*, I wrote, *that I have not forgotten his counsel to have ever present to my mind the duty due by us to our Maker*. I was not claiming to believe or to obey his solemn instruction, only to remember it. Like a Trojan horse, my words would I hoped open the gates of his heart to the ones that I wanted so much for him to hear: *with my love*.

PART THREE

INCREDIBLE

It was perfectly true to say that the crops of New South Wales were flourishing *in a manner nearly incredible*. In fact the flourishing was so *nearly incredible* that it was not credible at all. The reality was that the wheat had shrivelled and died, the corn had parched up into rustling dry leaves on creaking stalks, the barley had not even sprouted.

The prisoners had been described as making *rapid progress in building*, and that was another lie in truth's clothing. Yes, many things were being built. It was not a falsehood to withhold the detail: that what was being built were hovels made of crooked posts holding between them a few woven wattles daubed with mud, sad messes that a dog would be ashamed to live in. Oh, and *rapid progress in building* also involved mildewed canvas, some structures nothing more than a sheet of sailcloth flung over a rope between two trees, the edges of the canvas held out with a few stones to make—you could call it *build*—a small triangular space that a human might creep into.

That first morning in Sydney, looking at the place we had been allocated—a low, mean house with a roof of palm thatch—I saw that Mr Macarthur doubted for the first time. His lip curled, his brows drew together. It was the forerunning, like heaped clouds on the horizon, of a tantrum. Next would be the hard-heeled stalking to the governor, the raised voices, the hand chopping the air. *My wife,* he'd say. *My son!* That would cut no ice with anyone. Who would bring his wife and infant to such a place, when with a little humility he could have been sitting in some cosy barracks in Gibraltar?

– Much better than I expected, I said. And look, so superior to that other one!

I pointed to where an officer's backside could be seen as he bent to enter a hut even meaner than ours.

— They must respect you, sir, I said, to have given us this one, and look how conveniently close to the stream it is!

Providence now caused a commotion in the next hut. The owner of the backside stood rubbing his head where it had met the lintel, which was now dangling like a broken arm in the doorway.

— We could do worse, you see, Mr Macarthur, I said in my gayest tones. Quickly, best take possession before his envy of our better fortune causes him to eye off ours.

That was an argument I knew would strike home.

Sydney Town was a dusty ugly angry place, a sad blighted bit of ground on which too many souls tramped out their days dreaming of somewhere else. It had been two years since a thousand prisoners and two hundred and fifty of His Majesty's marines sailed into the bay called Sydney Cove and stepped onto a wild shore of which absolutely nothing was known. Since then they had been cut off, with no supplies and no exchange of news beyond those first, *nearly incredible* reports.

ROACHES

At the start everything was shocking to me. The prisoners were men and women whose lives had made them vicious enough to steal the bread from each other's mouths, and who seethed and schemed with plans for escape or revolt, and proved endlessly ingenious in the slyness they used to rob the storehouse or their neighbours. Certain of the marines were not much better, and seemed to take pleasure in the floggings meted out, as if they were punishing the prisoners not for their crimes alone, but also for causing the marines to be in this place. There were times when the screams could be heard in every corner of the settlement.

Hunger and desperation, anger and fear, loss and yearning for home, brought out all that was worst in everyone. It was a place of sniping and slanders and barbed rumours, everyone watching each other for weakness and concealing their own. The narrow steep-sided valley where we all lived was like a crack in a wall where the roaches scrabbled over each other.

At first I dreamed confused shadowy tumults of fists and whirlwind. It shocked me when I realised that the horrors committed by the convicts, and inflicted on them, were no longer giving me nightmares.

PRESIDING GOD

The presiding god of this unhappy place was a narrow lopsided captain of the navy, Arthur Phillip, who had led that first fleet of ships into this harbour two years earlier. As a naval captain he was used to being God and king combined, but little in his experience could have prepared him for what the governor of New South Wales had to contend with: to be in charge of a thousand felons desperate for escape or rebellion, and a restless body of reluctant guards. Alone, with no one who could share his dilemmas, a year's sailing time from any advice, his was the loneliest of situations.

Still, the authorities had chosen their man well. In a place where goodwill was hardly to be found, he was a person of goodwill and generosity, and hoped that his own honourable ways would set an example. When the food stores had begun to run low some time before our arrival, he had decreed that every person in this hungry place was to be served exactly the same ration, so that the meanest convict's fare was the same as the governor's. He had gone so far as put his own private supply of flour into the common store for all to share.

It seemed, though, that the people were not interested in his selfless example. In spite of guards and floggings, every carrot and turnip was stolen as soon as it grew as big as a finger. There was no honour among those thieves. Shortly after we arrived, a prisoner in desperation had exchanged his only pot for a handful of rice, but no one would lend him a pot to cook the rice in, and he died of having wolfed it down raw. As for the marines, and the new arrivals of the New South Wales Corps, behind the governor's back they seethed with resentment at being as hungry as the prisoners.

The governor knew how doomed his task was, and managed it with more grace than most would have found possible. Still, he was only human, in a circumstance that demanded something more than human. It was common knowledge that he suffered a nagging pain in his side that all the surgeon's efforts could not relieve, which left him easily exhausted, easily harassed. Under the splendid gold buttons and despite the sword that hung by his side, he could be seen to be a man not far from collapse.

The card inviting Lieutenant and Mrs Macarthur to their first dinner at Government House made it clear that—owing to the shortage of supplies—every guest was expected to bring his own bread, so when we arrived we had with us our rolls from the regiment's oven wrapped in a napkin.

– My dear lady, the governor exclaimed, pressing my hand in his. This was an oversight. I intended to make you an exception to the general rule. I assure you, there will always be a roll at my table for Mrs Macarthur!

By chance we were the last guests to arrive. Captain Nepean gave Mr Macarthur and myself only the coolest of bows before turning away to Captain Hill. Captain Collins the deputy judge advocate was deep in conversation with the surgeon Mr White, and I exchanged a smile with Mr Worgan, the naval surgeon, who had been generous in lending me his books. A few of the officers of the marines stood in a group by the fire, including the always-smiling Captain Tench. He had introduced himself to Mr Macarthur within an hour of landing and had made himself useful to him in many small ways. It was evident to me that Captain Tench, like everyone else in Sydney Cove, had a fair idea of what kind of man Mr Macarthur was, and had made the wise decision to keep on the right side of him.

– If you see Captain Tench paying especially close attention, Mrs Macarthur, the governor said, it is because he has contracted to write a book about our little antipodean society.

Tench bowed and smiled. He was a small man when you saw him beside someone tall, but his sparkle and animation let him seem to take up more space than he did.

– Indeed, madam, he said, I could not resist the opportunity of writing the first account of this place—the novelty is such as to guarantee a readership, I fancy, no matter my sad limitations as an author. I am like the ant in the fable: I waste nothing, and store away everything that comes to me.

He might have said more, but the governor had moved on and introduced me to Lieutenant Dawes of the marines. He was a tall, awkwardly-put-together man who bowed but did not meet my eye.

– You are fortunate to meet Mr Dawes, the governor said, smiling to fill the pause in which Mr Dawes seemed not to realise that the niceties required a *Delighted, Mrs Macarthur*, or a *How d'you do, Mrs Macarthur*.

– Our Mr Dawes is by way of being our resident astronomer, the governor went on. So he is seldom able to join us after sunset.

Mr Dawes bowed again, but the moment for *Delighted, Mrs Macarthur* had passed, and there was a sense that all of us wanted to put him out of the obvious misery he felt at being the centre of attention.

– Now, Mrs Macarthur, the governor said, let us take our places. We must not keep the feast waiting!

At this there was a rustle of polite amusement, which Mr Macarthur and I had been in Sydney Cove long enough to join. Every man and woman and child in this place could look forward tonight to the same *feast*—a mean portion of salt meat, pease pudding, and bread. Captain Tench had told me, though, that the governor's gamekeeper bagged a wild duck or a kangaroo now and then, and I was prepared to hope.

The plates were put before us: salt meat and pease pudding, with a leaf or two of the plant they called Botany Bay parsley. A silence fell as the hope of duck or kangaroo was extinguished in each breast. Across the table I saw Tench's mouth twitch up in anticipation of what he was about to say.

– Ah, the daily diabolical morsel, he exclaimed, and the company laughed, even the governor.

– Thank you, Captain Tench, he said. That is a jest that will not grow old until the supply ships arrive.

Clearly he had heard it before, perhaps once too often. As if recognising the hint of asperity in his tone, he smiled and turned to me.

– Captain Tench is by way of being our Sydney Cove humourist, he said. In a place that cannot be said to lend itself to comedy.

He leaned down the table towards Tench.

– I can assure you, my dear sir, that I for one am grateful for your efforts.

Oh, those dinners! The grand gold-rimmed plates were splendid, but they dwarfed the small serving, and the salt meat was unpleasantly rank. Still, the motions of splendour were gone through. Wine in crystal glasses, though no more than a few mouthfuls. A dazzle of silverware, as if seven courses were waiting to be served. Damask napkins, silver candlesticks, a wordy grace boomed out by Reverend Johnson.

From the other side of the table I watched Mr Macarthur lay himself out to charm the governor, as only a man could for whom charm was another form of strategy. The governor's furrow-browed decency and his mild manner had stimulated Mr Macarthur's deepest scorn from the first, and in private he referred to him—a captain in the despised navy, rather than the army—as *our favourite auld salt* in his best mocking brogue. But now, with something of relief and something of contempt, I saw my husband smiling and nodding.

The governor would already have taken stock of who he had to deal with in Mr Macarthur. Would have heard from Captain Nepean of the events on board the *Neptune*. To my eye he was accepting Mr Macarthur's charm in the spirit in which it was given, and showed no particular warmth to him.

As befitted God and king combined, the governor was attended by a good number of servants: three or four convicts doing duty as footmen, buttoned into some version of livery, and a couple of convict maids. The housekeeper, a quiet woman in a neat grey dress, watched the prisoners' every move, visibly counting the silverware.

She did not allow the convicts near the governor, but served him herself. From my position beside him, I could see that something about the angle of her head suggested more than the courtesy of a servant, and something about his murmur of thanks suggested more than formal gratitude. The governor saw me watching.

— Mrs Brooks is a gem, he told me, smiling at the housekeeper. Has been with me for many years, on ships great and small, leaky and sound, is that not right, Mrs Brooks?

— Indeed I have, sir, she said, and a fortunate woman to be in your employ.

— Mrs Brooks is the wife of the boatswain of the *Sirius*, the governor explained. And is good enough to see to my wants on land as well as sea.

At the words *see to my wants* Mrs Brooks gave a slightly startled smile, and a tremor passed between the two of them, nothing more than a glance as fleeting as the brush of the least fleck of a feather.

I thought, ah, Mrs Brooks may be housekeeper, and wife to the boatswain, but if I am not mistaken she is something more as well.

COURTESIES

To me the governor was always kindness itself. After that first dinner he took the trouble to ease my life in whatever ways he could: by the occasional gift of fruit from his garden, eggs from his fowls, once or twice a wild duck. As soon as it was within his power, he made sure that the Macarthurs were given one of the better houses being built, so within a few months of arriving we removed into a brick house, with a sawn-wood floor and a shingle roof. Two decent-sized rooms, the larger with a fireplace, and more commodious services behind.

No doubt he calculated that it would be wise to keep on Mr Macarthur's good side by pleasing his wife. But his courtesies had real warmth about them. I believed then, and like to believe now, that they were not solely strategic.

WALKS

Anne had to be persuaded to venture beyond our house. Some mischievous person had assured her that he had—personally, with his own eyes—seen a pack of lions eat a man limb by limb in the next cove, and I could not convince her that he had been telling her a tale. In any case, I supposed it was possible. My assurances that there were no lions in New South Wales were accompanied by a silent proviso of *as far as we know*. On our walks she was full of alarms. Every stick was to her eyes a snake, every leaf hid a spider.

But I had to get out of the house—superior to our first, but still dark and damp—whenever I could find a reason. Edward provided a most welcome one, because in this place of privation he began to thrive. When we landed he was a few months beyond his first birthday but hardly bigger than a child half his age, a wan silent creature with eyes too big for his pinched face. Within a few weeks of landing he was walking strongly by the hand, prattling away, with cheeks that, if not quite rosy, were no longer the colour of candlewax.

On Mr Macarthur's instructions, our walks never extended beyond the last hut on either side of the cove.

– You must remember, my dear, this is not Devon, he told me, as if I could not see for myself.

We never walked without Private Ennis and his gun. Ennis, a cheerful lad, was there to protect us against the surly prisoners. Against the natives, too, who had begun to come and go in the township, protected by the governor's decree that they were to be treated with amity and kindness.

Mr Macarthur had no patience with the governor's sentimental views. He told me the natives were the lowest kind of savages.

He had been told they had no words in their language for *please* or *thank you*, no notion of husbands and wives, only male and female as with animals. He assured me that he had it on good authority that they were known to kill and eat their babies. He called them *our sable brethren*, and that never failed to amuse him, because for him *our sable brethren* were not in the least brethren. Those wild forest-dwelling people were about as much brethren, as far as he was concerned, as a parrot. But it was a way of denying fear, to wrap it up in an elaborate covering of irony.

The men were a little frightening, tall well-made naked warriors carrying themselves with assurance and authority, their spears held casually in their hands. The women did not frighten me, exactly, but their frank confident nakedness was alarming.

Our walks—each a slow procession, to keep pace with Edward—were always the same short round through the cluster of hovels among the trees, past sardonic prisoners watching Lieutenant Macarthur's wife and her entourage taking the air. Each day I would gravely ask Anne, would she prefer to walk from west to east today, or east to west? She would join the game, putting on a pantomime of solemn decision-making, and we would set off. Private Ennis had promised her, on his word, that there were no lions, and if one should be seen he would shoot it!

From the last hut on either side of the valley, we could stand and survey what was beyond the settlement. It looked to be a place that would repel a person on foot: rocky, lumpy, with outlandish trees, and bushes with leaves like needles, and grass with blades that—I knew from experience—cut your hand. It would be prickly and difficult, probably dangerous and certainly uncomfortable.

Every oak was similar to every other oak, but here every tree was a different shape from every other, telling perhaps how the seed had fallen on the stony ground and wound its way up. Some were ramrod-straight. Others sprawled. Some grew upright but with trunks twisted like rope. Mr Macarthur was like one of those. The seed had caught in some awkward thwarted way that shaped the man ever afterwards.

I played with Edward, fed him the dull food that was available, sent Anne away so I could enjoy the humble entertainment of giving him his bath. I sat by the aperture in the wall that did service as a window and attended to our mending. I read, and re-read, the few books we had.

But when the walks had been walked, the mending mended and the books read, the hours hung heavy. My hands itched to be doing. I remembered the blisters I had earned as a child at Grandfather's, chipping away with the hatchet at the wood on the block, or cutting the fleece of a sheep. Remembered the smell of dung, the smell of the farmyard, in this place where there were no farmyards and no dung. The prisoner who did the rough work for us languidly raked the yard at the back, taking an hour over it. I thirsted to snatch the rake from his hands, go at it till I could feel the muscles and bones, the sinews and joints all working away and the blood coursing strongly.

Life is long, Mrs Macarthur, that rough landlady had told me. *Life is long.* She had spoken more truly than she could have guessed, for in New South Wales each day was a succession of dull lengths. Yet we were surrounded by an entire new universe: the natives and their language, the plants, the birds, the outlandish animals. The very stars were so unfamiliar that Mr Dawes, as the governor had said, was kept too busy mapping them to appear often in the settlement. The place spilled its gifts out, an overflowing cornucopia of the new and the wonderful, but out of reach to Mrs John Macarthur on her ladylike daily round.

I could only *bide my time*, the one commodity I had plenty of, and wait for one of those corners that woman had promised me.

NEITHER PROFIT NOR PLEASURE

There were twelve hundred people in Sydney Cove, but, with the Abbotts sent to the secondary settlement at Norfolk Island, there was one woman, and one only, whose company was suitable for the wife of an officer: Mary Johnson, the wife of the parson.

Lord, but Mary was dull. Ignorant, narrow, and with a habit of bringing the Almighty into every sentence that was utterly wearying. Time spent with Mrs Johnson could offer neither profit nor pleasure.

Yet she was a good woman, and so was her husband, the two of them ministering to the sick from their own supplies and never despairing—in spite of all evidence to the contrary—of being able to open the hearts of the prisoners to salvation.

In their company I felt sinful, cold-hearted, selfish. When I mocked them in my mind I was ashamed. I recognised that their faith gave them a comfort I had never known, and that my mockery sprang out of a complicated feeling that I see now was very like envy.

Mr Macarthur had no time for the windy parson. Richard Johnson knew no Greek and little Latin, spoke the broad dialect of the Yorkshire farmer he had once been. Not a gentleman, then, and so of no account to my husband.

– Oh, my dear wife, he said, seeing me set out to pay a call on Mary. This is indeed a high price for our sojourn in New South Wales. Had I known the Reverend and Mrs Johnson were lying in wait, I might have reconsidered the plan!

He thought this excessively diverting.

One morning I found Mary pouring water on a pair of struggling rose bushes near her door. They must always have been there, because no ship had arrived that could have brought roses. But we had first come to Sydney Cove in winter, and now it was spring, and the bare stalks were bursting into leaf. Oh, to see a rosebush in this place of dull olive greens, drab greys, the strange hard leaves all around us! They were like old friends, friends promising that I would at last return to the place where roses grew at every door.

– My word, Mrs Johnson, I told her, your roses make me think of home!

– They are very fine, she said. But I must correct you. They are not *my* roses, Mrs Macarthur. These are God's roses.

I was rebuked like a child and like a child felt revulsion at the rebuke. Smug Mary stood smiling at me, certain that she would enjoy everlasting bliss in Paradise, while frivolous chatterers like Elizabeth Macarthur would not.

But it would have been discourteous not to visit Mary Johnson, and discourtesy, in this too-small society, would have had consequences. Besides, I learned at last how to squeeze pleasure from her company. Like her husband, she was from Yorkshire. When I lived in Devon, Yorkshire had seemed a place utterly foreign and remote, but viewed from the other side of the globe, Devon and Yorkshire were the closest of neighbours, and our memories of home were the one thing we could share. We told over the taste of raspberries, the look of mushrooms standing like solemn sentinels in the mist of early morning, the way the bushes in a field would be flecked with tufts of wool where the sheep had brushed up against them.

Mary did not yearn for home as I did, but she must have been as lonely for female company, and could put God aside now and then to indulge a little nostalgia for the sound of sheep's bells on a winter's morning.

I wrote to my mother and to Bridie. Here are the copies in front of me now, and oh, what dull things they are. Full of fancy phrases but empty of content. *At length I sit down to assure my dearest Mother that I am in perfect health, and to add to the pleasure of this circumstance both Mr Macarthur and my little Edward are in the full enjoyment of this blessing, and we only want, to complete the measure of it, to hear that you are equally happy and well.* They are like sentences out of a primer of elegant variations, or the circumlocutions of someone being paid by the yard.

Which, in a way, I was. It was proper for me to write to my mother and my dear childhood friend in a way that would show me to be perfectly content, and our situation to be splendidly promising. My letters would be shared with the neighbourhood. All the callers to my mother's house, and to the vicarage, would be entertained with Elizabeth's account of the extraordinary place she was now in. I wished no one to be anxious for me. What would be the good of that?

There was also the small matter of my pride. I would not have them pitying me.

At times, reading over what I had written and admiring the fiction of all that pious good cheer, I longed for a cipher known only to myself and Bridie. On the whole vast extent of the globe, she was the one person I would have liked to tell how things really stood, behind the bland words. But there was no way to say anything of the truth.

Mr Macarthur read the letters I wrote to Bridie and my mother. Knowing that, I took particular care to include nothing with which he might find fault. He showed me his letters, too, to his brother and his father. Like mine, they shone only the most golden light on everything. He never commented on how much more sanguine mine were than our reality, and I never voiced any doubt about his. In fact, more than once I copied verbatim some of his effusions, since that pleased him, and Mr Macarthur pleased was very much more agreeable company than Mr Macarthur displeased.

As I copied out his words I noticed that the word *we* never appeared. In Mr Macarthur's lonely cosmology, there was no such pronoun. Only *me, myself, I*.

Each morning, waking to the barbaric cackling of the laughing jackasses, I tried not to wonder when we would leave. The tour of duty of the marines was three years, of which half was already done, but the New South Wales Corps had been raised to replace them on a permanent basis. The length of our time here—our sentence, you might say—was a matter of how quickly Mr Macarthur could advance. Pay off the debt, put money aside and return home.

I had to accept the possibility that it might never happen. True, he was clever and ambitious. But he was also erratic, provocative, pugnacious, irrational. He could not be trusted not to destroy our hopes.

Lying beside him each morning, hoping not to wake him, I had time to think. My position—woman, wife—gave me no power, yet somehow I had to take charge of our destinies. The only way was to enter his needs and desires, the way I had watched him studying the needs and desires of the men he wanted to bend to his will.

What might he want, or be persuaded to want? What he always wanted, insatiably, was…I was going to write praise, flattery, but it was more delicate than that. He needed to be seen and heard. He needed attention paid: attention and respect. The son of the draper, the ensign on half-pay, had for so long been small in the eyes of others that he needed to be made big in his own. That was why he was willing to throw away any advantage in a frenzy of defending his honour.

It was up to me to be the cool one, the steady one. For our time here—for the rest of our lives, in fact—I would have to head Mr Macarthur off from the kind of destruction he had brought down on us, on board the *Neptune*. To do that I would have to learn how to match his cunning with my own. How to outwit him, how to outwait him. Judge when to disagree, but cleverly letting him think my argument was his own, and when to say *Oh yes, Mr Macarthur, what a capital plan*, and wait for his enthusiasm to burn itself out.

If I could learn those arts, there was some hope—something between zero and infinity—that we would be able to return home. If I failed, we might spend the rest of our lives in this exile.

From Mrs Borthwick I borrowed that little uptweaking of the corners of the mouth into a serene half-smile, conscious at first and then a habit. Only when alone could I relax, and at those unguarded times I knew the look on my face was a stern patience.

A HOUSEHOLD

It was one of the perquisites of this place that an officer might be assigned convicts as servants clothed and fed by His Majesty, and once we had a bigger house, Mr Macarthur took full advantage of this privilege.

On our arrival we had been assigned a grizzler called Sullivan. He was a young man but wore on his body the marks of a hard life, his face worn like an old shoe and his mouth full of gaps. Mr Macarthur told me he had been caught with the candlesticks poking out of his pocket while he stood there denying all knowledge of any such thing as a candlestick.

Some woman had given birth to him and had chosen what he should be called, but the only forename he would admit to was Smasher. He never met your eye. It was a habit they got in the way of, the felons, not to meet your eye. If you met the eye of your master, it could be that you considered yourself as good as he, and that would be *insolence*, and insolence was worth a dozen lashes. Sullivan always called Mr Macarthur *squire*, grinning a nasty knowing grin.

But when the *Atlantic* arrived with a fresh load of felons, Mr Macarthur was Johnny-on-the-spot down at the dock. An officer who cherished his position would not make do with one worthless idler.

William Hannaford was a big fair man with a frank open face. You could see the farmer in him even after the months in the hold of the *Atlantic*. Could see, too, that he was a cheerful person who would not go under, no matter what life threw at him.

– A sheepstealer, Mr Macarthur told me. But avoided the noose, God only knows how.

That first day, Hannaford was standing with Sullivan, talking away, and I heard the shape of words I knew to be my own. It was easy to picture him leaning on a stile in Devon with his neighbour, talking on and on, up and down the hills and dales of a conversation, the way Grandfather had loved to do. Sullivan looked around at me, and that made Hannaford look too, and get a fright when he saw me listening, Mrs John Macarthur in her good bonnet.

— I think you are from Devon, I said, trying to find the right tone to take with a servant who was also a felon. But the sound of those familiar vowels woke a longing in me to speak of the place we shared.

— Now which part, exactly?

This emerged somewhat more inquisitorial than I intended, and he looked wary. When I smiled—not too much!—I saw him ease.

— Well, Mrs Macarthur, he said, my farm was out of Bradworthy a piece. But an out-of-the-way place, you may not have heard the name.

— Is it over Milton Damerel way? I said. Or more towards Kilkhampton?

Seeing it all in the eye of my memory, the high-hedged lanes.

— More the direction of Sutcombe, Mrs Macarthur, he said. Solden Cross, then Honeycroft, and then my place in the elbow of Beckett's Hill.

A silence fell then, as we each saw those places in our mind's eye. He pressed his lips together and I could imagine the pain of regret. He would have lost whatever few fields he might have had, and perhaps a wife and children, and all the future that he would have planned, when he had put his hand to the horn of a sheep that was not his own, and been caught in the doing of it.

I saw too late that it was no kindness to exchange the names of places that had been his home, and bring to his mind the picture of them. With time and good fortune, Mrs Macarthur would return to those places. William Hannaford, transported for the term of his natural life, would not.

What was it like to make the decision that changed your life? To lead that sheep out of its fold, knowing that in the moment you put your hand to its horn you were a dead man? Was it despair, or a gleeful throw of the dice? To end here, standing on foreign dust, avoiding the eye of a woman who had the power, if she chose, to send you to the chain gang?

I might as well have asked aloud, for he launched into his story. I felt he had already told it many times, to anyone who would listen, as if telling it often enough might make it end differently.

— I had need of a ram, you see, Mrs Macarthur, he said. My sad little flock. I could see how to go forward, if only I had a good ram. Just the one.

He gave a rueful laugh.

— Other men had rams they wasted, rams they did not deserve. In my view.

He glanced again, as if to be sure I would not turn into someone who would have him whipped for taking liberties, but he saw that I had no wish to be that person.

— I'd learned from my father, you see, he said. What to look for. Got my eye on a fine ram at Crawley Fair. Far enough from home, and I had a cart and a thing on the back of it to keep him hidden on the road, had a story for the neighbours, a sad story about a fellow selling it off cheap, his wife had died. Oh, I had it all laid out. Have you ever, Mrs Macarthur, seen a thing in your mind so clear and strong you believe you have the right to it?

He did not want or wait for me to say if I knew that sense of right, but I did. It was that short time behind the hedge when I thought I had a right I did not turn out to have.

– How could I have been such a fool, he said in soft wonder.

No matter how many times he had told the story, it still sat in him undigested.

– But lucky, more lucky than a fool deserved, he said. To have in my hand the beast that belonged to General Watson, and him a good-hearted gentleman, he came to the judge, told him he forgave me and would not for the world see a man hang for the sake of one sad sorry foolish mistake.

See a man hang. His story made me see New South Wales in a new way. William Hannaford should be dead, and yet he was alive. But only here. The innocent body of England would not allow the canker of a sheepstealer to go on living in it, and without the fact of transportation, General Watson's pleas would have fallen on deaf ears. New South Wales was a prison from which William Hannaford would never return. But the very distance of this place, its very strangeness, even its unpromising aspects, might reveal itself as a door rather than a wall, and offer Hannaford a future.

HE HAS OFFERED

Anne came to me one afternoon a few months after our arrival, looking grave.

— Why so down in the mouth, Anne, I asked, thinking she was going to tell me that she was unhappy working beside Sullivan. I had seen the way he looked at her, leering from his broken mouth. I would happily send him back to government service if that were the case, hoped that was what she had come to say.

— I am ever so sorry, madam, she said.

— Sorry, I said. What is it, Anne, are you unhappy?

— Oh no, madam, she said, but sorry to be leaving you in the lurch.

Now she was blushing.

— He has offered, you see, she said. Private Ennis. And I have said yes.

Anne and I had gone through a great deal together, and I had come to rely on her, one dependable thread among so many that could not be trusted. And as Mrs Kingdon had promised, she was a morsel of home in this alien place. For a second the stuffing fell out of me. Imagine it, stoic Mrs Macarthur crying out, *Do not leave me!*

— Why Anne, I am delighted for you, I said. And what a dark horse you are, that I noticed nothing!

But I knew that I had noticed nothing because I had not been looking. Like another person in our household, I had never seen further than *me, myself, I*. Anne was not abandoning me. She was making the best of what fate had flung at her, turning a corner when it came towards her. She had been with me for exactly two years, for I had left Bridgerule in October and it was October once again. I looked at her now and saw what I had not bothered to notice before: she was no longer a gawky girl, but had become a young woman, her freckles and red hair maturing into beauty, with an air of calm cheerful competence. Private Ennis, that good-hearted young fellow, had done well.

– Dear Anne, I said, I could not be more delighted for you.

We embraced as we had done once before, but when we separated and she looked at me, I knew she could see through my delight to what lay behind it.

– I am sorry, madam, she said again, and hesitated.

I saw that she was trying to find words to tell me that she had seen at close quarters what my marriage was, and wanted to offer comfort. But there were no words, there could be no comfort, and all she could do was take my hand for a moment and press it between both of her own.

With Anne gone I was in something of a pickle, for I had no idea how to begin finding a woman I would want to have close by me, and I did not like the thought of some rough convict lass dealing with Edward.

Mary Johnson was like a great ear to all that went on in our little world, and within an hour of my conversation with Anne she sent word that I should call in. She ushered me into her cottage where her husband was in the front room, crouched over the table preparing his sermon, his Bible in front of him, a man in the ecstasies of composition. She and I went out into the second room, where a fire smoked on the hearth. Another woman sat there sewing, from her garments clearly a prisoner. When I came in she got awkwardly half to her feet and clutched the sewing to herself.

– Have you nearly finished, Agnes? Mrs Johnson said. Make haste there, finish up quickly.

– Yes, Mrs Johnson, the woman said, meeting no one's eye, and sat down again to her stitching.

She was not in her first youth, her cheeks were wan, her figure what you could only call skinny. In a word she was no beauty, and that had turned out to be the best for her, because Mary Johnson would not have shared her roof and the care of her husband and babe with a pretty prisoner. She was not too pious to be shrewd.

— She had a most frightful time on the voyage out, Mrs Johnson said in a whisper that would have been audible in every corner of the room. Most sadly lost a baby on the passage.

I kept my eyes turned away from the woman, who was bending over her sewing as if to disappear into it. Mrs Johnson marched on.

— I told her, Mrs Macarthur, and I am sure you would agree, that God has gathered up her little one into his bosom, and that she should not mourn but rejoice that her infant is gone before.

A sound came from Agnes, some small wordless utterance of protest or recoil. On her face was a depth of bleakness that it was an intrusion to witness. Like her, I knew how it was to lose a babe on board a prison ship. But I did not have to live with Mrs Johnson's conviction that the loss was a blessing.

— I could spare her, Mrs Macarthur, she said. There is a deserving woman come to my notice who could replace her. If you would like her.

I could already foresee how the debt of this woman's services would have to be paid in grateful warmth towards Mary Johnson. But it was a solution to my problem.

And she had made up her mind.

— Mr Johnson made enquiries as to her character, she said, and she has proved quite satisfactory. She is a thief of course, but not the worst kind, and clean in her person.

Agnes was keeping her head down.

— So I will send her to you on Saturday, Mrs Johnson announced. In the afternoon, will that suit, Mrs Macarthur?

MRS BROWN

There was a weightiness of spirit about Agnes Brown that made me unwilling to call her Agnes, so I found myself always addressing her as Mrs Brown, although to give a prisoner woman the courtesy of a Mrs was eccentric. Was she really a Mrs? Was she really a Brown? Neither, perhaps. It did not matter.

She did not speak more than she had to, though when she did I could hear, as I did with Hannaford, the sound of the west country. She seldom smiled, going about her duties with her outer self but as if the inner part of her were elsewhere. Her expression was always entirely neutral. Something must have taken place in Agnes Brown, in the getting of her baby, and the losing of it, and the crime that had brought her here, and her life as a prisoner, that had burned all distractions out of her. Life now flowed over and around her like a body of water.

In another world, Mrs Brown and myself would have been not mistress and servant but equals: she was clearly no cheeky trollop. I was curious about the crime that had brought her here, and could have found it out easily enough. I told myself I did not because it was of no importance to me, but the real reason was shame at the power I had to know her story, when she could not demand to know mine.

She had been with us only a few weeks when I surprised her with Mr Macarthur's Horace—left on the mantelpiece more for show than that Mr Macarthur ever read it—open in her hand. She put it down with a fluster.

– I beg your pardon, Mrs Macarthur, she said. It being so long since I looked into a book, that was all. But now I see it is not English, I beg your pardon, Mrs Macarthur.

Her fluster might have been the confusion of innocence, or the proof of guilt. I asked her could she read, then? And when she said yes, I took one of my own books and opened it at random.

– Would you be so good as to read a sentence or two, Mrs Brown? I asked.

– *In philosophy,* she read, *where truth seems double-faced, there is no man more paradoxical than myself.*

Yes, she could read, and I was ashamed.

A SAD BEAK

Never beyond the settlement, Mr Macarthur had said, but I was tired of that dull round of trodden earth between the dank huts. Once Anne was gone I allowed myself to redefine what might be meant by *the settlement*. Mrs Brown now came with me on the daily walks, and we were accompanied by Hannaford, Mr Macarthur having decided an armed guard was no longer necessary. Neither of them knew the bounds Mr Macarthur had set.

On the western ridge of the valley, convicts lived in huts and hovels and some in the caves that honeycombed the steep rocky side of the ridge, and between these improvised dwellings ran a complex of steep tracks. Near the top of the ridge was the last habitation, a cave with a flap of canvas hanging over its mouth. This was where Anne and I had always turned around and retraced our steps. The first time I walked with Mrs Brown and Hannaford, I led the way as far as the cave and then kept going as if it was our usual route. A convict woman pushed back the canvas and watched us pass.

– Mrs Macarthur, Hannaford said, and I glanced back at him. Oh he knew, I could see. Sullivan must have told him. And did I see on Mrs Brown's face, before it was hidden by her bonnet, surprise that Mrs Macarthur was leading the way beyond the permitted world?

– Yes, Hannaford? I said, and watched him hesitate.

– Begging your pardon, Mrs Macarthur, he said. It was nothing.

I turned and went on up the track, with the innocent look of someone to whom it has not occurred that she may be disobeying her husband.

At the top of the ridge, the damaged valley fell away behind us and the place opened out onto a broad platform of rock. As was never possible in the settlement, here we could see for many miles in all directions. To the east great fingers of land, furred with forest, lay across the path back out to the ocean, and to the west there was a panorama of unexplored peninsulas, islands, hills and valleys, with here and there the smudge of a fire telling of other lives, for which this land was not prison but home. Devon had never seen a sun such as this, slanting between the trees and laying their shadows down the steep slope, or this air, blowing in freely and making the bushes toss and the gulls wheel and cry.

– Oh, Mrs Brown said. My word, that is…

But did not try to finish the thought. I was not sure that the language had a word that could encompass such a place.

From the great open platform on which we stood, the ground fell away towards the water, and a thin track bent around rocks and trees. Down there somewhere was the observatory where Mr Dawes the astronomer lived.

I had no wish to venture down that track, but sat on a rock of a convenient height with a depression in it that was shaped perfectly for the human backside. Mrs Brown found another convenient seat, and Hannaford sat Edward down and the two of them began some quiet private play with twigs and leaves.

Here, as never in the settlement, I knew that nothing more substantial than air separated me from home. It was over there, in the direction of north-north-west. Beyond this unknown continent, beyond that ocean we had traversed, Devon must still lie under the same sun and moon, as Mr Macarthur had enthused, that illuminated us here: the difference being that there the first frosts would be heavy on the grass, while here warm days were giving a foretaste of hot weather to come.

If I were a bird like one of those soaring gulls, I could rise up and point my beak across all that wild land, all those tossing oceans, and glide down at last to perch on the gate of Grandfather's yard, where I had made that row of mud-blobs as a child. Like a Musulman facing Mecca, I turned towards home, the place that held every good memory of the past and every hope for the future. With the sound of foreign leaves rattling together and foreign gulls crying, I willed myself to remember the gentle breezes of Devon, the rustle of oaks and beeches, the twitter and warble of the shy birds of the hedgerows. It was the place I knew in my bones. I yearned for it as a child might yearn for its mother.

I had some superstitious feeling that if I told over the details of the place—the exact shape of the lane at Bond's farm, the exact murmur of the quiet silver river coursing through the meadow at the bottom of Lodgeworthy, the exact smell of rich Devon earth turned over beneath the plough—then I would be rewarded by finding myself there again one day. If I neglected those memories and let them grow dim, my punishment would be never to see them again.

It was as if I were inventing the idea of prayer, the comfort and need of it, from first principles.

To come to the present was a shock like cold water. I was here in New South Wales, with my backside cold from sitting on a rock that turned out, after all, not to be made for human comfort.

It seemed impossible to have any kind of conversation with Mrs Brown within the walls of the house, but out here I turned to her with the impulse to talk, one woman to another. Her cap had come off, she was holding it in her hand, and strands of hair danced around her head. She stood gazing out into the radiance of the afternoon, her face softened into something more like a smile than

I had yet seen. Out here in this wild gusty place she was quite unlike the woman who was always so shrunken.

– A glorious aspect, outlook, I said, stumbling and awkward with her. And how pleasant to be here taking the air.

– Oh yes, she said.

Then remembered.

– Mrs Macarthur, she added.

She put her cap back on and tucked in the strands of hair and I saw that my comment might have sounded like a reproach for her idleness. Her brow creased with the endless anxiety of the person whose time did not belong to her. Which I remembered, with a shaft of pain like a toothache, from those years at the vicarage.

I wanted to unravel our exchange and knit it up into a different shape.

– We are far from home, Mrs Brown, I said. You and I both.

Then realised this might appear to be the prelude to asking her how she came to be so far from home, and down that road I had no wish to force her. I hurried on.

– Where I was a child beside the Tamar, my father was thought to be on a mighty journey if he had to travel as far as Exeter, I said.

Saw that I had not left the thought behind at all, and went on again.

– He was a farmer, I said. Though he died when I was a child.

– Oh, she said. And if I may ask, Mrs Macarthur, where was the farm? Only my own father was also a farmer, in a small way of course. And died, as yours did. We were out of Whitstone two mile.

– Whitstone! I exclaimed. I went there with Grandfather, he bought a pig there. We were in Bridgerule, not so far away.

A silence fell while perhaps we both considered the possibility that as girls in pinafores we might have passed each other on the streets of Whitstone.

I guessed that her father's death had left her at life's mercy, as the death of mine could so easily have done. It was nothing more than chance that I had been protected by a loving grandfather, a playmate at the vicarage, and a parson generous enough to make sure that a Midsummer Night's mistake got patched up into a marriage. She had lacked those protections, I guessed, and a few harsh strokes from malign fortune had ended with her being a prisoner in a foreign land.

The unasked question hung between us.

— I am not a thief, Mrs Macarthur, she said.

Then frowned.

— No, I am a thief. That is, I was a thief...

She stopped.

— Yes, I thieved, she said at last.

She spoke like a person who in the gloomy reaches of sleepless nights told over the words she had to own, so that repetition might make a callus on the place that hurt.

— I thieved, that makes me a thief.

She was as disdainful as any judge.

— But I am no thief here, she said. I do assure you of that, Mrs Macarthur.

I could hear her breathing rather emphatically, and realised she was holding back tears. I wanted to touch her, but would not presume.

— Mrs Brown, let us put it that you were a thief, once upon a time, I said. But now you are simply a woman on a distant shore, where Christmas comes in summer, and other unexpected things may come to pass as well.

I was trying for a light tone to ease her through the moment, but was surprised at the words, springing out of some deep place in myself, where hope must live. I had hardened myself never to think about the shocking folly that had brought me here, the night of bonfire and darkness that was the start of everything else. I had shrunk my thoughts to nothing more than the present, the survival through one minute, then the next, so as not to see the large view of my life. Yet here were these words about *other unexpected things may come to pass* springing out of my mouth.

Mrs Brown heard it, the tremor of some greater meaning in the words, and met my eye, and for a space of time we were simply two women standing together in a great plain space swept by clean wind, eye to eye, sharing something without being able to put a precise name on that thing.

That expanse of rock, open like an eye to the sky, became the destination for all our walks through that first spring. Somehow it never became necessary to explain to Mr Macarthur exactly where his wife and son and servants went every afternoon as they paced away from the house.

Edward enjoyed our excursions as much as I did, for Hannaford knew how to play the kind of games that a boy of a year and a half enjoyed. Loved especially to be borne along astride Hannaford's shoulders, then swung down with a great swooping when we reached the open rock.

At home he suffered under the thumb of his father. With Mr Macarthur there was no indulgence. No weakness was to be shown and no complaint made. *None of that!* was what Edward heard from his father, crisp and snappy like a whip, if he grizzled to be carried, or took a tumble. *None of that, my boy!*

Yet he loved his son, after his own fashion. Called him Ned, his own soft name for the lad. And I had seen him watching the child sleep, with a look on his face I never saw at other times, a kind of mournful tenderness.

Tenderness, because Mr Macarthur was no monster, but a creature like any other, for whom love of one's children was as fundamental as breathing. Mournful, because, being sent away so young, he had never learned that a father could be as strict as required, while also being tender.

I surprised a softness, almost a pity, for this armoured man, when I watched him bending over the cot.

Nearly three years after the landing of Captain Phillip and his reluctant colonists, New South Wales was still nothing more than two specks that were Britain among the numberless miles that were not. One of those specks was the township at the head of Sydney Cove. The other, some fifteen miles inland, was called by the native name of Parramatta. Its better soil made it the centre of such agriculture as could be given the name. Convicts had been sent there to farm, and a barracks set up to keep order. There was a second house for the governor, and plans for streets to be laid out.

It was our good fortune that Captain Nepean had been sent for a time to supervise that settlement. After the first weeks of awkward encounters in Sydney, it had been a relief to know that he was fifteen miles away. Fifteen miles from me, and more to the point from Mr Macarthur. I had not forgotten the pages of notes my husband had made on board the *Neptune*, but I hoped most sincerely that he had.

When he heard Nepean was to be sent to Parramatta, Mr Macarthur gloated. He had been obliged to take his turn there, but had argued that his family needed him in Sydney, and his stay there had been brief. Among the officers there was a kind of shame in being obliged to do duty at the inland settlement. It was regarded as the province of a province, a place for men to rusticate who had no ambition, no sense of larger prospects: an antipodean Gibraltar.

But one night during that first spring he burst in to where I was sitting by a small fire, lit more for company than warmth. He was barely in the door before he was sharing his mighty rage, the angle of his head and shoulders caught in a peculiar tension, as if he were straining against a high wind.

– Now the knave is slandering me, he exclaimed. Back here in Sydney, and putting it about that I eavesdropped on him and Trail—actually listening at the door like a bootboy!

He was at the table in the corner, scuffling through papers, now turned with a sheaf of them in his hand.

– Look! Look here! I have it all, every lying word!

The papers from the *Neptune*, not forgotten as I had hoped. *Oh, why did I not burn them?* A chance gone that would not come again. Ten months had passed since the events on board, but the flame was redoubled by whatever troublemaker had reported Nepean's slander.

– But sir, I said, the events are in the past. A page has been turned. Much water has flowed under the bridge. What is to be gained now by telling over what is dead and buried?

I was treading in place, hoping enough tired figures of speech going on for long enough would dull my husband's rage.

– Oh, what is to be gained? You ask what gained?

His glare could have burned through brick.

– Oh, nothing, my dearest. Only my good name. My honour. Only such an insignificant bagatelle as that, my dear wife!

I had never been afraid of Mr Macarthur, but his savage tone silenced me.

– He must be brought to justice, he shouted. Let His Majesty see what lying dog is taking his shilling!

He shook the sheaf of papers at me.

– Look, I have it all here! What he said, what he did! Proof positive!

Separated a page and thrust it at me: I saw the words *monstrous and unprovoked* before he snatched it back and pulled out another.

– Look! Look what he said to me, and look here, my reply!

Verbatim! Noted *at the time*! You, my dear, can bear witness that I made a record *at the time*, you would remember that! If asked in court, you could swear to it!

A kind of congealing came over me.

— Bear witness, I said. But Mr Macarthur, I was not there, I did not see.

This was the wrong tack.

— So you will take his side! My own wife, betraying me!

— Not betraying you, no!

But there was no joy to be got in trying to deny something I had never said.

— In court, I said. So the officers—they would sit in judgment?

— No! No!

Mr Macarthur was smiling now, a rictus of glee.

— Not here, my dearest. No court martial could be enacted here against Nepean. None of these weaklings would find him guilty, no matter what the evidence.

He was calm now, saw a plain path ahead of him and, at the end of it, a destination he liked the look of.

— A court martial would not take place here, he said. It would, of necessity, take place at home.

To have come all this way, through such suffering, to turn around and go back after such a short time? On a fool's errand, Mr Macarthur laughed out of court? And where to then, for all of us, with his prospects in tatters?

Be steady, I reminded myself. *Be cool.*

— But Mr Macarthur, I said, very steady, very cool, you will not have forgotten that Mr Nepean's brother could ruin you at a stroke of the pen?

He said nothing. Ah, I had struck a nerve.

— And do not forget, I went on, that Nepean may also have

made a record of what went on. Bring his own witness. Mr Trail, for instance.

Well done, I thought, and took a breath for my next argument, but Mr Macarthur was ahead of me.

– A damned liar, he shouted. A pack of damned lies! I would be the worst kind of coward if I let them go unchallenged!

The words rang around the room. He struck a fist into a palm and strode from the fireplace to the table and back again, the blood high in his cheeks. I imagined Sullivan and Hannaford in their lean-to at the back, and Mrs Brown on her pallet in the kitchen, listening. Perhaps sniggering. I could imagine it of Sullivan. Could picture him later, regaling others with imitations of Lieutenant Macarthur's rage.

The evening was bursting out of the safe place where a husband made grand threats heard only by his wife. In the vibrating silence after the shouting, the thing was tipping into the irrevocable.

It was out of despair, not cunning, that I met his fury with my own.

– Oh yes, I said with savage irony. Oh, Mr Macarthur, how right you are!

What bliss to surrender, to let hot unconsidered rage sweep reason away.

– Naturally a man of *honour* could do no less!

Now I was shouting too. Let them hear! What did it matter, now that we were set on this course to disaster?

He shot me a sharp look and I thought he might turn on me, and in my reckless ecstasy I would almost have welcomed a blow rather than this dance of words. But he had heard no mockery. He was silent, staring into the fire. He leaned forward in his chair, moved a foot, pursed up his mouth.

Something had shifted in the room. In borrowing his own

wildness and displaying it back to him, I had accidently hit on a way to make a pause in its headlong flight.

Outwit, outwait, match his cunning with your own.

– Do not delay, Mr Macarthur, I said. Go to the governor tomorrow, in the morning.

He blinked as if surprised. As well he might be.

– The governor's sense of justice will of course make him put aside his friendship with Nepean's brother!

Mr Macarthur cleared his throat as if about to speak. But he said nothing, only picked up the poker and rattled it around in the fire. A piece of wood burst into flame and lit up his face so I could see his thrust-out bottom lip very prominent as he considered. *Stop now*, I told myself. The crackle of the fire, taking new heart from its rearrangement, was the only sound.

I began to find the quiet unbearable and pretended to have heard Edward calling out. Went in to him, sleeping soundly with both hands flung up beside his ears. I stood over him watching and listening. The house held its breath: the air in the rooms, the servants, the wife, the infant, all waiting.

When I returned to the other room, Mr Macarthur was warming his backside at the fire.

– Well, time we were in bed, my dear, he said, as easy and calm as if he had not, ten minutes earlier, been shouting loud enough to be heard by the whole household.

He went out of the room and as I followed him I glanced at the table. The papers on which he had enumerated every inflammatory detail of what had taken place on the *Neptune* had been gathered together and folded over themselves, the fold flattened under a book. Not put away, not exactly hidden, but set aside.

Captain Tench was not the only officer planning to publish an account of his time in the colony. Captain Collins and Mr White were doing the same, although, knowing those men, I thought that Tench's would be by far the most entertaining of the three. But their example gave Mr Macarthur the idea that I should do something similar. He had in mind a narrative under some such title as *Journal of a Lady's Voyage to New South Wales in the Year 1790 by Mrs John Macarthur.* I saw him imagining the powerful men in Whitehall reading it. Oh, young John Macarthur, they would say, a fellow to watch, and a wife with a fine turn of phrase. Make him a captain instantly!

Of course, it would not be an authentic journal, being written so long after the events it described. Our voyage had begun in November of 1789 and it was now a year later. But that was no obstacle: Mr Macarthur told me to lard it with dates to give it the appearance of immediacy.

— Who will ever check, my dear wife, he said, that it was the thirteenth of the month and not the fourteenth when you boarded the *Neptune*?

I had no idea of myself as an author and not the slightest wish to re-live that ghastly journey. I tried to beg off, claiming that I had been so ill, et cetera, et cetera, that it was all an unhappy blur in my memory. But then he brought out the notes he had made, that little folded bundle, and gave them to me as an *aide-mémoire*.

— My dear, he said lightly, I assure you I will not let you off this task!

Now I saw his real motive. He had not forgotten his plan to punish Nepean. Mrs Macarthur's *Journal* would stand as a record

149

of the iniquities he had suffered. Being written by another, it would have the appearance of an objective account. It was the *long game*, the game he liked best.

I could see he had his terrier teeth into this idea of the journal now and would not let go until I yielded. Refusing would only make his jaws grip harder. My best chance was to make the *Journal of a Lady's Voyage* so dull that the terrier would look for something tastier.

The first pages were as dreary as I could have wished. Of what interest could it be to anyone that we had hired a boat at Billingsgate, or that the ship lay at Longreach? Or that I could find no more original effusion about the cliffs of Dover than to say that I was struck with their *formidable and romantick* appearance? I went into uninteresting detail about the white-painted houses of the Dutch at the Cape, the remarkable sight of Table Mount, the amount I had to pay for a cabbage in False Bay.

But intent though I was to be dull, I could not rob our voyage of all interest. A duel, a nailed-up passage, the mid-Atlantic removal from one ship to another: these things had to form part of the account. And once or twice I caught myself writing with some humour, some wryness. Here I see that I described that ferocious storm in the Bay of Biscay by declaring with deprecating understatement that *I began to be a coward*. In fact I was crouched in the corner of the cabin keening like an animal.

Of all that had passed between Mr Macarthur and Captain Nepean and Mr Trail I wrote only in the most general terms. I made it as obvious as I could to a careful reader that I was not present when the soldier was struck, or the sergeant insulted, or the short rations discovered. I had heard only Mr Macarthur's account of why our access to the deck was nailed shut, and never knew the truth of how Captain Nepean was persuaded to arrange the transfer to the *Scarborough*.

What actually took place between those three difficult men was never recorded and must remain a mystery. The only certainty is that that frightful situation—which if not caused by Mr Macarthur was certainly made worse by him—must have brought him satisfaction. Some gripe deep within him was eased by the story he could tell himself, of one honourable man holding his head high, alone against the world.

When I had written as far as the price of a cabbage at False Bay, I showed my work to Mr Macarthur. He read the pages with approval and wanted to keep them, but I insisted that he give them back so I could bring the account of the voyage all the way to Sydney Cove.

My task now was to spin out my writing so that it would never be finished, could never be added to the tinder of Mr Macarthur's documents. As Penelope had woven and unpicked, woven and unpicked, I would make sure I never finished the *Journal of a Lady's Voyage*.

But as I began to write about Mr Macarthur's illness and the loss of Jane, I found sentence after sentence pouring out from some central part of myself that had been silent until now. I heard my own voice speaking back to me from the page, a voice I had never heard before, speaking of things that I had not quite let myself recognise that I felt. Grief and despair, yes, I knew of those. The surprise was the extent of my rage. At Mr Macarthur, of course. But beyond him was the cruel machine, made up of laws, of beliefs, of the habits of generations, that robbed a woman of any power to shape her own destiny.

For a dangerous week I kept those pages in the depths of my

sewing basket, a wild creature hidden from view. But a wild creature that I loved, that was my dearest companion. I woke up each morning with a private warmth at the thought of it waiting there for me.

Then I came to my senses. I kept the genteel first part, so safely tedious, but burned the pages after the Cape. I promised myself that I would live long enough, keep my wits and my freedom, and come at last to write it again.

Just the same, it was painful to tear up those pages and slip them into the fire. In them I had discovered how to make a companion where life gave you none, and heard—for the first time, it seemed—my own true voice.

Like every toad and every fly, dullness of prose has its purpose in the great scheme of things. Having read that vapid first part, Mr Macarthur never asked again about the *Journal of a Lady's Voyage*. The surviving pages remained in a tidy package until I untied the ribbon around them an hour ago. Reading them over, I mourn the ones gone for ever, the truthful ones that I did not dare keep.

AN AGREEABLE PUZZLE

Mr Worgan the naval surgeon had become my library. He was the only person here who had filled his chests for the voyage with books rather than flour and tobacco and liquor. In this place of deprivation, and although he was mocked for it, he still felt the bargain to be a good one, and was generous in lending them to me.

– Food for the soul, Mrs Macarthur, he said. The body can make do, but the spirit can perish. As we see all around us.

It was not only books that he considered more important than tobacco and rum. He had also brought a piano, but in his own rough quarters he had nowhere to put it. When we had removed into our bigger house, with its larger rooms, he suggested he might bring the instrument to us to be looked after. In return he would teach me to play it.

He was a jerky, ill-at-ease sort of man. His awkwardness had a way of communicating itself to me, and the idea of sitting beside him on the piano stool while I floundered did not appeal. But I could not decently refuse, and I came to look forward to the lessons, because as soon as Mr Worgan's fingers touched the keys, all his strain left him and consequently so did mine.

I could see he was a poor lonely fellow, as hungry for company as I was. He was full of praise for my musical efforts. In truth I showed no tremendous aptitude, but the puzzle of learning the notes was an agreeable stimulus, and so was the praise he gave. Our lessons became a pleasure, with a certain amount of laughter from both of us at some of the sounds I produced. I practised assiduously, not from any great wish to excel, but because fingering my way laboriously through *Foote's Minuet* and *God Save the King* filled many a gaping hour.

How strange it was to hear the plinking notes of Mr Worgan's little piano in this rough place. They travelled no distance before they were swallowed by the robust music around us: wind among leaves, the cries of birds, the shouts of men commanding other men. The bland tune of the *Minuet* came from another world altogether, and what would have been pleasant enough in a Devon parlour, here was somewhat ridiculous.

Mr Macarthur liked the idea of a wife who could add musical skill to her accomplishments, and he encouraged the lessons. But the piano stool was narrow, and there was a certain intimacy about four sets of fingers together on the keys. My husband had never yet had any reason to mistrust me. I had always been careful never to be too interested, or too interesting, with other men. I admired Celia Borthwick for the way she created a life-within-a-life with a man not her husband, but Mr Macarthur was no sluggish George Borthwick. The merest brush of suspicion would have let loose a cascade of horrors. During the lessons with Mr Worgan I began to feel uneasy, picturing how the hilarity and praise might sound to someone standing outside the room, listening.

As if he had seen the same picture, one afternoon without preamble Mr Worgan began a story.

– I could not accept who I was, Mrs Macarthur, he said. Not for the longest time.

I nodded, wondering what he meant.

– But met a man.

He laughed, a blurt of joy.

– Oh, a man indeed! And I had to. Face up to the fact of the matter. Who I was. What manner of man. He had no doubt, had always known who he was. By trade he was a dancing master. Carried his kit in the tail of his coat, scratched out a tune on it for the pupils, he had never had any agonies about it, taught me to lose the agonies too.

He glanced at me to see if I had understood. Yes, I had. I knew enough to know what he was telling me.

– And then? I asked lightly. What happened then, Mr Worgan?

Even as I was asking, I wished I had not, because there was something about this story, and the way Worgan was telling it, that made me feel that there would be no *then*.

– No, forgive me for asking, I said. There is no need.

But he spoke over me.

– He was set upon, he said. Somewhere in Liverpool set upon, a commonplace story, and died. Quickly, I was told by a fellow who was with him. Knocked down and struck his head on a doorsill and never moved again, for which mercy I would thank God, if I thought God had men like him and me in His eye.

He touched one of the keys, his finger stroking the ivory.

I was not going to share that story with Mr Macarthur but, in the spirit of forestalling a difficulty, I made a casual remark implying that Mrs Brown was always in the room with us during the lessons. Mr Macarthur saw where I was heading and let out a great crow of laughter.

– Oh, you are safe with that fellow, I assure you. Our dear Mr Worgan could be trusted with a whole harem of wives!

Mr Worgan never mentioned the dancing master with the kit in his coat-tail pocket again, but that companion was with us as he patiently corrected my notes, praised me beyond my abilities, and, when my Ceylon ran out and could not be replenished, brought me the wild leaves they called sweet tea. It was a rare friendship in that loveless place.

A HOUSE WITH A PIANO

All the officers in Sydney Town were lean and their uniforms were inclined to the ragged, but there was a pleased look about them, a brightness of eye that came from satisfied appetite. It was perfectly understood that, as a privilege of their position, they had their choice of doxies among the female prisoners. More than once I had glimpsed a woman backed up against a tree with her skirt around her thighs and a man in an officer's jacket nailing her with stroke after stroke. Like the endless supply of convict servants, the endless supply of women who were in no position to refuse was one of the compensations for being in such a post.

But it seemed that the officers hankered for more sedate pleasures too, and once we were moved into our larger house and the piano was installed there, the Macarthurs' became a place for them to visit. Mr Worgan was always there, usually with Captain Tench and Lieutenant Poulden, and half a dozen others visited whenever their duties allowed. Captain Collins came now and then, and the governor put in an occasional appearance out of courtesy, but knew better than to spoil the officers' fun by joining them too often.

Perhaps they were drawn to the rituals of home: a mother with her little lad running about, teacups and a silver teapot, a song or two. Perhaps something else, too. Every one of those men knew the story of Captain Gilbert, destroyed by his run-in with Macarthur. Gilbert would never again command any ship bigger than a rowing boat. And of Captain Trail, who was followed now by a stream of vitriolic letters to his masters. They all knew it was a good idea to stay on the right side of John Macarthur.

Whatever their reasons, I was pleased to preside over such a cheerful tradition, and tried to put out of my mind what I had glimpsed of the more animal aspect of these men.

I could not always offer my visitors real Ceylon, or a glass of Madeira, but for the moment the threat of actual famine had retreated. One or two government storeships had at last arrived from England, and private ships now and then called in to Sydney Cove with goods to sell, if you had the money to pay their exorbitant prices. In any case the officers did not seem to mind when the Ceylon ran out again and the teapot was full of the native tea. With Worgan rattling out tunes one after the other as men called out their requests, it was a convivial scene on the afternoons of that first spring. There were a few occasions when so many officers called on me that I needed to send Sullivan to neighbours to beg more chairs, and one celebrated afternoon when, from a shortage of cups, visitors had to take turns drinking their tea.

Someone—Captain Tench, probably—instituted the tradition of raising our teacups in a toast. The first was, of course, *To His Majesty the King*. The second was *To our return*, or *To Home*. In the silence when we drained our glasses, I guessed that every soul in that room was picturing his own particular *Home*. I saw the glistening eyes and knew the same tears glistened in mine.

My own image of *Home* was of a snug farmhouse nestling in the gentle hand of a valley somewhere in Devon. Fat sheep gorging themselves on fine pasture, and a narrow silver river purling tirelessly down the middle of the picture. Edward was there, and myself, comfortably thickened, in a striped pinny with a pocketful of pegs. Somehow there was no Mr Macarthur anywhere in the picture. I strained to see more clearly, but the vision had the flimsy improvised nature of a dream.

Mr Macarthur encouraged these afternoon tea parties, which surprised me until I understood that for him they were strategic rather than social. A gathering of his fellow officers allowed him to assess what pressures might be brought to bear on the men who made up his world: to read their characters, discover their strengths and weaknesses. When the time came for persuasion, he would be in a position to turn what he knew to his advantage.

With some of the more wide-eyed younger men the matter was as straightforward as to offer to relieve a temporary pecuniary difficulty.

– My good fellow, I heard him say, as a fellow officer and a brother Mason, I declare that no man shall call after you for a shilling!

Then he could tweak that string any time he pleased.

Others were hungry gape-mouthed fish for flattery: lay it on like butter on a scone, Mr Macarthur said, he will wait for more. Some could not bear the silence of their own company, were ready to fall in with any slander or scheme, if it meant agreeable company.

As for Captain Tench, the way to his heart was to flatter him as an author. He relished the best gossip, the colourful marvel, the grotesque detail. As he entertained us with some amusing anecdote, he refined each phrase, trying this word rather than that. We were his first audience, the stories he told us his first drafts.

We were an appreciative audience. Beyond the pleasure of Tench's company, none of us wanted to be presented in his account as anything other than amiable.

It had tickled his fancy in the beginning to refer to the modest space where the piano sat against the wall as my *ballroom*, but the joke had worn a little thin. On the day of the shortage of teacups, he found a better idea and raised the cup he was temporarily in command of in an ironic toast.

– My dear Mrs M, he cried, you must be congratulated!

We knew that he was about to try out on us a new witticism

that we would read between covers at some time in the future.

— In this remote corner of the universe, my dear lady, you have created an article never so much as dreamed of in this quarter of the globe, he said. An antipodean *salon*, worthy of Mayfair or the fifteenth *arrondissement*!

Mr Macarthur's features were not well adapted to laughter, taking on a strained screwed-up appearance that could almost look like tears, but he roared the loudest and clapped Tench on the back.

Mr Dawes, the astronomer, was one of the few officers who never visited my brilliant *salon*.

— He is a species of genius, Tench assured me. Though he lives like a hermit, or a monk. Now and then I interrupt his solitude by visiting him out at the observatory, however, and he does not object, for he enjoys the pleasure of trouncing me at chess. He is a mathematical prodigy, as well as a chap fluent in those useful languages Latin and Greek, and for whom the intricacies of botany are an open book.

Tench's friendship with Dawes was one of those surprising pairings that arise between people unalike in every way: Tench the suave man of the world and Dawes the social dunce. Still, Tench did not mind joining the amusement when other officers called Dawes *His Holiness*, in reference to his erudition and the fact that Dawes and the reverend went out together on the harbour to fish.

But I glimpsed a chance to get out of the jammed-in township where I was going mad with boredom.

— Would Mr Dawes give me some lessons, I asked Tench. Would he have time, do you think, to instruct me in some easy stars, or easy botany?

— For you, Mrs Macarthur, he would be delighted, Tench said. He loves nothing better than to share his knowledge.

I remembered the Mr Dawes I had met that night at the governor's, a man in something close to agony at having to manage what was required of a social event, and wondered whether Tench might be taking the liberties permitted to an author.

The immediate danger of my husband setting off a conflagration with Captain Nepean seemed to have receded. But there were two fiery men involved in the situation, and now that the captain was stationed in Sydney again, there would be few hopes of advancement for the Macarthurs unless both flames were dampened.

On board the *Neptune* I had regretted not having any direct dealings with Mr Trail or Captain Nepean. Had I been able to judge for myself how things stood, I might have been able to influence matters for the better. A few of the right words at the right moment might have been all it took.

Sydney was too small a place for people to avoid each other, so my path frequently crossed Captain Nepean's. He bowed, looking somewhere over my head, and moved on. I greeted him as warmly as his rapidly retreating back allowed, wondering each time whether I could find a pretext that would force him to stop and exchange a few words. None had ever suggested itself until now, but my *salon* offered a possibility.

– Why Captain Nepean, I exclaimed, all innocence, next time I saw him. On Wednesday a few officers will be gathering in my parlour and Mr Worgan has most obligingly undertaken to entertain us with some musical items. Will you not join us, sir, for a pleasant afternoon?

He was forced to stop, and courtesy required that he look at me as I made my speech. I was somewhat flurried and hasty in my anxiety to get his attention, but threw my most appealing smile at his wariness. I watched him consider the invitation, backwards and forwards, inside and out, his shapely, rather feminine mouth pursed.

– Mr Macarthur expressly desired I should invite you, sir, I said. He wished it most particularly.

A bald-faced lie, but Mr Macarthur was not present to deny it.

– After all, sir, you and I were born on the banks of the same lovely river, and whenever there is a gathering at our house there is always a toast to the Tamar.

It was true that Captain Nepean and I had been born by the Tamar, and so had Mr Macarthur. But no one at my *salon* had ever thought to toast the river. That was my own dainty invention.

– It would be an honour, sir, to have you join us in celebrating our home.

Captain Nepean was nobody's fool. While I was uttering this elegant speech, he was making his own calculations, concluding perhaps that it was better to have Mr Macarthur flattering than accusing. Wise fellow that he was, he pretended to let my charm work its magic. The shapely mouth finally smiled.

That evening I told Mr Macarthur of the meeting on the bridge.

– Captain Nepean asked after your health, I said. Very sincerely and with great consideration.

Since he had suffered that African fever, Mr Macarthur had been prey to episodes of painful joints and digestive upsets, so my embellishment struck the right note.

– He recommended the sweet tea, I said, and was most concerned to see you recover.

Whether Mr Macarthur believed me or not, he saw the sense in the fiction. When Captain Nepean arrived the next Wednesday afternoon, I made sure to spin at least one of the inventions into a truth.

– To the banks of the Tamar, I called out, lifting my teacup and meeting Captain Nepean's eye so he was obliged to join the toast.

– The banks of the Tamar, everyone echoed, Captain Nepean as loud as anyone, and he turned to the man next to him—Mr Macarthur, as it happened– and the two men touched the rims of their cups together in mock ceremony.

Across the room I caught the eye of Captain Tench, whose eyelid dropped for a fleeting instant. Under cover of the general hubbub he mouthed across the room to me. Was it *Well done?*

From then on, at least on the surface, it was as if the poisonous events on the *Neptune* had never taken place. Watching the two men chuckling at each other's wit, I reminded myself that *on the surface* was all that was needed. If the surface could hold, like a brimming glass of water kept together by its own density, perhaps Mr Macarthur would at last leave the idea of a court martial behind, and our fortunes might prosper.

I wrote to Mother, in a way that approached second or third cousin to the truth, that Captain Nepean was *truly a good-hearted man*. Oh, beware that word *truly*! I did not scruple from adding that *He has, I believe, a great friendship for Mr Macarthur*. Can a claim be called a falsehood if it is hedged around with *I believe*?

Behind that *belief* was calculation. The streams of connection ran deep in Devon and Cornwall. If my mother was convinced that Captain Nepean had *a great friendship* for her son-in-law, that rumour could pass up and down the banks of the Tamar. It could reach the ears of old Mr Nepean of Saltash, who might then relay it to his son Evan, sitting behind some splendid spread of mahogany in Whitehall. Evan Nepean would accept it as nothing less than the truth, and might make a mental note that this Macarthur must be a good fellow, and should be promoted forthwith. To give wings to the rumour, I told Mother that, should Mr Macarthur gain a promotion, *our thoughts will be in some measure turned again towards 'Old England'*.

But why the elaboration of syntax, the coy inverted commas? Looking at the page now, I see that the idea of England was coming to seem like a story that I knew about, could name the parts of, loved, but did not quite believe. The inverted commas were a way of removing myself from the place. They made the idea of England something jocular. Even ironic.

Captain Tench loved to nose out things that were not obvious to the eye. He would no doubt add them to his book in due course, but he had a more immediate use for them: as a currency that he paid out to chosen confidants. He had read my husband's nature well, and knew what kind of coin bought his friendship.

In a quiet corner of my *salon* one afternoon just before our first Christmas he sat with my husband and myself. A ship had recently arrived with supplies, so that, until the colony's stores ran low again, our cups contained actual Ceylon, and there was even a dish of scones, though no butter and little jam. The brief respite from famine gave the afternoon a festive air. Captain Tench glanced around to signal that he was about to share a secret. Mr Macarthur leaned forward.

– I happened to see the governor yesterday, Tench said.

– Yes? my husband said.

Like every good storyteller, Tench would not be hurried.

– We spoke of this and that, he said.

He smiled and gestured a greeting at someone on the other side of the room. Was he enjoying keeping Mr Macarthur on tenterhooks? His eyes met mine. *Oh, you tease, Captain Tench!*

– The governor was not well, he said. But you know how valiantly he conceals his weakness.

– I do, Mr Macarthur agreed. And your business with him? Was it satisfactory?

– Oh yes, Tench said indifferently.

Mr Macarthur cleared his throat and Tench saw he had better tease no longer.

– I suppose you have heard about Mrs Brooks, he said, lowering his voice.

– Mrs Brooks! No, what should I have heard about Mrs Brooks?

Mr Macarthur was torn between his annoyance at being ignorant of a fact that was, from Tench's tone, common knowledge, and his hunger to be enlightened.

– Oh well, only that, how should I say it, she is…

– She is what? Come, man, out with it!

– Mrs M, Tench said, smiling at me, you will have to forgive me, I seem to have got myself somewhere that a lady might not…

– Oh, Captain Tench, I said, as eager as my husband to hear about Mrs Brooks. Do not be concerned! It is a well-known fact about me that I am inclined now and then to suffer a sudden fit of deafness. In fact I feel one coming on at this very moment.

We were all smiling now, Tench looking at me with appreciation.

– Well, only that Mrs Brooks is by way of being companion to the governor, he said. And since Mrs M is suffering her fit of deafness, I can speak plain: she has been the governor's *inamorata* these last seven or eight years.

Mr Macarthur was avid for more.

– There is a wife, Tench said. Back in Hampshire. But not suited, it seems.

Was it my imagination, or was he pointedly not glancing at me?

– Mrs Brooks is the wife of the bosun of the governor's ship, he said. So there is nothing strange about her being more or less everywhere the governor goes.

– Oh, our saintly governor! Mr Macarthur said. I had wondered, of course. Whether perhaps there was some convict lass or other.

166

– Indeed, Tench said. Any thinking man must have asked himself that question. The governor could have his pick, but would risk scandal. He has chosen wisely, would you not agree, in having a comfort who can travel with him in plain sight?

– Oh, canny! Mr Macarthur said. A wily fellow, our esteemed governor. And what of Brooks the bosun? How is that managed? In the usual way?

Made the finger-rubbing-thumb gesture.

– That I cannot tell you, Tench said, smiling, so it was impossible to be sure whether he *could* not tell, or *would* not. But certainly Whitehall is not privy to this facet of His Excellency's domestic arrangements.

He knew my husband well. Knew that the way to make an ally of him was to share with him the kind of gift he valued above any other: a secret that could destroy another man. They chuckled together about the situation as if it were the most amusing thing imaginable.

How dare they snigger! Without a companion, anyone in the governor's position must have collapsed from strain and loneliness. The men in Whitehall might not have been able to name that companion. But they must have guessed that she existed, those masters of the blind eye. They produced masses of paper that appeared to nail every detail of New South Wales, yet as far as all that paper was concerned, Deborah Brooks was nothing more than wife to the bosun of the *Sirius*. The future will not have any inkling about Mrs Brooks, except that I am telling you now.

Her situation was not an enviable one. Mistress of an important man was a sleight of hand that condemned her to live in a lonely netherworld somewhere between lady and disgrace. But there might be compensations. The frisson of the double life she and the governor were obliged to live must keep the affection between them

167

at a pleasurable rolling boil. I had a pang of envy, remembering that moment I had caught, of the governor glancing at Mrs Brooks as she served him at table: that softening, that hardly perceptible warming of his lean features.

Oh, what it must be like to have a man look at you with such warmth and love that, try as he might, he could not keep his feelings hidden!

RISING TO THE SPARK

Like my husband, Tench clung by his fingernails to the status of gentleman thanks to his officer's rank, a good-enough education, and gallant manners, when rumour had it that he was the son of a dancing-master. Only he, it seemed, in this place of meanness and malice, remained a friend of all. Even Mr Macarthur had a good word for him. I thought of him as some fluid insinuating creature, a ferret or an otter, with his delight in his own sinuous being, and the way he could twist and flow out of anything. Something in me rose to the quicksilver quality in Tench: sly, quick with innuendo, every look and utterance lingering and teasing. In his company I felt myself to be large of spirit, amusing, warmly alive along every vein.

On the afternoon of our first Christmas Eve in New South Wales, with Worgan hammering away at the piano with such effect that two people in the corner by the fireplace could converse in private, I laughed freely, frankly, pleasurably, at some witty bit of nonsense Tench had come out with. Our eyes met, his very brown, full of warmth and fun, and I allowed myself to wonder what it would be like to be with him, woman to his man.

He was not handsome, his face too narrow, his chin with its black beard-shadow too weak, his eyes too close together. But the flicker and dash of his spirit drew me. With someone like him, I knew, I would be a different woman: less cautious, less conscious of every word and gesture, more reckless, more inclined simply to enjoy each moment.

Tench caught the unguarded glance. I saw the same question in his eye. *What would it be like?*

I was rehearsing some repartee for Tench's banter, but Mr Worgan was all at once beside us, somewhat flushed. He touched me on the elbow and when, interrupted in mid-word, I glanced at him—with irritation, it must be said—I saw that he was meeting my gaze in an insistent way.

– Mrs Macarthur, he said, may I call on you to turn the pages for me? Captain Collins has requested *Lovers' Garland*, and I fear I will not do it justice without an assistant.

Dolt that I was, I must have looked put out, but thank the Lord I was alert enough to see his eyes move, and I saw what he was warning me of: Mr Macarthur watching me with Tench.

– I would be delighted, Mr Worgan, I exclaimed, left Tench discourteously without a word, and stood beside the piano to turn Mr Worgan's pages—which he could perfectly well do by himself— and then allowed him to show off my accomplishments by sitting at the instrument and picking my way through *Foote's Minuet*.

For the rest of the afternoon I made sure the roomful of men was between me and Captain Tench. Still, I remained conscious of him, knew exactly where in the room he was standing, and knew that he was equally aware of me.

On the day of the first *salon* of the new year Captain Tench required my advice on the matter of repairing his silk cravat. We stood close by the window together, holding the worn little pretext up to the light.

— Mrs M, he said, I feel I must tell you something.

He laid the cravat on the window ledge and smoothed it with his finger, the satin obediently rippling under his touch.

— Tell me something, Captain Tench? What can you mean?

Was he about to press his case here and now? With my husband on the other side of the room? What would I say, if he suggested whatever a man who had glimpsed willingness might suggest?

— Something you should be aware of, Mrs M. Something of significance. To you.

I felt myself colouring up. I was afraid to have him go on, but hungry for it too. *What would it be like?* Perhaps as it had been all that lifetime ago with Bridie: two people pleasuring themselves and each other with affection and humour.

He watched my fluster and I caught the amusement in his eye. In a blaze of understanding I saw that this was what he had intended. As I had watched him toying with Mr Macarthur, so he was toying with me.

My fluster and willingness were snuffed out in an instant. Tench held out no affection and humour. He was nothing more than a flirt.

— So what is it that you must tell me, sir?

He caught the change in my tone.

— Only the name the people have for your husband, Mrs M, he said. Which, God willing, he will never learn.

– A name? A name for my husband?

– Jack Boddice, he said in a whispering hiss. Behind his back they call him Jack Boddice.

I had braced myself not to show any surprise, but I could not stop my face slackening in nasty glee. They were no fools, those people who watched us. *Apprenticed to a corset maker.* I had never believed that old rumour but, true or not, the barb could not have been more precisely sharpened to puncture the fragile pride of the draper's son.

My glee was nothing more than an instant, smothered as soon as sparked, because I saw that Tench had set me a test. How loyal was I to my husband? Some hint of *aha!* about him told me that he had glimpsed that flash of unguarded glee. If he had asked that question, he had his answer.

Captain Tench was more than a flirt. He was dangerous.

– Oh, I am shocked, I said. How vile they are!

I did not only mean those who so cleverly skewered my husband. I had looked on Tench as a friend. Had allowed myself the weakness of that private question. *What would it be like?* Now there was a sickened hollowness where warmth had been.

– Shocking indeed, Mrs M, he said, but watching me, waiting for more. I had to step backwards as quickly as possible, away from the dangerous moment where I had exposed myself.

– And am I Mrs Boddice, I said, or have I earned a name of my own? And you, sir? What name do they have for you?

– Oh, who knows? Tench said with a laugh. Who knows what you and I are to them?

You and I. There was an intimacy in that casual pairing of us together. If *Jack Boddice* had been the first test, *you and I* was the second.

All at once Mrs Macarthur needed to attend to her duties as

hostess, bustle out to the table, call for more hot water, splash tea about into whatever cup was close by, call praise to Mr Worgan for his playing, demand an encore.

Jack Boddice. I wished Tench had kept that to himself. The words were in my mind now. Their presence was a dangerous crack, creating weakness where I needed strength. It was a weakness that Tench had brought about, and deliberately.

As I sat, smiling, patting my knee in time with Worgan's new tune, I looked anywhere but at Tench. *What would it be like?* I was amazed that I had ever had that thought. It had flickered, like a sheet of lightning shifting through cloud. Now it had passed. I did not want Tench.

But the flicker had been there. A great deal had seemed to die in me, in the time that had passed since Mr Macarthur and I had looked at each other along a tube of air in the Bridgerule parsonage. Now, in wonder, I realised that it had not altogether died, only gone into hiding.

Captain Nepean had only ever been a temporary commander of the New South Wales Corps. The more senior officer, a Major Grose, had been delayed in England, but in the new year his ship sailed into Sydney Cove and he took up his duties.

Mr Macarthur lost no time in inviting him to his wife's *salon*. Mrs Brown and Hannaford were put to it to make everything shine that could be shined, everything straightened that could be straightened, and to hide whatever could be neither straightened nor shined. Sullivan swept the front path with a great show of sighing and putting a hand to the small of his back, was made to rake the yard at the back in case the new commander needed the privy.

Major Grose was a big flaccid thin-lipped gentleman with a faraway look in his eyes. At first I assumed that look might be the wise caution of a person lately arrived in a new place, but I came to see that he was listening to the various aches and pains of his body, damaged in the American war and still not properly mended. He was an affable fellow, but my judgment was that under his splendid expanse of chest he was a small irresolute soul, easily persuaded by whoever spoke to him last. He seemed to me to be the perfect product of the great chain of military rankings, obedient to those above, overbearing to those below, a man born for mediocrity and well suited to it.

He accepted with alacrity the chair Mr Macarthur offered, and did not budge from it the whole afternoon.

– I suffer from want of vigour, Mrs Macarthur, he said. To tell the truth, at any time of the day I would be happy to assume a horizontal dimension.

As commander of the Corps, Major Grose was deputy to the governor, and would step into his shoes should Arthur Phillip be unable to fulfil his duties. I watched Mr Macarthur exerting all his charm that afternoon, and when I bade Major Grose goodbye—he made a to-do of taking my hand and bringing it to his lips like some old-time gallant—I congratulated myself. *So far, so good.*

– My word, Mr Macarthur said, when the door closed on our last guest. Oh my very word, I have got him eating out of my hand!

– But kissing mine, I said, meaning that I had played a part in our success, but Mr Macarthur was deaf to that. I did not insist. The more he thought Grose's compliance was due to his own cleverness, the better he would like him.

– He was most struck with your clear-sighted view of things, I said, thinking of a useful phrase Mr Worgan had taught me: *ad libitum.*

– He told me most particularly how relieved he is, I went on. That he has at least one officer with such energy and knowledge of the place.

The major had not quite said that. Not in so many words. Not in any words, as a matter of fact. But there are times when to speak a thing is to make it come to pass, and I hoped this would be one of them.

Mr Macarthur laid himself out to offer every assistance to the major, who was soon announcing to all who would listen what a steady, hardworking and loyal officer my husband was. Oh, an old head on young shoulders! The major's right-hand man! In short order, Mr Macarthur was made captain, and paymaster to the regiment.

Promotion, in Mr Macarthur's view, was well and truly overdue: welcome but unremarkable. But paymaster was a coveted position, offering its holder many opportunities for lining his own pockets. For the first time since we had arrived in New South Wales, I began to believe that the move might, after all, have been for the best. If Mr Macarthur's erratic temper could be kept in check, there was a chance that we could make enough in a few years to return to England with a modest sufficiency of wealth.

Mr Macarthur's thanks to the major was to privately christen him the Dear Dunce. In public he referred to him as the DD, and if asked what it meant, explained that it meant the Dynamic Deputy.

A SPREAD OF ACRES

Land was the one commodity in which New South Wales was rich. This was a whole continent of it, and every acre without sign of ownership, like a flock of sheep on a moor with no markings on them. The governor, and behind him the thrifty gentlemen of Whitehall, was intent on the colony producing its own food. Crops were growing on a few of those infinite acres, but in amounts as yet too small and unreliable to compensate for the irregular supplies from England. Famine was never far away.

The governor had it in his power to grant land, and had made a few modest gifts of acres to such ex-convicts as held out hope of becoming productive farmers, to any marines who wished to settle, even to a few soldiers who preferred farming to soldiering. Anne had told me that she and Ennis had hopes of a little land out towards the Kangaroo Ground. Reverend Johnson had had land from the time of his first arrival. Tench reported that the reverend was the best farmer in the colony—had mistaken his vocation, in fact, since his potatoes were so much better than his sermons.

The one class of person barred from being granted land were the officers of the New South Wales Corps, for it was the view of the governor that the duties of those men lay in keeping order rather than farming. To Mr Macarthur this was a travesty. To give land—for nothing!—to men who were common thieves and withhold it from His Majesty's officers! It was tyrannical! It was—that dangerous word—an insult!

He ranted all one evening as we sat by the fire, treading around and around the same outrage while I bent over my needlework. Finally I tried to turn the mood.

– So do you plan to become a farmer, Mr Macarthur? Go up

against the reverend to see who can grow the biggest potato?

– Do not mock me, wife, he said. I would not expect you to have a grasp of the situation, but pray do me the honour of trusting that I do!

Any sentence beginning with *but* would send the evening over an edge from which I would eventually have to retreat, and since only sentences beginning with *but* occurred to me, I said nothing.

– At home, for even the worst estate, I would be paying not less than ten pounds an acre, he said. Here the price is much more favourable, being nothing more than a little fawning on the governor.

The worst estate. Now I understood. Mr Macarthur's father had paid for a gentleman's education, and paid or borrowed again for the officer's rank that allowed his son to insist on being *Esquire.* But only in New South Wales could Mr Macarthur hope to have the true, undeniable proof of the gentleman: a spread of acres, an *estate.*

– A thinking man, he said—ah, he liked that phrase of Tench's!—can take a long view, in the light of which the land of New South Wales, no matter how worthless now, is a species of currency, and might be exchanged in the future for the actual pounds, shillings and pence that will help us return to England.

Mr Macarthur had gone so far as to pick out the place he wanted, which was at Parramatta. He had previously despised it. Now he was full of reasons why Parramatta was a canny choice. The better soil meant it would soon become the centre of the settlement, Sydney Cove simply its port. The governor could see that: it was why he had a second Government House there. A shrewd judge—such as he himself—could see that this was the moment to seize the opportunity, quietly and without fanfare, before others got the same idea.

– I have paced out the spot for us, he said. Superior even to the Auld Salt's. A perfect aspect, with an eminence ready for a splendid house. Imagine it, my dear: yourself at Parramatta, the lady of the best farm in the colony!

And quicker than a mouse across a room, the picture came to me, of escape. It was that word *farm*. I could see it clear: a comfortable cottage, a garden full of flowers, the sun streaming into quiet rooms. A run full of hens, perhaps a milk cow, my own peas and beans off my own vines. And slow-moving quiet country days.

Quiet, yes—because I knew that I would have the place to myself from time to time. Land, though the *sine qua non* of a gentleman, and irresistible when it could be got for nothing, would always be secondary to Mr Macarthur's real passions. He would soon tire of a farm. His nature needed a density of other men to work on, like yeast on sugar. He would always be drawn to the centre. Sydney, that bustle of intrigue and scheming, was where he could use what he knew about his companions to get what he wanted. He had barely finished saying *Parramatta* before I had decided this might be the way to find a little daylight in the closed box I had been in since my marriage.

But I dared not urge. Urge Mr Macarthur and he would go backwards.

Parramatta! I exclaimed, allowing a note of incredulity into my tone. Are you serious, Mr Macarthur? Have you considered how far it is? How isolated ? The lack of female company?

He glanced at me and I feared I might have gone too far.

– I have not, my dearest wife, noticed any great yearning on your part for female company, he said. I am sorry, my dear, to take you away from your society here, but we must keep our eye on the target.

Ah! *Society*: was there another motive? It was a mark of how contagious his way of thinking was, that a new thought flickered through my mind: my husband might be pleased to have his wife far from the town. No woman, no matter how lively, could maintain a *salon* in the country wastes of Parramatta. He had not caught any whiff of my thoughts about Captain Tench. I was sure of that. But it was his nature to dart ahead to future possibilities. One woman surrounded by men vying to divert her was a circumstance he might come to mistrust.

From that thought another blossomed. My husband was one of the few officers in the place who did not have a pretty young convict doxy. Might he not feel that he was entitled to that pleasure too? To have a lady-wife, safely tucked away at Parramatta to breed his dynasty, but also to enjoy the pleasures of more frivolous company in the town?

It was a welcome thought.

I pretended to sigh, a sigh that I pretended to stifle. Took a few stitches at my needlework, gave the angle of my neck a victim's humility. Allowed myself a little moue of displeasure.

– I am surprised, Mr Macarthur, I said. But I see you have your reasons. Of course I bow to your judgment.

– Oh my dear wife, do not be down in the mouth about it, he said. Picture us there, taking our ease before a splendid marble fireplace! Perhaps blue wool for the livery, do you agree? Brass buttons with a crest—what would you say, my dear, to an olive wreath, plain but distinguished?

– Oh, not a made-up crest, for heaven's sake, Mr Macarthur, I said. I am not ashamed to be a farmer's daughter.

– My dear wife, he said. I watched him casting about for a final persuasion.

– I will name the place Elizabeth Farm, my dear, in recognition of your perfection as a wife.

I smiled as if I was tempted by this bauble.

– I am sure it will work out for the best, Mr Macarthur.

Mr Macarthur was not planning to do anything as straightforward as simply to ask for land. Oh no. This would require what Mr Macarthur so enjoyed, the long game. Piece by piece, he would put his troops in place for a subtle flanking movement that, when it closed, could not be resisted.

The first, innocuous, move was for him to be appointed commander of the Parramatta garrison. A word in the DD's ear would achieve that. The commander would be obliged to live at Parramatta, naturally, and at this point Edward and I would be brought up from the rear and pressed into service. An officer could live in the rough quarters at the Parramatta barracks, but a lady such as Mrs John Macarthur, with a young child, could not be expected to do so. Nor could she be left alone and unprotected in Sydney. The only way out of this dilemma would be to provide the Macarthurs with an establishment appropriate to a family, close to Parramatta. The government had too many demands on its resources to do this, but should Mr Macarthur be granted a parcel of land, he would do the rest.

I was divided in my sentiments between scorn, that he would use myself and Edward so ruthlessly, and satisfaction, that the escape I hoped for might come to pass.

At no point did my husband imagine that the governor would refuse him. It was only a question of whether he should settle for fifty acres or hold out for a hundred. His ambition, like a fine hunter with a pink-coated gentleman on his back, sailed untroubled over any obstacle in the present, landing lightly on some sweet pasture in the future.

I was not so sure. The governor had right on his side. Why should men who were paid to do government service be given land in order to farm on their own account?

The first part of the plan went off without a hitch: the DD named Mr Macarthur as commander at Parramatta, to take up his duties when circumstances permitted. But the Auld Salt was not such an easy mark. He let it be known that, while Major Grose could make such arrangements of his officers as he thought best, permission to grant land was in his own hands, and on that matter he would not be budged.

I expected the familiar rage, or its polar opposite, black gloom, from my husband, but he brushed the subject aside when I questioned him, as if nothing could matter less. To have his will denied by another threatened to damage the very deepest, most brittle part of his sense of who he was. Rather than feel the pain of failure, he grew a crust over it.

– Oh, trust me, I have it in hand, was all he would say. The Parramatta estate will be ours, have no fear.

Still, there was a pulled-tight feeling about him, and that night in the darkness he came at me with an extra edge of force that was not quite the right side of painful.

One evening a short time later Mr Macarthur joined me in the parlour, perching on the front of his chair to lean forward persuasively.

– Now tell me, Mrs Macarthur, he said pleasantly, what is there that folk here would give any money for?

There was a trick in the question, I knew, and would not please him by giving an answer that would be wrong. But the evening would not progress until I obliged.

– Well, flour and axes, I said. Shoes. Pots. Tobacco, nails, rope. I thought of my own particular needs.

– Tea and sugar. Anything and everything, in fact.

– Exactly! He sat back, electric with excitement, his fingers drumming on the arm of the chair.

– Word has got around among those villainous greedy captains. Go to New South Wales with a hold full of—as you put it—anything, and you may charge what you please.

That was true. On the few occasions when a ship came into the cove there was an undignified rush for its goods, and those with money—the officers and a few others—were prepared to pay the scandalous prices demanded. Who knew when the next ship might call in? But the generality of the people—the ticket-of-leave men, the emancipists, the small farmers—continued to go without.

He leapt up and began pacing. His steps were crisp, then muffled, as he walked from rug to boards and back again.

– What is needed is for us, the officers, to charter a ship ourselves and send it to the Cape, he said. Take the selling of the goods into our own hands. Break the monopoly of those rogues.

I took a breath to say, You would simply be replacing one monopoly with another! But he was forging on.

– With a boatload of goods to sell we cannot fail to do well.

The ghost of *five hundred pounds* floated in the air between us.

Mr Macarthur himself proposed—using the regimental purse—to make the largest subscription. He would keep the records, oversee the selling of the goods, allot all of the subscribers their returns. And in there, you could be sure, he would have a finger in every part of the pie, underneath where no one could see. Mr Macarthur might be the grandson of the Laird of Argyle, but when you stripped away his haughtiness he was the son of a shopkeeper, and it was profit and loss he understood.

There was only one problem. Like everything else in the colony, the scheme would require the governor's permission, and the terms of his appointment prevented him giving it. Whitehall's instructions were that the governor was not to engage in any trade, or permit others so to do, within the area of influence of the East India Company.

But Mr Macarthur was confident. With due modesty, he explained the true genius of his plan: that it exploited the governor's own goodness of heart. Hunger and want still haunted the settlement, men and women falling down in the street from lack of nourishment. A man such as the governor would not refuse the offer of a boatload of supplies.

– Mark my words, he will yield, my husband said. And, once having gone against his instructions, he will be...vulnerable.

He savoured the word like something delicious. In the fire's glow his face was light and dark by turns, shadows moving across it as he paced, and the spit glistening as he smiled a wolf's smile.

– I will have him on a plate, he said. He will find himself in no position to refuse us any reasonable request.

– Such as fifty acres at Parramatta, I said.

He shot me a look: part surprise, part contempt.

– My dearest wife, he said. Indeed you would make a poor villain. Fifty acres! A hundred at the least.

He showed his very eye-teeth in his pleasure.

– Why not two hundred?

When, in due course, the *Britannia* returned from the Cape, there were casks of flour and rice on board. There were axes and cooking-pots, hoop-iron and paper. But the bulk of its cargo was barrel after barrel of that most profitable commodity, rum. Five or six hundred per cent was the premium the officers asked, and in a place where none but the officers' consortium had the capital to import, that was the price people would pay. Profit flowed in on every hand. Mr Macarthur already planned another charter, and his fellow officers were happy to go along behind him filling their pockets. He made sure that they were all involved in the great volumes of liquor pouring off the ships into the gullets of the people. All were equally implicated, should anyone ever make any trouble about it.

In among the casks of rum on the *Britannia*, space had been made for a few comforts that found their way to the Macarthur household. Oh, that first, exquisite cup of Ceylon after a time without! I drank the tea, I closed my eyes in pleasure at the sweetness of the sugar. I will not try, in this account, to make myself look better than I was. If I had to suffer the fact of being married to this man, I was craven enough to enjoy the fruits of his villainy.

Mr Macarthur leaned hard on the Dear Dunce to lean on the governor on the matter of that piece of land at Parramatta. The DD was willing enough, but the governor continued to hold out. That good man could be seen every week to be more harassed, more beset by problems of which the demanding Mr Macarthur was only one. The pain in his side never left him, and his honourable nature was being flayed by the malice all around him. He did not seem to mind hunger, but his footing on the world was undermined by ill will.

It was a matter of general knowledge that he had requested permission to return to England. Had in fact done so more than once, with increasing urgency. Sooner or later that permission would be given, and he would sail away. At that point the colony would be left in the hands of his dynamic deputy until a new governor arrived.

Mr Macarthur was in no hurry. There was nothing more patient than my husband with his mind made up. There was something not quite human about it, like a hawk hovering, hovering, hovering, only its cold eyes watching.

Writing home to Bridie I was conscious that she was still unmarried. She had hinted in one of her letters that there had been a person of interest to her after Captain Moriarty, but evidently nothing had come of it. *To write of what has been would afford you no pleasure*, she wrote, *and occasion me some regret.* She referred to herself as an *old maid*, as though she had given up all hope. This caused me some anguish for my friend, like myself in her middle twenties, with the cul-de-sac of spinsterhood rushing up at her.

In my letters I had never wanted to emphasise the difference in our circumstances, and of course there was no way to tell her privately how little there was to envy in my marriage, so I had written nothing on the subject of my life as Mrs Macarthur. I had hoped that the silence might itself be a hint to her of what I could not say. But that had caused trouble. Mr Macarthur had seized a letter and flown into a rage that it was so full of news about the settlement, its geography and economy—hardly the letter of a wife at all!

Next time I took a different tack.

I have hitherto in my letters forborne to mention Mr Macarthur's name, I wrote, *lest it might appear in me too ostentatious.*

Oh, you ingenious woman, Mrs Macarthur!

No two people on earth can be happier than we are, I went on. *Mr Macarthur is instructive and cheerful as a companion and universally respected for the integrity of his character.*

Like so many of Mr Macarthur's own utterances, this one had that fleck of truth. Yes, he was *instructive*. Wearyingly, obnoxiously so, instructing me in the matter of ships' bonds, of the value of a Spanish dollar, of the amount of water in rum that would alert a drinker to its dilution. I hoped *no two people on earth* would signal my real feelings to Bridie. Surely, knowing me so well, she would recognise that hyperbole as excessive to the point of irony. As for *universally respected for the integrity of his character*—well, that was fiction pure and simple.

Still, though marriage was no bliss for me, it was not a cul-de-sac. My life would surely offer me corners to turn, and although they might turn for better or for worse, there was a degree of freedom—or at least of elasticity—in having those corners in one's future. There could be no corners for an ageing spinster in Bridgerule.

My dearest friend, I wrote impulsively, *abate a few of your scruples, and marry. Few of our friends, when I married, thought that either of us had taken a prudent step. I was considered indolent and inactive: Mr Macarthur too proud and haughty for our humble fortune or expectation.*

Then I saw that I had been overly frank. Between the lines the truth could be read: I was telling Bridie that even a bad marriage might be better than no marriage. Quickly—I remember the way my pen hastened over the page—I went on to smother that truth.

Judge then, my friend, if I ought not to consider myself a happy woman.

Oh, you poor dear woman! Reading it now, I see that I was determined to write the plain lie: *I am a happy woman,* yet I could not quite make myself do it. There it is, in that *ought* and that complication of negatives: the truth peeping unbidden through clouds of falsity.

I plunged on. *Whenever you marry, look out for good sense in a husband. You would never be happy with a person inferior to yourself in point of understanding.*

This letter was becoming too complicated in its purposes: I was writing for Bridie's eyes, but I was writing for Mr Macarthur's too, and my grasp on the two-headed truth I was trying to tell was slipping. In the course of a line or two, I see that I talked myself around, from urging Bridie to marry at all costs, to warning her of the misery of being yoked to the wrong man.

Watching my instructive and cheerful husband's mouth soften as he read, I saw that he was right in his view that it was not possible to lay flattery on too thick. Had a pang of something like pity, that there was some need in him so great that it made him as willing to believe as any of the men he mocked. He was armoured in every way. Yet there it was, exposed to the air: the emptiness in him that craved to be seen and heard and yes, loved.

He did not complain again. And it did no harm to boast. All of Bridgerule would read the letter, and if any of them still spoke of me with pity, let this lying letter silence them.

PART FOUR

SOME BASIC STARS

When Mr Dawes finally appeared in my parlour in the hot days of our first January, it was clearly because Tench had waylaid him in the street and more or less dragged him in.

– May I introduce our resident genius, Mrs M, Tench exclaimed. Our scholarly stargazer, Mr Dawes the astronomer. Mr Dawes, may I introduce Mrs John Macarthur, our very own Madame d'Epinay.

Mr Dawes was frowning in response to Tench's raillery and looking about with an air of desperation. I was going to ask who Madame d'Epinay was—the quickest way to tell Mr Dawes that I did not see myself in any such company—when Tench spoke again in his amiable, amused way.

– Mrs M has expressed a great desire to learn some easy astronomy, Dawes, he said. I told her, I had no doubt but that you would be delighted to give her some instruction in a few basic matters, stars, planets and so on.

Mr Dawes shot me a startled look.

– Delighted, he said. I would be delighted, Mrs Macarthur. Some basic stars, yes, I would be delighted. Yes.

In spite of so many words of delight, it was easy to see that *yes* was purely for lack of immediate reason to say *no*. In Tench's mouth my wish sounded frivolous, even insulting, and I tried to explain.

– I am a woman of scanty education, Mr Dawes, but great curiosity, I said. Here we are, in a place so strange that the very stars are unfamiliar. It would seem a missed opportunity to remain ignorant of them.

All the same, I was wondering if the idea of astronomy was a mistake.

He slid me an oblique glance at the word *curiosity*. What train of thought took place I could not guess, and what he might have said will remain a blank, because Tench did not wait.

– That is settled then, he said. Next Thursday, let us say, in the afternoon, for the first lesson! And I will be most interested to hear what progress you make, Mrs Macarthur, so Dawes, do not fail to inform me.

Mr Dawes raised a hand like an awkward benediction, murmured something I did not catch, turned away and was gone.

– Never think our Mr Dawes is impolite, Mrs M, Tench said. But his orbit is a fraction eccentric as it passes through our merely human sphere.

The Thursday afternoon following, Mrs Brown and Hannaford and Edward and myself set off as usual towards the top of the western ridge. Arrived there, we stood in the wind blowing in from the sea, looking down at where that faint foot-track through the bushes made its way towards the unseen observatory. I had a sudden compelling hunger to be alone, as I had never been, in this mighty landscape.

— I wonder, Mrs Brown, if it might be best for you and Mr Hannaford to stay here with Edward, I said. You will still be in sight of the settlement.

The truth—my longing to be alone in this broad airy place—seemed too eccentric to be spoken, but Mrs Brown's wishes were travelling in the same direction as mine.

— Yes, Mrs Macarthur, she said, the track will be too rough for the lad's little legs.

No rougher than the track we had just climbed, we both knew.

— And he is heavy to carry, when he gets too tired to walk back up, I said.

It was not a difficult matter to carry the child. Hannaford would swing him up onto his shoulders as easily as putting on a cloak. But between Mrs Brown and myself we had put together some semblance of a story.

It would never happen in Devon, but this was not Devon.

I took only a few steps before there was a sudden falling-away of everything familiar. I knew Mrs Brown and Hannaford were barely out of sight. But it was as if I were the only person on the surface of the globe. Human life receded into irrelevance. Here I was in the kingdom of leaves, rocks, wind. The branches of those barbaric trees tossed and twirled as if in play, birds swooped from one to another, and down below, in a tangle of bays and inlets, the stately waters of Port Jackson glittered and glinted.

I stepped down the track from rock to rock, unbalanced, ungainly, as if in a dance with this landscape for which I had not yet learned the steps. I felt it watching me, a woman clumsy in too many layers of clothing, her boots catching on stones, her skirt snagging on low whippy branches. I paused on a ledge of rock, taking great gulps of that roistering blast of clean air, feeling as if I might be lifted clear off the ground and carried away.

Each step revealed a new marvel: a view through the bushes of a slice of harbour rough and blue like lapis, a tree with bark of such a smooth pink fleshiness that you could expect it to be warm, an overhang of rock with a fraying underside, soft as cake, that glowed yellow. The wind brought with it the salt of the ocean and the strange spicy astringency given off by the shrubs and flowers. There was an almost frightening breadth and depth and height to the place, alive with openness and the wild energy of breeze and trees and the crying gulls and the brilliant water. Alone, a speck of human in a place big enough to swallow me, I looked about with eyes that seemed open for the first time.

It was not a long track, but it was a journey into another land-scape, another climate, another country.

Down the slope, facing around somewhat to the west so it was out of sight of the settlement, was a clearing in which stood a strange construction: a hut like any other of the township, but with a stubby tower attached to one end, its lopsided pointed roof covered with canvas that puckered and gaped around a shadowed vertical slit.

And there was Mr Dawes. He was wearing a checked shirt

and a pair of sailor's trousers, turned up around the calves. He was stirring a bucket of something—whitewash, I saw as I came closer—and had a big coarse brush in his hand. The canvas gleamed with preparatory wet and he was about to apply the whitewash. He had clearly forgotten the arrangement Tench had made. He would not want a visit from an idle woman who had toyed with the idea of wanting some instruction in a few easy stars. I stopped, intending to go back the way I had come and return another time.

But he must have seen me out of the corner of his eye, for he looked up and I was obliged to come forward. I bustled down the slope as quickly as I could, blundering in my thick boots, hoisting my skirt and petticoats clear of the bushes and wiry grass. Alone with him here I felt a shyness. We both stared up at the strange canvas structure.

– The carpenter grizzled, Mr Dawes said. The awkward angles, you see, necessitated by the peak of the roof. Needing to be off centre to allow for observations at the zenith. And the difficulty involved in causing it to rotate for the measurement at the azimuth. While at the same time needing to be able to be closed in inclement weather, to protect the instruments. Which are of course the most precious and fragile objects in this place, possibly the most precious and fragile on this entire continent of New Holland, whatever its extent, which of course is a dimension as yet unknown.

At last he stopped, having been unable, it seemed, to stem the flow of words that I could see functioned by way of wall or barrier. But now they had abandoned him.

– A good carpenter likes to make a tidy job, I said, trying to offer rescue, but it was not the most promising entry to conversation.

– Some instruction on the matter of the heavenly bodies, Captain Tench mentioned, he said.

197

His lack of enthusiasm was so palpable that I was angry at Tench, angrier with myself for having got myself and Mr Dawes into this awkward thing. I might have simply retreated from any thought of learning about the stars, but I could not bear the weeks going on and on with not enough to think about.

He glanced at the whitewash in the pail. The stuff smelled foul and had a nasty grey sheen. I guessed that for tallow Mr Dawes had had to use fat from the rancid salt pork or beef that was the colony's only meat. The whitewash was ready, the canvas wet so the stuff would stick. He wished me gone. If he was forced to stand here playing gentleman to my lady, the canvas would dry and he would have to wet it all over again.

I had words prepared, but they were not the words that came out.

— You are much in demand, Mr Dawes.

He smiled slightly, his teeth crooked in a way that made his smile look rueful when perhaps rue was not intended.

— And here I am, with one more demand, I said.

His eyes went back to the canvas, the pail of whitewash.

— Yes, he said. If I can be of service.

— I see you are at the vital moment here, Mr Dawes, I said. I will come back another time.

I had schooled myself for years in calmness, and was surprised that now I was all awry, snapping my skirt off where it had got caught on a twig and stretched out beside me like some ridiculous flag, revealing those workmanlike boots. I turned, in a flurry now to be gone, speaking over my shoulder in a way that in another situation would have been rude.

— Another time, Mr Dawes, a thousand pardons.

I felt him watching me go, unsteady with haste, reaching out for a bush that turned out to be sharper than it looked.

That word—*azimuth*—had frightened me. It told me that I might be biting off more than I could chew. But by insisting, Tench had made it as awkward to retreat as to go on.

The next Thursday, Mrs Brown and I did not need to construct any flimsy coracle of story. We arrived at the open space, she took off her cap and sat on the rock shaped for the human behind, Edward ran to the cleft where the twigs he had played with last time were still lying on the rock, and Hannaford got out his pipe.

I took the track slowly, learning the dance. There was plenty of time. All the time in this new world.

Mr Dawes heard me coming, came to the door of the hut, rolling down the sleeves of his shirt and checking the button at the neck.

— Good afternoon, he called, his voice cracking as though it was some while since he had spoken. Good afternoon, Mrs Macarthur, welcome to the observatory.

This time I had my words ready.

— Mr Dawes, you are a busy man, I said, and it would be presumptuous of me to intrude on your time. It is kind of you to meet my idle fancy, but do not consider yourself under the least obligation. Come next week to what Captain Tench pleases to call my *salon*, I will give you a cup of tea, and let us say no more about instruction in the stars.

I spoke as matter-of-factly as I could, to give him a graceful way out. All the same, now that I was here again, I hungered to go into the canvas structure, to look through the telescope, to learn what an azimuth was. I hungered for that, as I never hungered to learn another bar of *Foote's Minuet*.

But I was ashamed, too. Mr Dawes did not pretend to erudition, the way so many did. He possessed deep and authentic learning. It would be foolish to think I could understand a thousandth of what he knew.

– I mistook, Mr Dawes, I said. I blush at my error.

Could, in fact, feel myself blushing, knew my cheeks were hot and ugly with flame. I put a hand up, that pointless gesture of trying to cool a blushing cheek with a hand equally hot. Now I was the person unable to meet the eye of another.

– Truly, Mrs Macarthur, he said, I would be delighted…

He seemed to remember this was the hollow form of words he had used before.

– Truly, it would give me great pleasure to share.

He coughed into his hand as if the words were an obstruction.

– The stars have been my companions since I was a friendless boy, he said, and smiled that rueful smile. It would give me great pleasure to introduce those companions to another who may enjoy their company.

Now, ridiculously, I felt tears come to my eyes. This awkward stranger had spoken to a part of me that I allowed no one to see. Brassy Mrs Macarthur, that lady of the banter that could amuse Tench, charming Mrs Macarthur for whom Worgan would do anything—that brittle carapace of a person had been surprised, in what had seemed nothing more than another part of the social game, by a man speaking from his heart to hers.

BLIND AND DEAF

In his hut, using bits of twig and gumnuts laid out on the table between us, Mr Dawes started on our first lesson. He talked about the sun, and the planets running around it in their orbits, and one planet, our own Earth, having as if its own planet, the moon, running in another orbit, its own shadow causing it to wax and wane—and at that point he saw that he had lost me. I stared at the gumnuts and twigs but I did not follow, had not followed from the first.

I knew I was not a stupid woman, but nothing in the learning Mr Kingdon had thought suitable for girls had equipped me for this. Easy arithmetic, enough for household accounts. Dot and carry one, long division. But what Mr Dawes was trying to explain had no numbers to add and subtract, had nothing at all except these gumnuts, these twigs, making ovals as he moved them around the table, and these words that I did not understand.

— You have done no geometry, I think, he said at last, gently, as if not having done geometry was like being blind or deaf.

— No, Mr Dawes, I have not, I said.

I sat miserable with myself. I had truly mistaken this idea of learning.

— You have been good beyond measure, Mr Dawes, I said, trying to snatch back some shreds of dignity. But the stars and planets will have to go on circling without the understanding of an ignorant woman.

He looked at me with some strong feeling that looked close to anger.

— Do not denigrate your abilities, Mrs Macarthur, he said. No one is born knowing geometry. Being a woman, you have been denied the smallest education in such matters, and it is to your great credit that you wish to remedy that lack. Come back again next week and I promise we will make better progress.

SLY MAGIC

When I arrived at his hut the next week there was a strange spindly contraption on the table. I thought it was a machine to spin or skein, and said so before I stopped to consider.

He laughed, that strange half-swallowed laugh of his.

– My word, Mrs Macarthur, he said, the Astronomer Royal himself would be hard put to it to recognise this. I call it an orrery, though its relation to any orrery I have ever seen is tenuous.

When he smiled, his features fell naturally into the shape of good humour, creasing around his eyes and mouth in lines worn by frequent amusement. Mr Dawes might be called His Holiness behind his back, but he was no sobersides.

– I cannot wonder at you not recognising this, Mrs Macarthur, he said, it being such an inept contrivance, but it is supposed to show our solar system, this ball in the centre the sun you see, this one here the Earth.

He turned the handle at the side and the planets jerked around, each at a different speed. It was a sly magic, that the mechanism caused all the planets to travel around their different paths, some slow, some fast, but all impelled by the same single action.

– Oh yes, now I see. Spinning indeed!

I could hear my anger at myself, that I might have lost my chance, that he would dismiss me as nothing more than a silly bored woman. But he ignored my mortification and embarked on an explanation. Not of what the orrery was for—that was so familiar to him that it was of no interest—but of how he had made it. The carpenter had given him an offcut for the central capstan and the planets, he explained, and he had gone to various acquaintances until at last Lieutenant Bradley of the navy had been able to supply him with the wire for holding each planet at the right distance from the capstan. The result was that this antipodean variety of orrery was a strange spidery affair of crooked wires and not-very-round carved wooden planets trembling on their extremities.

He invited me to try, holding the base steady while I turned the handle, our heads close together watching the miniature planets travel around their tiny sun.

— You could imagine yourself God, I said, and humankind down here, thinking ourselves to be choosing, when we are not choosing at all.

Remembered too late that he was a friend of the reverend, and might not take kindly to a woman telling him she imagined herself God.

— You are speaking my thought exactly, Mrs Macarthur, he said. Making it, I had to remind myself that even His Holiness the Lieutenant cannot walk on the water out there.

It was an agreeable surprise that Mr Dawes knew he was an object of ironic amusement. He promised to be better company than Tench, for all Tench's rehearsed wit. Sharing that amusement with him, years dropped away from me. I was twenty-four, a mature woman, but was again the girl I had been with Bridie: flightier, livelier, expansive with confidence, laughing fearlessly over nothing in a world not yet shrunken.

THE ONLY QUESTION

What astronomy taught was perverse: that what might appear to be true was not. My feet, which seemed to be so solidly planted on the earthen floor of Mr Dawes' hut, were in fact dangling from it, feet and hut and continent and oceans all being whirled around at a tremendous speed through some kind of nothing.

The idea was so absurd that I spoke without thinking.

– But how do they know?

Then heard how childish the words sounded and wanted them unsaid. But Mr Dawes seemed delighted.

– Well done, Mrs Macarthur, he said. You have asked the only question that matters.

Was he mocking me? He saw my uncertainty. I watched him pick his way among words to find the ones that would most closely resemble what was in his mind.

– We decide what we think we know, he said. From such evidence as we have. In the absence of more evidence, we can do no other. But we must be humble. You know, to question that evidence and know it to be partial. Most particularly to be humble about the conclusions we draw. Not to be too sure.

He seemed to doubt his own words, was staring away as if to find better ones. But they were exactly the words for a truth I realised I had always known, without knowing I knew it: that the world, and my own part in it, was a surface that might be enjoyed, but should never be quite believed.

Before I could learn the most fundamental fact about the heavenly bodies, it seemed that I needed to understand some even more fundamental fact, and behind that was something more fundamental still. But Mr Dawes was a patient teacher. What was a baffling set of words one week became straightforward the next, beads strung along a filament of understanding. I began to see that bafflement was not a reason to despair. On the contrary, bafflement was the beginning of wisdom.

When we came to the end of what I could follow of astronomy, we turned to botany. In the settlement, the names given to the local plants made them an inferior second-hand copy of the familiar. *Native cherries, wild spinach, Botany Bay parsley.* Now I was learning to see them, not for what they failed to be, but for what they were in themselves. The trees, although misshapen compared to an oak, and giving but poor shade on a hot day, had their own good reasons for being the way they were. Mr Dawes showed me how the shining hard leaves cleverly hung edge-on to the sun so as to retain as much moisture as possible. Explained why the trees had no seasonal yellowing and falling of leaves.

– The leaves are too hard-won from this poor soil to waste, he said. They have learned how to stay alive in hardship.

Through his eyes I came to recognise the trees as having a vigour and variety that no oak had ever had. Once I stopped expecting them to be like the trees of my childhood, I could recognise the delicacy and grace in the way their shining leaves played with the sunlight and their crowns tossed and coiled in the breeze. Yes, the soft pale bark of one—neatly layered, like leaves of paper stacked page on page—was strange enough to seem impossible, or creation's joke, but Mr Dawes showed me that there was a reason for that too: the piled pages resisted attack by fire or flood.

I loved to peer at these leaves, that bark, through Mr Dawes' fat lens, where they sprang into view as an entire secret landscape, a bright crisp-edged world hidden inside the one I inhabited. I came to see that, if a person had learned even a smattering of botany, her days could never be empty. Wherever she might be, there would always be plants bowing and nodding and holding themselves up for her to understand.

Not since those far-off lessons with Mr Kingdon had I known the pleasure of straining to comprehend. And oh, the pleasure of being praised for comprehending at last! The first time I managed to class and order a plant without help from Mr Dawes I was ridiculously proud of myself. So much that I was capable of, that I might never have guessed I could achieve!

– Thank you, Mr Dawes, I said. For pulling me and pushing me. To do more than I believed I could, and see more than I ever dreamed of.

I felt my throat closing and could not go on.

– Well, Mrs Macarthur, he said. You are a most apt and eager pupil, and I can only say that if I have opened any, let us say, *doors* for you, that gives me the greatest pleasure.

The poor bit of wordplay saved us both.

One afternoon, as I made my way down the familiar track, I saw that Mr Dawes had visitors, a group of native women and their children, with one or two men, sitting around a fire outside the hut, Mr Dawes among them. I hesitated, but one of the children saw me and called over to the adults, so all faces turned to me and I had no choice but to continue down the hill. Mr Dawes got up and came to meet me.

— Allow me to introduce my friends of the Sydney people, he said.

He went around the circle like any gentleman in a drawing room.

— Werong. Milbah. Patyegarang. Baringaroo. Daringa.

Each name was a burry blur of sound to me but he saw my difficulty, repeating each name and making me say it after him until I had it. Once you made the little effort to hear them properly, the names were as straightforward as *James* or *Mary Ann*.

Then he said a sentence I did not understand, but I caught my own name in the middle of it: *Mrs Macarthur.* Through the ears of the people listening, I heard it as if for the first time, a set of sounds considerably more complicated than *Werong* or *Daringa*.

The men, strong, upright, enclosed, acknowledged me by a look somewhere to the side of me. They were not unfriendly, but they were not especially welcoming either. They cared nothing for chat, for social smiles, for cheerful prattle. They were not concerned to *take an interest* or *put anyone at their ease*. There was a weighty power about them, an authority that seemed to come not from the weapons that lay beside them, but from some assured world of knowledge they lived within. They reminded me of no one more than my grandfather, that man heavy with his faith, who lived always under the shadow of eternity.

The women did not exactly look at me, either, but there was a sense that I was greeted. They had found my attempts to say their names hugely amusing, that was obvious, while my own came easily to them. They spoke to each other and laughed, very clearly about me, but there was a subtle shifting of bodies that felt like an invitation to sit beside them on the clean dust. I was pleased to accept, but was unused to it and awkward, my legs and skirt tangling so that becoming a part of the group was something of a business.

Beyond their names and mine, exchanged between us as a token of all we might have liked to say, we fell back on the language of the body. I found myself paying attention to Mr Dawes' visitors in a new way, as if my skin, rather than my ears, was listening to them.

Daringa showed me her baby, wrapped in that soft powdery bark that looked so much like paper. Admiration of a baby is one of those things for which no language is needed. I peeped at the child's face in among its strange but effective blanket, stroked a cheek, said the praises that are usual to please a mother.

Daringa laid the child gently down on the ground and unwrapped her so I could further admire. The babe lay solemnly staring, her fists gesturing, her thighs strong, the woman already in the making. Daringa's long shiny fingers smoothed the baby's body as if the feel of that soft skin was an irresistible pleasure. She was a queen to this princess, her hands firm and sure, authority and love together.

No one ever talked about *our sable sisters*. And yet Daringa, a mother like myself, alive with love for her child, dandling her babe as I had dandled mine, the babe chuckling up at her just as Edward, for all his sickliness, had chuckled up at me—Daringa was surely as much a sister to me as any woman I had known.

But this was the woman whose people, I had been solemnly assured, ate their babes. The conviction passed from mouth to mouth, and no one ever asked, *How do you know?* A few guesses could become an entire story that, once in place, was as watertight as a barrel. Falsehood could travel around the world in a barrel like that, and down into the future, without ever springing a leak.

When the women talked to each other and to Mr Dawes, their speech was a rounded liquid flow of words with none of the jerkiness of English, and with a different cadence, the words starting firm and easing away as if not to insist. It was hard to imagine a scolding in such a tongue. Mr Dawes' questions were slow and laborious. Still, the women understood and replied. He had a little blue notebook and a pencil, and made jottings as they spoke, but although he was clearly trying to learn the language, what was happening remained a conversation.

When the baby had been sufficiently admired and wrapped again in her shawl of bark, and Mr Dawes had written down enough words, the women got up, called to the children, and slowly made their way around the slope of the headland towards the next cove. The men were already gone, so quietly I had not seen them walk away. From my own society I guessed that they believed men had business with each other, and women were not part of that.

– As you saw, my friends here are good enough to be sharing some of their language with me, Mr Dawes said. Most remarkably, the language is inflected! Exactly as Greek is!

Inflected, I thought. What in heaven's name is *inflected*? And why might it be so remarkable?

– You think you will remember the words as you hear them, Mr Dawes said. But you will forget. Or you will think you heard something easier, something that seems familiar.

He riffled through the pages of the notebook, so eager for me to see everything at once that I saw nothing.

– Slow, Mr Dawes, I said. Let me look!

Some pages were headed with a letter of the alphabet and ruled up in two columns containing pairs of words: *Karingal—Hard, difficult to break. Karamanye—the stomach ache. Korrokoitbe—to swallow.* On other pages there was a verb, and below was the mostly empty shell of its parts. *To see—Naa. I see—Ngia Ni. Thou see'st. He sees. We see. Ye see. They see.*

– I thought it would be no more difficult a matter than filling the blanks, he said. Such was my presumption. Now my method, if you can call it that, is different. You see here, an exchange between myself and the child Patyegarang. Transcribed as I heard it. What I said, what she said. So that I might take in the living body of the language rather than a fingernail or earlobe, and hope for understanding to come in its own time.

Patyegarang had been part of the circle of women, a child on the threshold of womanhood. He told me that, in spite of every obvious difference, she reminded him of his younger sister.

– Patyegarang has my sister's quickness of mind, he said. And her bright humour, her curiosity. I feel almost as if I have Anne's company here, when I speak with Patyegarang.

He pressed his lips together in a grimace of regret.

– My sister would make a good astronomer, he said. But she will have to marry.

I had nothing to console him with. I knew the scant possibilities of happiness for a woman who would make a good astronomer, but whose acquaintance with the stars would never go beyond walking out into her yard and looking up only until the husband and children in the house needed her.

PARTICULAR FOLK

Mr Dawes did not call his visitors *natives*, much less *sable brethren*. He told me that to call one of these people a *native* was like calling an Englishman a *European*: accurate only in an offensively general way. The particular folk who sat down with him were mostly Gadigal, he told me. Beyond the next cove were the Wangal. Across the water were the Cameraygal. Inland at the head of the river, at the place we called Parramatta, were the Burramattagal.

— You can hear that the suffix, *gal*, must have the meaning of a particular tribe, or people, he said.

He smiled.

— You see, not such a great difficulty. And what a lovely word it is, Parramatta, and one with a very particular meaning: the Place of Eels.

Parramatta. I had heard the word, and said it, dozens of times, without thinking. It was nothing more than *the native name for the place.* Now I would never have the word in my mind without thinking of what it meant. It was more than a set of agreeable sounds. It told you about the place, and in telling you that, it told you which people belonged to its intimate life, and which did not.

One afternoon, leaving Mrs Brown and Hannaford at the top of the ridge as usual, I made my way down the track and approached the hut. I could hear music from within and pictured Mr Dawes happily singing to himself, enjoying his privacy, and thought to come back another time. But as I hesitated the singing ended and I heard his voice speaking in the Gadigal tongue, and a light voice answering. I knocked on the door and heard Mr Dawes call to me to come in, come in! He was sitting on the chair, pencil in hand, with the notebook on the table in front of him. Patyegarang was standing by the fire, and a little boy—her brother, I thought, though I had never managed to catch his name—was sitting beside her, toasting a morsel of bread on the end of a stick.

– I have been trying to teach Patye here that fine old tune of *Greensleeves*, Mr Dawes said. And she was trying to teach me one of hers, but the difficulty is mutual.

He sang: *Greensleeves was my delight, Greensleeves my heart of gold.* This was a song I knew better than I knew any music in the world, one that my father had sung, sitting at the end of my bed, his weight warm beside my feet, his big gnarled hand resting on my shoulder, the wind outside and the quiet jangle of the sheep's bells as they shifted in the fold. It was the most familiar song in the world, but watching this girl, for whom it must be so strange, I heard it as if for the first time: a series of sounds high and low, some extended, some brief, swelling like a gesture towards resolution.

As Mr Dawes sang, his voice thin but true, his features became soft around the music. He watched the girl as he sang, making a connection between them along that unravelling thread of sound. But when he was finished, no amount of coaxing from him could get her to copy him. Was she embarrassed, I wondered. Or puzzled?

When she lifted her head and began to sing, I could follow the first sounds: high, strainingly high, then plunging down to an insistent chanting monotone with a deep thread of pulse through it. I groped for a tune, strained to find a rhythm, then simply gave myself up to its power. It was not music in the way that *Foote's Minuet* or *God Save the King* were music. But it was music, because it came from the place all music must come from: inchoate yet disciplined, public and yet utterly personal, a language that spoke without any need for effort of understanding, a gift from one person to another.

She stood foursquare on to us, and when she was finished she stood watching the echo of the music on our faces. Around us the sounds of the world resumed: the cry of the gulls, the murmur of the trees shifting in the breeze, the chip and chop of the waves against the rocks at the foot of the headland.

– Thank you, Patye, Mr Dawes said. That was a gift we will not forget.

He smiled at the child and she smiled back, but then her eyes shifted to me. I smiled and nodded my appreciation of her song, but it was not praise she wanted. The little boy had toasted the bread and eaten it, and was now watching me too.

– Well, Mrs Macarthur, Mr Dawes said. I would say you owe the two of us a song, I believe the lass has that in her mind?

Until I opened my mouth I did not know what I was going to sing. *As I was a-walking one morning in May, 'twas down in the meadow among the green hay, my true love he met me the very same day, 'twas down in the meadow among the green hay.* There was my mother, singing over her saucepan, stirring a custard that, she explained, you could not leave for as much as a second, and, she said, would not curdle if you sang while you stirred. Of all the music stored away in my brain, why that?

IS HE HEAVY?

On a particular Thursday, Mr Dawes had embarked on another attempt to explain the arcana of retrograde motion, and I felt rescued when Daringa and Milbah and their children came trailing down the track. We greeted them, Mr Dawes brought out a few embers on his shovel, and in short order we were sitting on the ground in front of one of their small tidy fires.

I was now able to say *bujari gamarruwa*, good day to you, in some version of the women's language, and understand when they returned the greeting. They were the first words of any other tongue I had learned, apart from the Latin on the Kingdon coat of arms. It gave me more pleasure than I could ever have imagined, to enter the words of another world far enough to exchange a greeting.

Daringa addressed me, a short string of words I did not understand, even when she repeated it. It was clear that she was teasing, gesturing to Mr Dawes and then to me, and whatever she was saying was vastly entertaining to the others. I turned to Mr Dawes, whose look suggested he understood, but for once he was oddly reluctant to translate.

– Come, Mr Dawes, I said. Is my linguistic education to end so soon?

His mouth screwed sideways in that universal signal of doubt, but he was too serious a teacher, and too honest, to go on refusing.

– She is asking, *Is he heavy?* he said.

– Heavy? Is he heavy? I repeated.

I could feel an intensity of meaning in the air around us that I did not understand, only saw that Mr Dawes and I were the subject of keen scrutiny and much amusement.

And that Mr Dawes was blushing. Actually blushing red to the roots of his hair. It was the blush that told me what was causing such amusement. As quick as a lightning strike I understood that the women thought, or were pretending to think, that Mr Dawes and I came together for more than instruction in astronomy. And now they were watching us, to see if what they thought was true.

Mr Dawes met my eye, the blush still high in his face, and that look, charged with strong and private feeling, told me what I had known all this time, but had not let myself know that I knew. His Holiness the Lieutenant was no monk. On the contrary, he was very much interested in the female of the species, and perhaps especially in one in particular.

That understanding blazed into another: that I was as interested as Daringa in the question of whether Mr Dawes might be heavy.

Now she was calling out something that made the others crow with hilarity, pointing with her chin at Mr Dawes. She used English this time, saying 'that feller all right', but there was another part of the sentence that was lost in her laughing.

– Well, Mr Dawes, I said, my voice unsteady from my own laughter, or some other cause, there is something Daringa wants to tell me, but you will have to help me understand!

He hesitated, then his face relaxed into humour.

– It is a reference to a story they have, he said. Based on the Pleiades, the Seven Sisters, they too have a tale about them that involves the chase of a man after women. What Daringa is saying, I fear with regard to me, is, *that one all right, but take care with his friend.*

– Your friend, I said. Who is your friend, Mr Dawes?

He glanced down at himself. I followed his glance and now, married woman that I was, it was my turn to blush.

After the women left there was a space of silence between us. I was calm, in an attentive radiance, peace and intensity both. There was no hurry.

— I have a place I would like to show you, Mrs Macarthur, Mr Dawes said, and took my hand. I felt the warm dampness of his palm, and a strong tremor of feeling travelling from his body into mine.

His bed, I assumed, and drew back from the too-direct move from where we were to where we were about to be. He felt the reluctance, took my hand more firmly.

— Down here, if you please, he said, and led me past the hut, down the steep slope towards where the harbour glittered and danced.

— I call it *mon petit coin à moi*, he said. Do you have French, Mrs Macarthur?

But did not wait for me to say no, I had no French.

— *Mon petit coin à moi*, he said, and I saw that he was in the business of filling silence. It did not matter whether the silence was filled with English or French or Gadigal.

— It means, my little corner of mine. My very own little corner. *Mon petit coin*—my little corner. *A moi*—to me.

And now, scrambling down between the bushes, we came to a halt in a space enclosed on three sides by greenery. The fourth, facing the harbour, was obscured but not closed in by more branches, forming a private space: a room made of leaves.

— *Mon petit coin à moi*, he said. But now perhaps I may call it *notre petit coin à nous*. Which means, of course, our little corner of ours.

It was like that first afternoon, when he had not been able to stop talking about the canvas and the azimuth and the grizzling carpenter: Mr Dawes covering the forward movement of a new direction with whatever words he could summon.

He groped under a ledge of rock and brought out a blanket and spread it out on a chair-height, or bed-height, space of smooth rock.

– You see, he said, *mon petit coin* is equipped with every comfort, since it is a place where I spend many hours.

– *Mon petit*—how do you say it, Mr Dawes?

Hearing the foreign words in my own mouth, and copying each syllable as he sounded it out, made me feel part of him. As much as the words, we shared the feeling behind them: the pleasure of having a small private place where you could simply be who you were. *A moi.* Mine alone, my own.

It was no clap of thunder, but as quiet and unforced as ice melting on a stream, unseen until at last the surface cracks and is borne away, showing what was there all the time: the relentless pouring of desire.

Our relationship was always one of the greatest simplicity. Between us there was fondness and pleasure. He was a warm and eager companion. I heard him laughing, a pulse of breath against my ear. I was always *Mrs Macarthur,* no matter what might be going on, and he was always *Mr Dawes.* We took a great deal of pleasure in the formality of our address, as well as all that we did with each other.

I felt my skin go out to meet him, felt my blood warmed by his nearness. The habit of being Mrs Macarthur—proper, courteous, reserved—had grown around me like a long-worn garment, every stitch familiar. Yet here it was, unravelling to show me what lay beneath. With Mr Dawes, that surprising man, I found myself becoming the possessor of a body that could crave the body of another and cry out from sheer delight.

On the blanket there was no room for two people to lie other than close together, feeling one another's heat, hearing one another's hearts. A person barely had to breathe for the words to be heard.

– You said, I blush at my error, he whispered. And when I looked I saw that you were indeed blushing. Cool Mrs Macarthur was blushing.

He touched the cheek that had blushed.

– A blush becomes you, Mrs Macarthur.

A GIFT

It was a puzzle that Mr Dawes, as guarded in his own way as I was in mine, should recognise me. I think now that he recognised the shield. He knew what a shield looked like and what it was for, because he lived behind one too.

He was not handsome, but I came to find him so. He was from Portsmouth, his father a clerk with the Office of Ordnance, and had been a scholarship boy bullied for his humble circumstances. His consolation had been the stars and planets, the gloriously indifferent grandeur of their movements the only comfort to his loneliness. Had become a lieutenant of marines because every ship needed a man who could calculate by the stars exactly where the vessel was on the blankness of the ocean. Had learned how to hide who he was, a strange creature his fellow officers thought him, with strange enthusiasms. Was thankful, he said, that his stargazing duties gave him a reason to be away from the settlement.

Portsmouth was a fair step from Bridgerule, but not the other end of the country. It gave me a painful pleasure to dream a little, of how things might have been if it had been Mr Dawes and myself behind the hedge.

Within the bounds of forgivable human stupidity, we came to know each other. For a short stretch of summer months, peppered always with the pungency of danger, we made each other happy. How simple, to write the word, and to remember the feeling. To enquire too deeply into that happiness is unnecessary, another kind of stupidity. All I can say is that the happiness we had was a gift, and I am grateful.

From our room of leaves we heard waves slapping at the

shore, watched gulls wheeling and floating on the breeze. From that spot, if you looked to east or west, the water of the harbour seemed to end, closed off by enfolding points of tree-furred land, as if that mighty body of water were nothing more than a lake, a space that belonged only to us. Now and then we saw people of the Gadigal and Cameraygal in the slips of bark from which they fished. Now and then the packet boat laboured past on its way to or from Parramatta, the sail flapping or the oars dripping and knocking hollowly against the wood. Once the reverend drifted by in a dinghy, a fishing line over the stern. But behind our screen of branches it was possible to forget that there was a world beyond, where Mrs Macarthur and Mr Dawes were tangled in nets of impossibility.

As the afternoon drew towards evening we watched the glow of the late sunlight on the water, that soft glinting and twinkling, the light hanging among the leaves of the bushes, and the stillness watching us. When the evening star—Venus, to astronomers like ourselves—began to separate itself from the sky, it was time for me to go. Then I had to promise myself that I would be back. In the meantime Venus would be there, every evening, to remind me of that other world.

We never spoke of Mr Macarthur. Never spoke of the future. We knew there could be none.

Shortly after Mr Dawes and I discovered each other, I embarked on an awkward conversation with Mrs Brown. She was a shrewd woman, and our Thursday routine—Mrs Macarthur disappearing down the track alone—was peculiar. From week to week it was more urgent to find a way to say *Do not tell Mr Macarthur.*

Hannaford was ahead of us on our way up the ridge, Edward on his shoulders—we could hear him piping out a parody of the shouts of the sergeant-at-arms, and Hannaford playing up to him, quick-marching, to the right about-facing, pausing to present imaginary arms.

– Mrs Brown, I said, I must tell you, Mr Dawes is an unusual soul. A solitary, you understand. Not much for company.

Seeing in my mind's eye Mr Dawes with his Gadigal and Wangal friends, playing the fool as he added to his vocabulary: now pretending to eat, now to everyone's entertainment creeping on all fours or scratching his armpit.

– Yes, Mrs Macarthur, Mrs Brown said.

– Which is why he prefers…

I groped for words. *To be alone with me* was much too blunt.

– Prefers that we are not distracted. I am a poor pupil, Mrs Brown, and distracted all too easily!

– I understand, Mrs Macarthur.

I wondered if that was amusement I could hear in her voice, but her face was hidden behind her bonnet.

– It is not what is usually done, I said. A married woman…

Ahead of us Hannaford had turned, Edward still up on his shoulders, and was waiting for us. Briskly, as if impatient with me, Mrs Brown made my complication simple.

– I understand, she said again. As far as Hannaford and myself go, I can assure you, Mrs Macarthur, lessons are between a pupil and a teacher and no one's business but theirs.

She turned and looked me fair in the eyes. For the space of several heartbeats we were not servant and mistress but two women who understood each other.

– You can trust us, Mrs Macarthur, she said. Hannaford and me. To understand what you are saying.

Us. Hannaford and me. I had been too full of my own affairs to take note of what I saw every Thursday when I walked back up the track: Mrs Brown and Hannaford sitting beside each other on the backside-shaped rock, quietly talking, Edward playing at their feet, the model of a sweet family scene. These were two people whose hard lives had not erased the same urge Mr Dawes and I had, to find a companion. I could trust them. They would not want to forgo their afternoons on the rock.

I could hardly believe that Mr Macarthur did not see what was happening. Could he not tell how bliss-softened I was when I returned from my lessons? But he understood only the animal aspect of relations between the sexes, and so could not recognise that tenderness in another.

In Mr Macarthur's eyes, as in Tench's, Mr Dawes was a clever buffoon, an awkward machine of mathematics. The stars, and a place to view them from, were all he appeared to need. To have so few wants was contemptible. He had no ambition, did not delight in scheming, took no pleasure in besting a rival. In the eyes of Mr Macarthur, those lacks made Mr Dawes hardly a man at all.

In the beginning the orrery had been a good pretext, essential for the lessons but too difficult to transport. When botany was added to astronomy, Mr Dawes' headland was the best place to examine the delicate plants that had been trampled out of existence closer to the settlement. The pretexts were accepted, and Mr Macarthur made no difficulty about me visiting the observatory every week. I let him assume that Hannaford and Mrs Brown were with me there, and he did not show enough interest for any outright lies to be necessary.

Still, on the rare occasions when my husband enquired after the weekly lessons, I wondered if there was a recognition that he was not aware of behind the questions. I made sure I shared only the driest husk of the riches I was being given.

– Such an interesting fact, Mr Macarthur, I would begin, I wonder if you know that those plants which produce a pod like a bean are of the family called *Papilionaceae*, so called because the flower resembles a butterfly or *papilio*?

Mr Macarthur never found it necessary to be instructed beyond a single sentence. He always found a reason to leave the room, or become engrossed in a book, and that was the end of botany or astronomy for another week.

WRITING HIS NAME

I sailed close to the wind in one of my letters to Bridie, written at the time when Mr Dawes and myself were in the full blaze of our friendship. I have the letter in my hand now. At the time I wrote the words, I thought I was simply telling Bridie about the various people who were our society. But now I remember the dangerous pleasure I took in manoeuvring my news to include a particular name again and again. *Mr Dawes and Captain Tench and a few others are the chief among whom we visit.* Innocent enough, and so is the next: *Under Mr Dawes I have made a small progress in Botany.* But here I can remember smiling to myself: *Mr Dawes is so much engaged with the stars that to mortal eyes he is not always visible.* At last I could not resist a private joke: *I had the presumption to become Mr Dawes' pupil, but I soon found I had mistaken my abilities and blush at my error.*

I blush at my error! Reading the faded old ink I am smiling, remembering my pleasure in telling my secret but—as I thought— disguising it. I considered myself very clever. Now I see that this letter shouts the truth from the rooftops.

I trusted Mrs Brown and Hannaford. But I feared there could be no secrets in a community of a thousand souls packed into one small clearing in the forest. Most particularly when one of them was writing a book. An author was a dangerous acquaintance. When Tench and I encountered each other down by the bridge one afternoon and he stopped to speak to me, I smiled my blandest smile. *Go carefully*, I told myself.

— Well, Mrs M, how are your studies in astronomy progressing, he said. The labour it took me to arrange your lessons—I hope it has proved worthwhile?

Innocently, it seemed, but Tench was never innocent. *Does he know?*

He moved closer.

— I was at pains to persuade His Holiness, he murmured, as if telling me a secret. No easy matter, I assure you, but for your sake, my dearest lady, no task is too onerous.

His tone was solemn and went along with a yearning look. No, he did not know. He had stopped me at the bridge to quiz me about my lessons in astronomy, not with any suspicion, but to give himself the chance to act the lovesick swain. I thought of making some satiric remark—would he now kindly slay a dragon for me?—but changed my mind. Any response, no matter how mocking, would arrive at his ear as the next move in the dance of flirtation.

After the shock of *Jack Boddice* I had been a little cool with Captain Tench. But he was not a man to believe a woman could resist him, and I knew by the arch looks he gave me that he judged my coolness to be simply part of the game of advance and retreat. There had been no more tests. Tench had been all gallantry, all courtliness, all courtesy. But waiting for the next move in the game.

I would have liked to pay no more attention to him for the rest of the marines' time in New South Wales, but I could not be too chilly, because I had come to see that I needed something from him: his silence. Perhaps he guessed nothing, but I could all too easily imagine him, in his book, describing Mrs Macarthur's weekly visits to the observatory in such a way as to awake a certain reader's suspicious attention. That might not happen until far into the future, but whenever it took place, the consequences for me would be dire. Captain Tench did not know it, but he had in his hand a tool that could bring down disaster on me. In some way or other I had to ensure that there would be no mention of me in his book.

– Mr Dawes and I have lately returned from an expedition into the interior, Mrs M, he said. And I assure you, without a gentleman of his superior skill in navigation, we would still be there! At night by the fire he was able to cast up our courses and work them by a traverse table to pinpoint our exact location: a most remarkable feat, which I will not fail to record in my little account of the colony.

Remarkable, but his tone and smile said *entertaining*. I could imagine how he would present poor Mr Dawes in that book of his: as a ridiculous instrument of tedious erudition.

But I saw my opportunity.

– Oh, Captain Tench, I cried, with what I hoped was playfulness. I see you will stop at nothing in search of the entertainment your readers hunger for!

– Indeed, my dear lady, you are correct as always, Tench said with a bow.

There was a brightness to his eye. I could see him thinking, *Ah, she is coming around!*

– But I must tell you, sir, I said, that some of us are shy of being mentioned in your pages. If I suspect that you are tucking away in your memory anything I tell you of my doings, to bring out later for your book, I will become sadly mute in your company!

I had worked to toss this remark off in the most unconcerned way, but he caught something in my tone.

– Even mute, madam, you would be a most delightful companion, gallant Tench said.

I could feel his entire intelligent attention on me.

– Ah, but I would rather be free to speak, I said. Could you not give me an undertaking to forgo any mention of me in your book?

– Why, my dear Mrs M, anyone would think you had something to hide, he said. A lover hidden behind a tree, perhaps!

And made a show of looking around, laughing, it was the best joke imaginable. But was still watching me.

Do not become earnest, I told myself, *or he will catch a whiff of mystery*. Too late I realised that in asking for his silence I had put into his hands the very weapon I feared. A great heat of panic rose into my chest.

The best defence against a teller of stories is dullness, but it was too late for that. Captain Tench would not believe I had become Mary Johnson so quickly.

I lowered my voice, speaking as if reluctantly.

– My dear sir, I said, I think you are aware of my position here as a woman. With so few of us, I fear any mention of one will sound like a shout. You know how you men love to—let us say—make mischief with the fairer sex.

That was a good attempt. *Make mischief with the fairer sex*. It brought us back to the ground Tench liked, where men and women sized each other up behind a screen of banter. I gave him a small warm smile, at the same time hoping my situation was not about to become more complicated by Mr Macarthur catching sight of us deep in private conversation.

The charmed suitor returned the smile, but I could see that the inquisitive author still had his nose to the wind.

– I am in your hands, my dear sir, I said, and spread my own in a gesture of helplessness that by chance brushed against his arm. I can only appeal to you *as a gentleman*.

The son of the dancing-master could not resist this.

– Oh, indeed, you have my word as a gentleman, Mrs M, he said, so fervent I feared he might go down on one knee. Instead he fumbled for my hand, touched my hip as he fumbled, grasped the hand at last, but awkwardly, catching my thumb. I drew my hand away. Here on the bridge we were as exposed as if on a stage. This was a dangerous game. He came close to murmur into my ear.

– My dearest lady, your helpless admirer will obey, he said. Not a mention, not a single mention of you will appear in my text. Upon my honour.

Not a single mention of you will appear in my text. I have his book here on the table, with its inscription: *To my dear friend John Macarthur, with the greatest admiration and esteem.* Captain Tench obeyed the letter of his vow, for I do not appear in the text. But he could not resist finding a loophole whose ingenuity is worthy of the *esteemed* John Macarthur himself: he includes me in a footnote. It is no more than a passing reference, nothing more than the fact that I was present at a certain dinner at Government House. In fact, a person in a questioning frame of mind might wonder why he bothered to name me at all, but I can imagine how he smiled to himself, composing that footnote.

There is no mention, anywhere in the book, of Mr Macarthur. My husband does not even rate a footnote. Which might have caused offence but for that fulsome inscription. In any case, if Tench calculated that Mr Macarthur would not bother to read the book, he was right.

Mr Dawes was seldom seen in the settlement, but one morning I saw him walking towards me along the dusty track that went past the barracks. Even from a distance I could see his smile, white in his sun-browned face, and as we came closer to each other I thought that he was going to embrace me then and there.

Of course he did not. He stopped and took off his disgraceful hat with the sweat-darkened band and the split where it had been creased once too often, and we bowed to each other, sedate as a pair of churchwardens.

– Good morning, Mrs Macarthur, he said, and the cleverest soul alive could not have guessed that the afternoon before he had been closer to Mrs Macarthur than any man save her husband had ever been. In fact he had been closer than her husband. Mrs Macarthur's husband could do what he wished with Mrs Macarthur's legs and arms, but he could not touch her being.

Only when we were safely past each other did I wonder who might have seen. In this place there was always someone to see, even if it was no one as dangerous as Captain Tench. Nothing had happened, nothing had been said. Nothing was visible. And yet the air rang and swooned. It was hard to believe that others did not feel the world humming when Mr Dawes and I were near each other.

The thing was madness. It was true that Mr Dawes had few visitors from the settlement. True, too, that he and I were safely hidden in our leafy refuge, and Mrs Brown and Hannaford guarded the path. Still, I knew that Tench visited now and then, and perhaps there were others.

We were mad to think it was possible. But we did not think,

only floated from one meeting to the next. I look back now with amazement and a tingle of remembered fear. Fear, and passion too. I have not forgotten what it was like to lie with him. Sitting here, an old woman, I feel my blood stir at the memory, a blush that tells me I am not dead yet.

What an unfathomable thing, like a strange warped orrery, all this business is, the puzzle of desire. Each man runs along his own orbit, and each woman runs along hers, each thinking they have set their own course. And yet we are all being cranked by the same invisible handle, impelled by the same forces: the urge to join with another, the yearning to find a fellow soul. All of us moving, but the distance between us never decreasing.

And for myself, what was the force turning my handle? Desire: what a discovery that was. Ambition, too: I loved meeting again that bold young woman who had thought herself in command of her destiny.

And, if I may tease you, my unknown reader, let me remind you that you have only my word for any of this. This story, of the tangling of two hearts in Sydney in 1791, is recorded nowhere but in the document you are reading. It may appear to speak with authority, but might it be nothing more than the mischievous invention of a sly old woman?

SLANDER

I was wearied of my *salon* now, and the tightrope it obliged me to balance along, keeping Captain Tench charmed into silence but at arm's length. As I handed the teacups around, my smile felt as brittle as porcelain.

He was like a cat, quietly relentless. He knew by now that he would make no headway with me, and I did not think he truly wanted to. It was the game of romance that energised him, or rather the game of power: to create little secrets between us that forced me into complicity.

On this particular afternoon as I handed him his teacup he took it in such a way that his fingers overlapped mine on the saucer. His fingers were smooth, cool, lingering. I could not drop the cup, could not protest. Anyone watching would have thought his smile one of thanks for the tea, appreciation of the hospitality, those blameless reasons to smile. But the feel of his skin against mine revealed his satisfaction in having drawn me into a secret touch.

When he finally took the cup I turned away with the impulse to wipe my fingers on my skirt. He followed my turned head and murmured in his confiding, close-to-the-ear way.

– Oh, by the way, Mrs Macarthur, he said. I was out at the observatory yesterday, visiting Mr Dawes, your friend and mine. We spoke of you, my dear Mrs M, and your doings together.

Your doings together! He knew! This time he knew. But I must not show my fluster! Must not slop the tea I was pouring or betray myself by any muscle of my face! There was still time to deny everything. I smiled my social smile, but my legs were trembling, my heart was beating unpleasantly hard. I could feel something in my throat trying to get out, and what was trying to get out was a nausea of fear.

— He tells me you are making great strides with your astronomical studies, he said. And that your aptitude with botany is truly remarkable.

I glanced at him but he was turned away, helping himself to sugar, carefully replacing the lid on the sugar-bowl. Was he playing with me, the way the cat likes to keep the mouse alive?

— Oh, I am a wondrously dull pupil, I said, forcing jocularity into my tone. But can tell you the order of the planets, as they stand in relation to the sun.

And began to do so, with the thought of creating a weight of plodding fact that would push the conversation away from where it must be going. But I had only got as far as Mars when he interrupted.

— My word, I see that Dawes is quite right, he said. You have made great strides indeed. But I wonder, has he introduced you to his friends among the natives?

— Oh yes, I said. I have met them, they are often at his hut.

The words *Is he heavy?* rose into my mind and I pressed them down. Dared not speak again, in case they were the words that came out. But he was stirring his sugar, carefully putting the spoon back in the saucer, nodding in the way a man nods who is not listening. I saw that he had a plan for this conversation, and his question was nothing more than the means of moving it in the direction he wanted it to go.

— I wonder, he said, whether you might have met a native who is a particular friend of Mr Dawes?

Now he met my eye. He winked.

— A young girl, a particular and private friend? He calls her Patty, I believe.

I was not a good enough dissembler to disguise what I felt: outrage, disgust, contempt.

– Oh, Captain Tench, I cried. I am shocked!

Shocked, yes, at a man who could create such a grubby lie.

I opened my mouth to prove him wrong, thinking to bring as evidence the sister that Mr Dawes had told me of. But arguing would only give the lie greater substance, and in any case I would be wasting my breath. Tench had forgotten that he was speculating. A guess had shifted seamlessly into something that, as far as he was concerned, was now plain fact. And the lie had enough appearance of truth to be convincing. That gave it a malign power that the actual truth was not strong enough to defeat.

How the mind can leap, in less than the time it takes to blink! I had hardly spoken the word *shocked* when I saw that I could do something better than protest. If Captain Tench thought he already knew what was going on at the observatory, he might not look too hard in that direction. His nasty little invention could serve as a screen or decoy. All my ingenuities could not produce a better way of turning his eyes away from *your doings*.

– Oh, our good Mr Dawes, I said. Who would have imagined such a thing?

I could hear the richness of relief in my voice. Tench heard it too, and I saw him wondering.

– And indeed I have seen him with the natives, I said, trying to smother the tone of relief with one of reproach. He told me he was learning their language!

– I am sorry to shock you, Mrs M, Tench said earnestly. And the girl still almost a child.

He shook his head as if in sorrow, but there was an excitement running under his skin. Salacious, and triumphant too. From the moment he had slyly caressed my fingers, this was where Tench had wanted our exchange to travel: as with the business of *Jack Boddice*, he wanted to share a dirty secret, and draw me intimately into the dirt of it.

Never mind. He thought he had trapped me in his secret. He would never know that, to the contrary, he was trapped in mine. The more he told his story of Mr Dawes and Patyegarang, the safer Mr Dawes and Mrs Macarthur would be. Captain Tench could caress my fingers and murmur intimately in my ear all he wished. I would not be afraid of him again.

He was the last to leave the *salon* that day. I saw him to the door and when he took my hand and bowed over it, I allowed him to kiss it. He went off whistling. I watched him disappear towards the barracks, a man entirely happy to have a secret, even if it was the wrong one.

NOTHING NEEDED TO BE EXPLAINED

The story of Mr Dawes and Mrs Macarthur did not end as it would have in a romance. We were not discovered. No other woman usurped my place. No one died. What happened was at once simpler and more mysterious. It was that one morning, lying in the dawn beside Mr Macarthur, I knew that this was not a proper way to live.

During my time with Mr Dawes, a new Elizabeth Veale had begun to take shape, a secretive shoot preparing itself deep in the soil, complete with leaves and roots, biding its time until it was ready to push upwards through the heavy earth, into the sunlight of its proper life.

In the company of Mr Dawes I had found a woman I liked, even admired. Had learned things about myself that I had never guessed at. Our friendship had taught that life was not extinguished in me. Under the bland courtesies of Mrs John Macarthur lived another woman entirely, one I was happy to greet.

The world had given us this one brief space, a few months as an antipodean summer eased into autumn. It had been a time not of the pleasures of the flesh alone, but a deeper wisdom that might be with me for the rest of my life. I could so easily never have learned things that would stay with me now until I died: that I was complete as I was, with all my flaws and all my strengths. That I took up space in the world, and that I was entitled to that space.

Having met the woman that I was, I did not wish her to hide like a rat in a drainpipe. I was my truest self with Mr Dawes, but I had to exist in the hard light of the life I had been given. What he and I had made together was honest and important. But his

237

orbit, like mine, lay elsewhere. We had been given a gift from the universe, a momentary precious conjunction. It was not meant to last, only to be valued and its lesson taken to heart.

I could not imagine what space the world would offer me in the years to come. But the astronomer's perspective would give me patience. To shrink to the size of a distant star, to slow to the speed of planets that took centuries to perform their serene dance: these were the arts of the astronomer, and I would make them the arts of a woman. I was destined to an orbit I had no power to alter, that of being Mrs John Macarthur. It was my task to find a way for the velocity of that orbit to create a space for my own.

Mr Dawes hardly needed to be told. Nothing needed to be explained.

– We have been fortunate, Mrs Macarthur, he said. I count myself lucky beyond deserving.

We sat for a long quiet time across from each other at his rickety table, watching the fire on its hearth, like a comforting companion who knew better than to try to speak.

He reached for my hand and led me out of the hut, down towards the water. Neither of us wanted to lie together. That would be too heavy with *the last time*. We simply sat together in our *petit coin*, side by side on the rock from which one could see all the way to the east where the sun rose over the headlands and bays, and all the way to the west where it sank behind the body of the continent. Gulls came. We watched as one dived into the water—with such a smack, it must have hurt—missed its prey, wheeled up, smacked down again, staggered into the air. We watched it circle and take aim, smack down once more and this time bob on the water, tossing its head to get the fish down its throat.

We laughed at the bird, at the sparkle and energy of it all, the way water and sky, fish and bird, wind and tide all worked together in exactly the way they were supposed to. Yes, something was over, but something would always be with us: this life, this world, and what we had given each other.

It was in the sweet days of early autumn that Mr Dawes and I sat for the last time in *notre petit coin*. By the beginning of the following summer, the *Gorgon* was being made ready to return the marines to England. By the time of our second antipodean Christmas my whole society would have departed: Mr Dawes, Captain Tench, Mr Worgan, and all the other marines who had become my friends. The governor remained, but it was an open secret that he would soon be gone, leaving Major Grose in charge until another governor could make his way here.

There were some new arrivals, and they were pleasant enough men, happy to continue the tradition of tea at Mr Macarthur's. Colonel Paterson—an agreeable gentleman, second-in-command to Major Grose, and like the governor a protégé of Sir Joseph Banks—had brought an agreeable wife, but after only one or two appearances at my *salon* the Patersons were sent to the Norfolk Island settlement.

In any case, there was a bond between those of us who had shared the earliest, hungriest times that no new arrival could match.

Mr Worgan left me his piano, with exhortations to continue my splendid progress, instructions as to the instrument's tuning, and the tool to do it with. I have it still, although the piano is gone. Here it is, an odd-shaped bit of metal with no meaning to anyone in the world except me, but I keep it in memory of that friend.

Captain Tench made no secret of his impatience to be gone.

– I could say, my dear Mrs M, that I contemplate our departure with mingled sensations, he said. But the fact is that I hail it with nothing but rapture.

I watched him hear how this made a lie of all his earlier yearnings and hankerings.

– Other than my parting from you, dear lady, naturally! That is a true grief. A person for whom I entertain such deep affection, and whose exquisite presence will always burn bright in my memory and my heart.

This might have sounded overwrought even to his ear and, perhaps to make it seem authentic, he asked me for a keepsake. He picked up a piece of ribbon that had come loose from my hat and was lying on the windowsill waiting to be sewn back on, clearly the thing he had in mind. But I did not want Captain Tench taking that bit of ribbon away, keeping it in his breast pocket and making a story out of it. *Oh, yes, I was given this by a lady very dear to me*, I could imagine him telling someone. *Very dear. Very close to my heart.* I ignored his hints and presented him instead with nothing more intimate than a handful of sweet tea in a twist of paper.

Mr Dawes might have stayed, as a few of the other marines were doing, but had been ordered by the governor to return to England. He had been involved in some act of insubordination, Mr Macarthur told me, something to do with a punitive expedition that had been mounted against the Botany Bay tribe. He was being sent home in high-minded honourable disgrace. According to Mr Macarthur, he was to face court martial.

No one had ever questioned the ending of the lessons in botany and astronomy. Captain Tench had been too busy making eyes at me, and Mr Macarthur was glad to be spared any more lectures on *Papilionaceae*. I had encountered Mr Dawes on a few occasions in the township since our time together, but we bowed to each other and walked on without meeting each other's eyes.

By the time the departure of the *Gorgon* was announced, I was almost certain that I was with child. I did the arithmetic of the months, then did it again and then once more, but always with the same result: Mr Dawes could not be the child's father. I was grateful for the certainty. Watching the child for traces of the man would have been too painful a pleasure. Certainty was harsh, but it was the truth.

Mr Dawes was obliged to come to the *salon* for the farewell gathering Tench insisted on, but the two of us performed an unhappy dance of avoidance, moving around the room so that others were always between us. Tench tried to cheer what was a rather strained afternoon. Raised his cup as he had done so often and proposed the toast: *To His Majesty!* And then: *To Home!*

I should have envied the marines, for whom the toast would soon be a reality, but in truth the picture of *Home* had become a little stale. I could no longer imagine the house, the land, myself in a striped pinny. There was nothing but a blur of rain and fog.

To Home! I exclaimed with the rest, but the word rang strangely in my ears.

Mr Dawes sent a messenger to the house with the orrery, carefully wedged in a box, and with a stiff note—written with a consciousness that it could be read by other eyes—hoping that I would continue my studies. The orrery, humble and half-broken though it was, became precious, a reminder of the best of myself. I have it still.

Bridie had written to me, with what might have been a hint that she had read between the lines of mine. Told me she had always thought Mr Macarthur *would make an excellent husband, if he met with a woman whose disposition and accomplishments suited him.* Thank you, dear friend, I thought, for this gossamer tissue, transparent only to my eyes, behind which you tell me that you understand.

Now, on the eve of the marines' departure, my feelings could not be contained as I composed a letter back to her. My letter would travel to England on the *Gorgon,* Mr Dawes and the letter on the same ship, both carrying a little of myself away with them.

My spirits are at this time low, very low, I wrote. *Tomorrow we lose some valuable members of our small society and some very good friends endeared to us by acts of kindness and friendship.* I remember the bleakness I felt, the conviction that nothing would ever be different. Reckless in my despair, I let my pen go on. *From this you may be led to question my happiness.* For God's sake, question! I hungered to be heard, to share, for once, my true feelings.

Seeing them bald on the page I knew how dangerous those words were. I had to take them by the hand and lead them back to safety. *But this much I can with truth add for myself, that since I had had the powers of reason and reflection I never was more sincerely happy than at this time.* Oh, you poor dear woman, postponing, by one unnecessary phrase or another, the moment at which the lie would have to be told. *Sincerely* told.

A flicker of truth insisted on being heard again. *It is true I have some wishes unaccomplished.* I watched myself straining to keep the balance between revealing and concealing. *When I consider this is not a state of perfection I am abundantly content.* Yes, relative to death or dismemberment I was of course content. *Abundantly* content.

I see that, contrary to my usual practice, I have underlined many words. *Sincerely* is emphasised with a somewhat wavering line, and in the phrase *than at this time* each word sits on its own dab of ink. *Perfection* has four, as if to spell out the word in firm syllables. *Abundantly* and *content* are both bolstered with a strong line. My nib paused with a thickening of ink at the end of each underlining, as if I did not trust the words to do the hard job of persuading.

GORGON

All that morning I was aware of the *Gorgon* in the cove, rocking on the water, ready to turn its bow to the east into the vastness of the ocean. I had determined not to watch it sail away, but half an hour before it was due to raise anchor I left the house and hurried down to the cove. To the accompaniment of ragged huzzas and a blast of disorganised noise from fifes and drums, the last few marines were being piped on board. The anchor was being raised, I could hear the sailors' song as they ground the capstan around, and the rattle as the sails were set. The ship was too far away for faces to be made out, but as it slowly got under way I waved my handkerchief, watching a few white specks on board flickering in reply.

As the ship disappeared and there was no longer any point in waving, I looked across the cove and saw a figure at the foot of the headland where Mr Dawes had lived. She was up to her knees in the water, gazing at the ship: Patyegarang. It was too far to be sure, and yet I was sure. She was not waving, but fixing a beam of attention on the ship as if sending a message by the sheer power of feeling.

Captain Tench had told me that Mr Dawes was hoping to return. Sell his commission, apply to emigrate as a schoolteacher, something along those lines. Certainly the place could have done with a teacher of his abilities. Why none of that eventuated, I do not know. Only that I have never seen him since and do not expect to, though few days pass when I do not think of him.

THE EVENING STAR

What Mr Dawes and I had shared was not like the love that triumphs at the end of novels, with a great complacent silence after the last page. Let me be truthful. We were like any other humans, fumbling for the sense of each other's selves through clouds of obscurity. There were great shadowed masses of me that he would never know, and of him that I would never know.

Just the same, Mr Dawes, how much—oh, how much!—I would like to sit with you on that rock by the water one more time, watching the evening star, its brightness by the moment announcing, like a bell tolling, that it was time to return to the complicated and dangerous business of being the wife of John Macarthur, Esquire.

PART FIVE

The *long game* tested even Mr Macarthur's patience, for the governor went on resisting all pressure to grant land to the officers of the New South Wales Corps. But a year after the marines sailed home he followed them. No new governor had yet arrived, and until then the role would be filled by Mr Macarthur's greatest admirer, Major Grose the Dear Dunce.

It was not a matter of the long game now, but of speed. The new governor might arrive at any time, and overnight the DD's power would evaporate. The Auld Salt's ship was barely out of sight when the DD signed the paper Mr Macarthur had been pressing so relentlessly for: a grant for the chosen hundred acres at Parramatta, plus convicts to work it. At one stroke of a compliant pen, Mr Macarthur had what might have taken him a lifetime to achieve back in England.

But the difference between Mr Macarthur and other ambitious men in the colony was that, as soon as one of his ambitions was realised, another formed.

– The ink was barely dry on the grant, he said. He was still blotting his signature when I played my next card. The idle fellow did not take much convincing that a man was needed to take into his own hands all the pettifogging details of his new position. Inspector of Public Works was the title I suggested.

What would Mr Macarthur have done without a wifely audience to nod agreeably at his triumphs?

– He leapt at the idea, he said. Saw himself free to lie on his sofa all day—I saw his eyes go to the cushions. Until with a grand show of grief I mentioned how unfortunate it was that the post could not be remunerated without sanction from Whitehall. Poor fellow, all was woe-is-me!

Mr Macarthur had not forgotten how to mimic another man's weakness. There to the life was the poor major, his face furrowed like a bloodhound's in deepest dismay.

– Then, with becoming diffidence, I offered myself for the post.

– Without payment, I said. Then what is the advantage?

It was like a game of shuttlecock: he lobbed me the shuttle and was waiting as I lobbed it back.

– My dear, he said. My dear clever wife.

He was taking his time, enjoying himself.

– Whitehall cannot refuse once the work is being done, he said. The post will be handsomely remunerated in due course. But it is not a matter of the money. Can you, my dear, name a single action in this place that does not come under the heading of a public work? Any permission to own, or clear, or build, or assign, or reward, or punish?

He was right, I could not name one.

– Governors may come and governors may go, he said. But the Inspector of Public Works is a fixture beyond the reach of their whims.

The Inspector of Public Works lost no time in assigning himself ten, then twenty, then thirty convicts victualled by His Majesty, and set them to work clearing and planting his land. The Inspector of Public Works was also in a position to allocate bricks and timber towards his own farmhouse. Six months after the governor sailed away, enough land had been cleared for a promising crop of corn to be growing. Six months more and the house was ready to live in.

By then I had been safely delivered of a daughter. Like her brother she was a sickly babe, and for many months I feared my second daughter would go the way of my first. I held her to me as

I had held Jane, this time without hope. I could not bear to hope again, was reconciled to this one making her little whimperings, puckering her little mouth, and fading as the other had done. But she clung to life. Every day there was the surprise of her continuing to breathe, and her stillness was more like a person husbanding her few resources than someone easing her way into the hereafter.

Mr Macarthur insisted that she was named Elizabeth. I would have chosen a different name. She was herself, not a copy of her mother. But Mr Macarthur was determined—it seemed to tickle him to be surrounded by Elizabeths—and what could it matter what she was called, as long as she lived?

She was eighteen months old, Edward a lad of four, when at last we removed to Parramatta. She was still not a strong child, would have looked puny beside Daringa's robust princess, but I hoped the move to Parramatta would give her new strength, and I had begun to trust that she was with me to stay.

NOT A SINGLE PANG

Sydney had been my home for three years, but I left it with not a single pang. After the departure first of the marines and then of the governor, it had changed beyond recognition. Thanks to the officers' speculations, the place now ran unashamedly on rum, and rum fuelled every manner of corruption. The officers strutted about, lords of all they surveyed, and under them men scrabbled for crooked advantage.

Even before Mr Dawes left, his headland had become a military battery, with cannons pointed towards the sea, and his hut and observatory had been absorbed into the military structures. The delicate track I had taken such delight in springing down was now a broad path trundled over by carts and gun carriages, and the next cove, where Mr Dawes' friends had once had their camps, was a muddle of wharves and cockle-pickers' huts.

All around the settlement, grants were being made by the DD, fifty acres here, a hundred acres there. Every settler with a deed in his pocket felt entitled to chase away the tribes from the land that he thought now belonged to him by virtue of that piece of paper.

But they obstinately remained. It was as if they were bound to the place by something stronger than comfort or preference. They went on perching, unwelcome and unhappy, on what we had claimed, as if determined to believe we would soon depart. They did not thrive, though, in the slivers of space we allowed them. Ailments that were no more than a week of discomfort for us proved fatal to them. The general sense among the settlers was that it was only a matter of time before, in a natural way like the turning of the seasons, *our sable brethren* would obligingly disappear.

Among the natives who frequented the town I looked for the people I had come to know with Mr Dawes. Now and then I saw Daringa and the other women, and once Patyegarang too, sitting by a small fire at the water's edge. I stopped, said the greeting I had learnt: *bujari gamarruwa*, and they greeted me in return. But they did not make room among themselves as an invitation to join them, as they had done when I knew them at the observatory. If they had, I might not have done so. Mrs John Macarthur, down in the dirt in front of the whole town with some native women? I will not pretend: that would have taken a woman braver than I.

It was sadly clear to me that my acquaintance with the Sydney people had depended on Mr Dawes as intermediary. With him gone I could see no way to continue it. That time, that place—those few months, that headland—had been a neutral space, a momentary suspension of all the usual ways of being. People who stood on either side of a great chasm had come together to make a flimsy bridge. But it had been only a moment, and now it was gone.

It was a relief to make the move to Parramatta, away from the reminders of those more innocent days. I turned my back, closed my eyes, looked only to my own advantage. Let me say it plain: I was no better than any of the others.

THE FIRST MORNING

The house at Parramatta stood on a sweet slope looking out to the north, the river at its feet. The township was a few minutes' walk away, the governor's house less than a mile. Mr Macarthur took great satisfaction in pointing out to me that our house was two feet longer than Government House.

The first morning there, I walked from room to room, not a tremendous journey by any means, but from each of the main rooms I could see down to the brook, sparkling over stones as it ran to join the main river glinting between the mangroves. Sun came in at each window like a friend, and there was something about the spot—on the brow of a gentle rise, with a further rise at its back—that filled me with peacefulness. It was, of course, the echo of Grandfather's house on its green Devon hillside, with sun pouring in and a great receptive quietness all around.

Edward ran in and out, getting under the feet of the men bringing in boxes and chairs and tables. Little Elizabeth, that sweet dreamy child, stood in a shaft of sun in the parlour, her fine pale hair a crown of light around her head, lost in a trance as she stared out into the newly planted garden. She is too young to remember this, I thought: the sun, the hollow sound of the men bringing the boxes in and putting them in the empty rooms, the singing voices of the place we were in, of breeze in leaves, and birds, and all the unseen things that lived in the grass and spoke to each other. She would not remember how the sun felt on her face, and the feeling of a new beginning. But I would.

Hannaford was put in charge of the labourers and proved more than a match for those truculent men. Knew when to be open-handed with Mr Macarthur's liquor, when to withhold. Mr Macarthur stood in front of the new men, laying down the law about what would be done to them if they took it into their heads to thieve, or utter profanities, or idle their way through their work, or offer insolence. Hannaford stood beside him, his expression obscured by his hat. After Mr Macarthur strode off, I heard Hannaford translating.

— No back-talk from any of you buggers. And by God no effing and blinding or he will have your guts for garters.

We left Smasher Sullivan behind in Sydney. He had served his time, got his ticket. I was glad to see the back of him. There was something about him I shrank from.

Mrs Brown had the house servants under her. She had poor enough material to work with—girls who had been subjected to God alone knew what abuses before they had washed up here—but learned the ways of each, the way Grandfather knew the ways of each of his treasured milking-cows. One girl might respond to gentleness, another had to be chivvied. One could work from dawn to dusk if she did not have to think about what she was doing, while another rose to a challenge.

— They are not bad girls, Mrs Macarthur, was all she would say when I praised the way she managed them. They are not bad girls.

REPRIEVE

As I had hoped, Parramatta was a reprieve from Sydney, where too many people were packed unhappily into too narrow a place. The sky was bigger here, bigger and cleaner and more open, the river lovely with drooping she-oaks, glistening mangroves, wild fowl dipping and gliding. The township was nothing more than a track with convict huts lined up along each side, and the modest patches of cultivation were sad scratched-over bits of dirt. But no matter how shabby the settlement was, and no matter how feeble the farming, the place had a comforting orderliness that compared well with the mud and squalor, the broken-down trees and bushes, the flayed look of Sydney.

Edward and Elizabeth and I could walk about our own acres and each day see some new shoot, some flush of green. It was by no means Devon. But there was the familiar sound of a rooster at dawn, and the comfortable bustling of hens in their yard, and pleasure in watching them flap and fluster back into their shelter as the sun set, as if they could picture the teeth of the native dogs. I loved that flock of mine, the complacent fat hens gossiping to each other as they scratched, the rooster standing up on his dunghill announcing how important he was.

Mr Macarthur had bought a pair of peacocks that had been sent on a ship from the Cape. I found them to be insolent, boastful birds, with their bullying screams, and the cock draggling its tail in the dust or quivering it upright. They were a boast by their owner too. Peacocks were part of a gentleman's estate.

ATTACKS

In Sydney it was possible to imagine that the natives were a temporary inconvenience, but those of us who lived away from the town could cherish no such illusions. Here the wild lands were not out of sight beyond hills and across water. Starting a few yards beyond the outhouse, immeasurable miles of what was strange dwarfed the speck of what was familiar.

The township of Parramatta was so heavily defended that no trouble was likely to come to it, nor to our house, within earshot of the barracks. But out in the new farmlands to the north there were attacks. Not every week, but like a headache, always returning. Crops were burned, stock killed, huts robbed. It was thought that many of the attacks were led by a man named Pemulwuy, but there were other leaders too, their names unknown to us. Whoever the warriors were, their talent for warfare was evident. They knew how to do the most damage to the settlers at the least risk to themselves, quickly raiding an isolated place, then disappearing back into the forest. They never made a direct massed charge and never attacked a township. They left a farm alone if there were soldiers stationed nearby, or if the farmer had a gun. Never struck twice in the same place.

Now and then a farmer was speared, but everyone knew that out on the isolated farms many more could have been killed. The warriors did not seem concerned so much with killing their enemies as with striking at the very foundation of their existence, and for this they had the perfect weapon: fire. In late summer, fields of corn ready to be harvested were burned out, the labour of the past year and the food for the next destroyed in half an hour. The power of the weapon lay in its simplicity and the way it worked hand-in-hand with nature. A fire sparked on a day of hot wind was unstoppable.

Thieving, with or without violence, was an activity the people here were uniquely qualified to understand. What was happening out beyond the settlements was something else. Corn burned rather than stolen, hogs slaughtered but uneaten, huts robbed of clothing when the natives had little use for it: in the eyes of the settlers this was proof that the natives were irrational, childish, spiteful. How else could their behaviour be read?

The general instructions from Whitehall remained as they had always been, that bloodshed should be avoided when possible. Natives should, when practicable, be taken prisoner and brought in to be dealt with like any other criminals. Buckshot should be loaded in the muskets rather than balls, to terrify and wound rather than kill. But the Dear Dunce was happy to leave the details to his commanders' discretion, and the people on the farms made up their own minds about how to defend themselves.

My husband had arranged to be appointed commander of the Parramatta garrison only as part of a larger strategy, but it soon became clear that for once he had miscalculated. Until now his military duties had demanded very little of him. Now they threatened to take over his life.

As commander at Parramatta, it was Mr Macarthur who was responsible for dealing with the *attacks and depredations* on the outlying farms. After each attack he was obliged to send men out to track down the perpetrators, though no one had any illusions about the likely success of this, as the natives did not stand still to be caught. Detachments had to be organised to stand guard over the most vulnerable farms, even though the natives were not blind, and wherever the soldiers were, the natives attacked somewhere else.

Still, the motions had to be gone through, the appearance of control maintained. My husband was kept busy, moving men around from one place to another and trying to guess where the next attack might be made. A serious fear was that runaway convicts would join the natives and add muskets to spears. The situation smouldered on, neither bursting into frank flame nor being extinguished, but taking up more and more of Mr Macarthur's time and energy when there were other, more profitable uses for them.

He refused to dignify what was happening with the word *war*. It was the erratic and malicious actions of savages, he maintained, essentially pointless and ultimately futile. It was true that this was not the kind of war that soldiers like him meant by that word. In their tradition, not to stand in formation and fight an orderly battle was called by another name: *treachery*. Men guilty of *treachery* deserved no mercy.

In any case, he assured me that he had no intention of losing sleep over depredations led by men he dismissed as naked savages. Parramatta was in no danger whatsoever, he said, and he brushed off the attacks on the farms.

– Oh, let them burn out a few crofters, he said. We cannot protect every hut and every cob of corn. But I take the long view, my dear. Make no mistake, Pemulwuy and his fellows will not occupy our time for much longer.

There was an edge to his tone that made me look at him, but he only gave me a tight bland smile.

BURRAMATTAGAL

I had been told that, in the first weeks of settlement at Parramatta, there had been the beginnings of cordial relations with the Burramattagal. A commerce had been struck up, an exchange of bread and salt beef for fish. But at some point things had gone wrong, some business of a native canoe wantonly destroyed by one of the convicts, and there was no more trade.

A few Burramattagal families still lived around us, in the ever-smaller places where grants had not yet made them trespassers. These people chose a strategy different from Pemulwuy's: they simply became invisible. Two or three men might be seen down by the river's edge with their fishing spears when the eel were plentiful, and groups of women with their children hunted crabs among the mangroves. I would have liked to get close enough to greet them, thinking that the words Mr Dawes had taught me might be understood. But they always saw me as I approached, and had disappeared before I reached the spot where they had been, leaving nothing to see but shifting leaf-shadow. We were two sets of people inhabiting the same space, each set going about its affairs as if the other were not there.

One afternoon soon after we removed to Parramatta, I surprised some women down by the river who disappeared in their usual way. When I got to the place where they had been, I found a hidden fire, hot embers without smoke or flame, and nearby, left behind in the haste to be away, a stick of the kind I had seen them using to dig. When I picked it up, it seemed still warm from the grasp of a hand.

A person had to hold it to see how cunningly it had been

wrought. The wood, darkened as if from a fire, was hard and dense like metal, but the weight balanced itself sweetly in the hand. One end was shaped into a rounded bulge that you could lean on to give yourself leverage. The other was a sharp flattened blade. And there was the place where the hand grasped it, polished to a dull gleam. I could see that it was the product of many hours of labour, as beautifully and knowledgeably made as any carriage wheel or dining chair.

There was an urge to keep it. To walk away feeling it balanced in my hand. To take it home, show it to others, display it on a mantelpiece, steal some of its glory for myself.

But there was an intimacy about grasping it where that other woman grasped it, her hand smoothing it to a fine gleam over the years. It put me in mind of the big spoon my mother had used to stir her custards, one side worn away from so many years of stirring against the bottom of the pan, leaving its mark on the shape of the spoon as if she had signed it with her name.

I was ashamed of my urge to take. I laid the stick back down beside the fire. She would come back for it and be glad to see it still there. She would recognise that I could have taken it away, and had not. It would be a communication between us. A friendly greeting, perhaps even the start of a conversation.

As I lay that night waiting for sleep, I mused about the trade of fish for salt beef that we had been told of. I thought of those Gadigal women I had come to know, whose insight about Mr Dawes and myself had far outstripped mine, and whose subtle humour had needed to be explained to me as you might explain something to a child. Those women would never have been so dull as to believe sour salt beef was a fair exchange for fresh fish. Why would their neighbours the Burramattagal be any less shrewd?

261

Another possibility occurred to me with a feeling like relief, a puzzle solved. *Trade* was our word. But what the Burramattagal were doing, when they exchanged their fish for our beef, was perhaps not commerce. Perhaps it was something more like education. *Look*, they might have been saying. *I am showing you the proper way to do things: I give to you, you give to me. And in accepting your inferior food, I am teaching you grace, forgiveness and generosity. Perhaps also shame.*

When the exchange of goods ended, it may have been because the pupil was too dull to learn. Too coarse-grained to feel shame.

I had been pleased with myself for using the stick as a friendly message to its owner. But was it possible that it had been left as a message for me—one that I had been too obtuse even to recognise as a message? *This is my place, and this object shows that it is my place.* As one of its manifold uses, the stick might be a title deed as clear and unambiguous, to a person who knew how to read it, as the piece of paper on which was written *J. Macarthur 100 acres.*

It was a shadow at the edge of my life, the consciousness that I was on land that other people knew was theirs. On the days I walked without glimpsing any of the Burramattagal, I was glad to pretend that there was no shadow.

THE FIRST SHEEP

A hundred acres was not a fraction of what Mr Macarthur wanted, and we had not seen out a year at Parramatta before he was trying to buy the land of the man on our western side, an ex-convict by the name of Ruse. But it turned out that, on board the *Neptune*, Mr Macarthur had delivered himself of some particular insult to the convict woman who was now the wife of Ruse, and Ruse had not forgotten. He steadily refused any price that Mr Macarthur offered, and in the end, to make his point, he sold it to someone else for half what it was worth. Ruse was the only man I knew who had ever bested my husband.

Mind you, I heard later that the poor fellow had fallen on hard times, and I wondered. The Inspector of Public Works was a dangerous person to cross.

The way to get more land by government grant was to show that you had made the most of what you already had, so Mr Macarthur drove Hannaford and the convicts hard. But crops were slow. Clearing the land required too much labour. If a man had his eye on a big spread, he needed sheep or cattle that could simply range between the trees and eat the native pasture. As their numbers multiplied, so would the acreage they needed. Mr Macarthur's eyes shone with the arithmetic of procreation.

In short order he bought the only stock he could get, which was sixty Bengal sheep off the *Atlantic* out of Calcutta. Accustomed to the great woolly tubs that had made up Grandfather's flock, I could barely recognise these ugly creatures as sheep. They were sad scraggly things, no better than goats, covered with coarse wiry hair in dirty colours, twitching their strange dangling ears. You have been diddled, Captain Macarthur, I thought. Someone has spotted a draper's son coming along who has never seen a sheep at close quarters.

— It is what we can get, he said indifferently. I will look for a chance to obtain better, but for the time being they will serve.

The sheepstealer Hannaford went to inspect the new arrivals the first afternoon as they huddled together on the grassy rise behind the house.

— What do you think, Mr Hannaford, I said, they are a sad apology for sheep, are they not?

— Ah well, Mrs Macarthur, he said.

I had laid a trap for him without meaning to, for what shepherd criticises the animals belonging to his master? He eyed me from under his hat-brim.

— Indeed they are not sheep such as I am familiar with, he said. But they may surprise us yet, Mrs Macarthur, I will do my best with them, you can be sure of that.

He turned to catch one of the sheep. It was apparent from the understanding authority with which he handled the animal that Mr Macarthur may have been diddled with respect to the sheep, but not with respect to the shepherd. This was a man who knew what he was about.

Soon after the Bengals arrived, Hannaford came up from Sydney with three Irish sheep, two ewes and a young ram. The big-framed Irish were a pleasure to look at, solid and creamy-woolled in spite of the months on the ship. *A leg in each corner*, as Grandfather had said of his strongest sheep. They joined the Bengals up on the hill and set to straight away on the tufty grass as if they knew nothing of sweet Irish pasture.

It became a daily pleasure to stroll up that slope in the late afternoon with Mrs Brown and Edward and Elizabeth as the sheep were being walked back down to the folds. I called the place the Fairview, from the way the land eased up into a natural stage, the ground falling away on every side, trees standing solemnly among the grass as if planted to enhance the beauty of a gentleman's park. From there you could see as far as the line of distant mountains that marked the perimeter of our world.

To step out—the birds making their music from every tree, the air with that damp, rich end-of-day thickness, each grass stalk with its own halo of light, its own thread of shadow—that was a humble delight. I loved to watch the blue of the mountains grow deeper and more mysterious, waited to see the sun slide down behind them. I tried to explain to Edward why the last pale light on the slope was wiped away by the shadow crawling across it. We were moving, I told him. We were on a great ball turning away from the sun, like an orange held up to a candle. But I was no Mr Dawes. I could not convince my dear little boy. Never mind, I thought, he will come to it in his own time, and might remember with a smile how his mother had tried.

Hannaford was there too, making sure the shepherd lad did not try to rush the sheep on their way down to the fold, or leave any behind. Had a piece of string to make the tally, and I liked to watch his big fingers sliding, knotting, sliding, knotting, as Grandfather's had done.

Mr Macarthur told me he had got the Irish in order to put some meat on the skinny Bengals. Mutton always fetched a good price. I doubted that the Irish ram would recognise these goatish creatures as his own species, and wondered whether the light-framed Bengal ewes might be outraged at this heavy stranger approaching them. But one afternoon we walked up the hill earlier than usual, and I could see that the ewes were skittish, ready for the rams.

Hannaford was watching them.

– Good afternoon, Mrs Macarthur, he said. And to you, Mrs Brown.

The sheep were moving uneasily, the rams wandering to one ewe, then another, as if they had mislaid something and were asking for help to find it. The Irish ram was scouting around a Bengal ewe and one of the skinny Bengal rams challenged him, but the Irish did not hesitate to see him off and the Bengal did not stay to argue.

– They are, that is, they are, Hannaford said, awkward for once.

– The ewes are ready, are they not, I said, very matter-of-fact, to tell him that a ram covering a ewe was not going to shock me. Watch this now, Edward, I thought. It will be your turn one day to sidle up to some woman and try your luck with her.

– I am curious to watch Irish meet Bengal, I said. How do you think it will work itself out, Mr Hannaford?

He spread his big strong hands in a gesture of making no pronouncements.

– Never in the history of the world has that been done, Mrs Macarthur, he said. We are here at the world's unknown end.

I knew he was thinking *arse-end*.

Mrs Brown heard the unspoken word as clear as I did, and I felt her shift and cough as if to smother amusement. Hannaford's eyes went sideways towards her, and the three of us stood with faces lit with humour suppressed, not quite glancing at each other.

Now the Irish was nosing at the ewe's backside and shaking his ears at her. Pawed at her side, his foreleg scratching at her, while she took no notice, only stepping forward as if she had spotted a better tuft of grass, so he had to follow after, still pawing away at her side.

In my mind it was Mr Macarthur tickling at my arm, which

was his way of telling me he required my services, and the ewe was myself, thinking, oh, must you? I made some sort of noise as I saw the resemblance, and Mrs Brown looked at me, our eyes met, and we were two women joined in amusement at the antics of men.

It turned out that the Irish ram was by no means too proud to mount the Bengal, no matter how ugly she was, and she took him as placidly as if he were an old habit.

When Hannaford came to tell us that the Bengals were lambing, we all walked up the hill—Mr Macarthur came with us for once, to count his increase—on a clear still morning with a thick selvage of grey cloud hanging above the horizon, and the sun gleaming through the pearl of it.

Already, even with some of the ewes not yet delivered of their lambs, the increase in the flock was remarkable. Grandfather's sheep generally had only the one lamb, but most of these Indian sheep stood with two lambs nuzzling at them. Some had three, and a few of these unpromising ewes had produced four healthy lambs, as if they thought they were bitches dropping a litter. They were in good heart, had thickened up on our rich pastures, and their lambs were strong as they ran about among their shadows.

Mr Macarthur, having less knowledge of sheep than Hannaford and myself, was not astonished at the fecundity of the Bengals. But was as proud as if he himself had sired the things.

– Lord Irish has done his best, Mr Macarthur, Hannaford said. Served mightily, among so many. But any chance you might get, sir, for a few more good rams might be an opportunity you might think of taking.

I heard him going carefully. Who was a convict, to tell Mr Macarthur his business?

WOOL AND HAIR

You could tell where the Irish ram had been among the Bengals. As the lambs grew and their coats developed, among them were some with a smoother coat and of a different shape.

– Look at this beauty, Mr Macarthur, Hannaford said, holding one for us to see. Such a strong big bugger, pardon me Mrs Macarthur. And look at this here.

He parted the lamb's short dusty hair.

– See here, sir, he said. Under the hair d'you see, right on the skin, something near wool.

Mr Macarthur did not care to touch, but I did. Hannaford was right: under the hair was a secret second skin of something like velvet, the imprint of the Irish on the hairy Bengal.

– The good blood coming out, Hannaford said. The good blood for wool.

But Mr Macarthur cared nothing for wool or hair, only about the numbers. Hannaford and I watched him trying to count the sheep, losing count, trying again. Hannaford had his tally string in his hand.

– A hundred and fifteen lambs by my count, Mr Macarthur, he said. The whole flock a hundred and eighty-seven.

OF THE SPANISH BREED

The colonel's grants had allowed Elizabeth Farm to expand as far as it could: further expansion was now blocked on every side by other men's land or by water. For Mr Macarthur this was the spur to a larger ambition. Some thirty miles away there was a piece of land superior to any yet seen, on which the cattle that had escaped in the earliest weeks of the colony had made their home. Mr Macarthur, in his capacity as inspector, had ridden over it, glimpsed the cattle, recognised the uniquely splendid nature of the place, and decided that Cowpastures, as it was called, must become his.

He was not discouraged by its distance from the settlements, although that would make it difficult to defend against *attacks and depradations*. The more immediate obstacle was that Cowpastures had been set aside in perpetuity by the first governor as Crown land, never to be granted away. But for Mr Macarthur this was not so much an obstacle as a stimulus to ingenuity. Like a general arraying his troops, he made preparations for the long game.

The first step was to acquire more stock, any animals at all, their only function to give the man who owned them an argument for needing more land.

His next purchase was four ewes and two rams. They were skinny and slope-shouldered, with no chest to them and not a good shape as to the ribs, but even bedraggled after their time on the ship their fleece was softer and finer than the wool of the Irish.

— Merinos, so called, Mr Macarthur said. Waterhouse bought them at the Cape, someone spun him a tale about these being bona fide Spanish merinos. A good tale, so he wasted good money on them. Well, they may once have been Spanish, but admixed since then. I told him, these are no more the pure Spanish than I am a Dutchman!

The memory of which witticism amused him considerably.

Grandfather had spoken of the mythical Spanish merinos, sheep so precious, their wool so fine, that Spain kept them locked up for itself alone. I was glad he was not here to see the myth in the flesh.

Why had Mr Macarthur bought these unpromising things? Oh, that was easy—to spite the new parson, Mr Marsden, who fancied himself as a farmer.

— I wanted them all, he said. But Waterhouse had already shaken on the deal with Marsden. I leaned on him, but the obstinate fool would only sell me half.

He watched the sheep mill and bleat.

— Had the satisfaction of seeing the parson's face fall, he said. Not the only one in New South Wales to have merinos of the Spanish breed! The fool has some grand fantasy of fine wool, imagine.

All the same, I could see that he regretted the purchase.

— We will keep them apart, he said. Keep them pure.

He spoke as if he had a hundred Spanish, not six.

— Keep their impurity pure, he said, and laughed. So I may call them Spanish for the next man who comes along wanting some pure merinos.

Hannaford was not impressed by the new sheep. Told me the Spanish were reputed to be slow to multiply, and poor mothers. Was not convinced, either, by the notion of purity. Six sheep kept pure would soon become a sickly flock. Still, he did everything as Mr Macarthur wanted, and at great labour fenced off the miserable-looking Spanish in their own field.

TO BE DOING

When the Spanish dropped their lambs, Mr Macarthur was disappointed: from the four ewes, only three live lambs.

Hannaford was in the fold with one of the mothers, I could see him trying to persuade her to stand still so the lamb could suckle. The mother did not look at her lamb, but as fast as it approached she moved away, as skittish as if it were a stranger, leaving the poor little mite straining up to nothing. We watched it stumble, fall, stagger after its mother again.

– Mrs Macarthur, if I hold this one still, would you bring the lamb over to her, Hannaford said, taking hold of the ewe.

The lamb was featherweight in my arms, a lamb in need of a good suck if ever there was one. But a winsome thing like a child's toy, its coat smooth and soft. I crouched with it beside its mother, stroked the ewe under her chin and held the lamb to her, and finally she stood still long enough for it to latch on. How I loved to be doing again, among the sheep, smelling the wool up close, remembering what Grandfather had showed me.

– It could break your heart, Hannaford said. Somewhere down the line, the blood that makes a good mother and the blood that makes good wool went their separate ways. Give me a good Leicester any day of the week.

The lamb had drunk its fill and lay down exhausted from the chase after its mother.

– If we were to mix some of this Spanish blood back into those others, I said. The crosses, when they are of an age. I wonder would the blood for mothering stay, and the blood for wool come out?

I was following a thought and speaking it out loud, but when Hannaford was silent, bending over the ewe intent on getting a prickle out of its fleece, I realised I had made a difficulty for him. It was not up to him to remind me of my husband's order to *keep them pure*.

– I could not say, Mrs Macarthur, he said at last. I am just an ignorant fellow.

– Nonsense, Mr Hannaford, I said. You are no ignorant fellow, but a sheepstealer, and what greater expert can there be in the matter of sheep than a man who came within a whisker of paying with his life for a good one?

He laughed, glad not to have paid that price, and I was happy to leave the moment of difficulty behind. The little puzzle of good wool against good mothering had been a quick flare of curiosity. The pleasure of that puzzle would not be worth setting myself against Mr Macarthur.

But Hannaford was standing by the ewe, his hands smoothing and parting her fleece. Soft, fine, creamy, it sprang up strongly under his fingers.

– The rams, Hannaford said. You know, Mrs Macarthur, a ram can spread its seed, if you pardon my language. And not lose anything. Not lose any…

He was avoiding saying *purity*. We did not look at each other, only down at the wool opened up under his hands. *Crimp*: the word came to me in Grandfather's voice. Tight, densely packed, this was better crimp than Grandfather could ever have imagined.

– Of course the Spanish ewes must be kept separate, I said.

– And so they would be, Mrs Macarthur, certainly, he said. The Spanish gentlemen to do their duty with their countrywomen. Then have at as many of the others as they have the vigour for.

Now at last he looked me in the face.

– No purity would be lost, Mrs Macarthur. I assure you. None whatsoever.

Oh, he knew what I laboured under. They all knew.

LAMENTABLE

Land, though irresistible when it could be got for nothing, was secondary to Mr Macarthur's real passions. It was not sheep or corn that interested him, and certainly not his unexpectedly onerous military obligations. What was uppermost in his mind was trade: the *Britannia* had been only the first of many charters. It was not only the gigantic profit to be made from liquor. It was that his nature made him crave to be at the heart of a complicated tangle of other men's greed, fear, sloth and malice, directing them by plotting, scheming, luring, threatening, coaxing. More than the money, more even than the power to shape events, was the pleasure he took in his own ingenious schemes.

We had not been at Parramatta more than a few months when he came to me full of endearments.

— It is regrettable, my dearest wife, he said. Nay, it is lamentable. But it is essential that I spend some time in Sydney. I must ensure that the DD's favour continues to run in my direction.

It was what I had hardly dared to hope for, but I pouted, for form's sake, and to tease. I watched him cast about for another argument.

— Those rogues in the Corps, he said. If I am not on the spot, some other man will be convinced he can do as good a job of the new charter. I must be there.

— Oh, I said, and may I not accompany you, and enjoy the novelty of society?

— Oh well, he said.

I let him flounder before I rescued him.

— On second thoughts, I would not feel easy in my mind to leave the children in the care of the servants.

His frown cleared, and there it was: two people pretending a thing was *lamentable* when in their hearts they both rejoiced.

That first morning as he rode off to Sydney I stood with Elizabeth's hand in mine, watching the horse grow small in the distance. When I turned back into the house I walked with her from room to room. The air in every corner seemed more still. The light gleamed along the boards in a more serene way.

I had come to hate the marital bed, and even the room it was in. Can a person fear a marble mantelpiece, the particular shape of the cracks in the ceiling? I flung open the French doors—he liked a closed-up bedroom where I loved a flow of air—and let in the outside world. There was the garden, and beyond that the yellow-green of the bush, pale trunks like Chinese writing in among the blur of leaves as the sun shifted calmly through its day.

How quickly a person could reclaim a space! How little it took!

That night I lay savouring a joy no more complicated than the certainty of being alone. I could not sleep for the novel pleasure of it, and another novelty occurred to me. I slipped down from the bed and stood on the verandah, barefoot on the flagstones, letting the dewy darkness of the night enter me. My body felt alive along every morsel of skin, my feet on the cool paving were aware of every grain of the stone.

A dog barked, far off, a hollow sound, the dog unhurried, unworried, its barking as if for the sake of hearing its own voice. Chained somewhere, its sound carried miles, not filling the silence but making it bigger. That hollow distant sound told you how vast the night was, like a speck on a white sheet that showed you how white it was. The dog was doing what I was doing, simply being in the darkness, greeting the hidden world.

Beyond the flower garden a light gleamed between the cracks in the hut where Hannaford lived with the shepherd lad. I was seized with an impulse to walk out across the grass, slip up to the wall of the hut, and place my eye to one of those cracks.

Why did I want to peer through that tempting chink? It was nothing about Hannaford, or the shepherd lad. It was a curiosity that was the other side of ignorance. Having come to myself, and in the freedom of being alone, I wanted to watch another life, to watch other people when they thought no one was looking. I had seen surfaces only, all my life. I had presented only surfaces to others. Now I was consumed with wanting to see beyond surface. Who are other people when they think themselves unobserved? What is it like, to be a person?

I crept up to the hut, trying in a confused way to prepare what I could say if I were discovered. Could I convince someone that I was sleepwalking, staring and muttering like Lady Macbeth? But Lady Macbeth would not stand on tiptoe to peer through a crack, no matter how fast asleep she might be. Nor would she have had the idea of pulling on her blue wrapper to hide the white of her nightdress. I had no story, no pretext however mad, as I approached my eye to the crack.

In the flicker of the fire I could see nothing clear at first. Then something moved and someone murmured. There was a sound like a contented sigh. I squeezed myself sideways to the chink and saw that the movement was a bare leg, and that the leg belonged to Mrs Brown, and that it was entwined with an arm that belonged to William Hannaford.

I stepped away quickly. *More than I bargained for*, I thought. *Oh, more than I bargained for!* I was laughing, although what was so amusing? I was doubled over around the mirth, or whatever it was, as I went silently back across the grass to the house. Of course I knew that Hannaford and Mrs Brown had found each other. And of course they would arrange a way to be together. Easy enough, when they wanted time to themselves, to tell the shepherd lad to make his bed in with the other men. But somehow I had not followed the knowledge further. Had not considered what I might see, had only wanted the freedom to look.

Back in the house I slid into bed and lay coiled up, my heart-beats slowly calming. There was a pang, no question, a wryness that twisted around in me like a small unhappy animal. I had once been where those two people were now, in the tenderness of two bodies and two spirits coming together. But it was gone, gone, gone. I did not think it would come again.

At the same time, the thought of that leg, that arm, made me smile. That joy would always be part of who I was. What I had shared with Mr Dawes was a flame that passed from person to person. For a time it had alighted on William Dawes and Elizabeth Macarthur. Now it had come to rest with Agnes Brown and William Hannaford. It was a gift we might have a share in, but it was for passing on, not for owning.

I lay curled around myself in a confusion of smiling and wryness too mixed to be separated. Lady Macbeth had crept to that crack in search of something, and perhaps she had found it: that when life offered delight it should be enjoyed. Here I was, alone, and what a delight that was. How much better to have your own true self for company than to be lost in the solitude of an unhappy marriage.

I never knew how many nights I would be alone in the bed, for Mr Macarthur returned unpredictably.

You may imagine, I wrote to Bridie one day when he had just arrived, *how great was my joy on the return of Mr Macarthur.*

Oh, how I loved to find a two-faced form of words. That private pleasure never staled.

It is possible that Mr Macarthur treated himself to some pretty young doxy in Sydney. But I did not want to know then, do not want to know now.

COMING FORWARD

Nothing was spelled out between myself and Mr Macarthur, but as he gradually withdrew from the workings of the farm, I gradually came forward. Compared to Grandfather's modest place, this was a gigantic enterprise and in the beginning I was alarmed at all that I had to understand. I had no experience, no confidence in my judgment, no knowledge of working men and how to wield authority over them.

But I was not alone. Every morning Hannaford came to me, then Mrs Brown. Each stood courteously over me beside the table telling me all that was needed, while like a pupil I wrote down the lists of things to be seen to, money to be laid out, projects to be planned, problems to be addressed.

I never told Mrs Brown and William Hannaford that I knew they had found a way to be together. That was their business. But they knew that I knew. It was a warmth between the three of us, like a friend in the room that we were pleased to have among us.

At first I went to Mr Macarthur, papers in hand, for him to advise or approve, but he would run his eye down the pages without interest, and I went to him less and less often. Now and then, to remind him of how dull the farm affairs were, I pretended a dilemma, and obliged him to sit while I laid out endless details and he fidgeted for me to be done. It was *Papilionaceae* over again.

The farmer's wife that I might have become, and that Grandfather had taught so well, came tiptoeing out from behind the gentleman's wife. My time with Mr Dawes had showed me how keenly I loved a problem, loved to wrestle with difficulty. As mistress of Elizabeth Farm, every day had its vexation. But each new vexation brought the memory of the last, and the fact that it had been solved. Vexation was vexing, but idleness was like death.

FINE WOOL

Hannaford and I said nothing more to each other about putting the Spanish rams to the crossbred ewes, and certainly nothing to Mr Macarthur. But it was done, and as the lambs from those pairings grew, it seemed that, yes, the Spanish ram had given his fine wool to his offspring, and the crossbred ewe had given her robustness. We had hardly dared to expect such a miracle.

– God must feel like this, I said to Hannaford one evening as we leaned together on the fold watching the woolly lambs we had somehow created from hairy sheep.

I had once, in that other life, said something similar about an orrery, and smiled at the memory.

– Indeed, Hannaford said. God might. And we could help Him along, if we went about it right, to breed the hair out of the whole flock.

There was a flicker of apprehension then, as if he was thinking that William Hannaford, convict, and Mrs John Macarthur should not be spoken of so casually in the same sentence, as *we*, or that he should speak so lightly of helping God. But I was happy to be *we* with him, and agreed that God's work was not always so perfect that it would not benefit from a helping hand.

– Breed for the wool, are you thinking, I said. Not the meat?

– That ram I put my hand to, it was his fleece tempted me, he said. My thinking was, breed for the fleece. Not trust that Spain would always sell us theirs.

He turned his head away as if to spit, but did not.

– When I say *us*, he said, with a curl of scorn, I meant England. But why not here? Give this place something to go to market with.

At my urging, Mr Macarthur came up to the field with me,

and had to agree that the wool promised to be very fine. But after a cursory look he turned back to go down the hill.

– Yes, well done, my dear, he said. Very satisfactory.

– But Mr Macarthur, I said, putting out a hand to stop him, is it not true that wool can be sent to London for sale, where no other commodity can come out of the hold after six months and still find a market?

– Oh yes, he said. I suppose that would be so.

There was an extra degree of the casual in his tone but his face had tightened. I realised that Hannaford was still within earshot, and my husband felt the need to show that his authority was untroubled by a wife piping up at him.

– That fellow Marsden has some idea of growing wool here, he said. But what is needed is meat. Only a fool would think otherwise.

His silence let it sink in that I was the *fool*.

– My dear wife, your enthusiasm is to be applauded, he said. But let me convince you by means of a little arithmetic. The price of wool is measured in pence, that of mutton in shillings. A difference by a factor of twelve, you see.

Hannaford had all at once become busy leading one of the ewes away and getting out his knife to scrape at her hoof. Called to the lad to help him, Look sharp, lad, look sharp now!

– My dear wife, Mr Macarthur said, and patted my arm in an excess of condescension, I think you will find your idea is nothing more, *au fond*, than a desire for the fields and sheep of home.

I did not try again to speak to him about wool, but his indifference freed me to picture for myself the culling and the keeping Hannaford and I might do, so that each generation of lambs would have finer wool. I was dizzy thinking of all the combinations and permutations of Bengal and Irish and Spanish that we would have once we went down that path. *In-and-in*, Grandfather had called it, but you could not do *in-and-in* unless you knew what every sheep's parents were, and its parents before that. The way to keep track would be to write it all down in tidy columns like the blue notebook in which Mr Dawes had begun to chart a language new to him. That way you could keep order, so the mounting of ram with ewe was not chance, but system.

I saw myself striding up the hill every morning to the flock to feel the wool on this one, the chest on that. In the same image, there was Grandfather on the hillside with me, proud of his clever grand-daughter, looking about him with pleasure at what she had done. He might even find it in himself to forgive William Hannaford for stealing a ram that did not belong to him.

MON PETIT COIN

Down beside the river I had a spot of my own, where now and then I could slip out of the skin of Mrs John Macarthur. It was screened by bushes that framed a view up and down the stream: another airy room made of leaves. In that lovely place I often wondered what harbour, what river, what street, Mr Dawes might now be looking at. Wherever he was, he would find himself another *petit coin*, and perhaps, sitting there, remember the woman who had found it so difficult to get her mouth around the phrase. *Mon petit coin à moi.*

One evening I went down there, in a musing frame of mind, thinking of the year past and the year to come, and the surprising corners that had led me to this peaceful place. There was a fallen log that, like the rock at the top of Mr Dawes' point, was as if made for a backside. I sat on its familiar shape and waited for the air to flow in around the disturbance I had made, until I became just one more object in the landscape and the creatures around me resumed their lives.

A black waterbird stepped across a patch of grass, head bobbing earnestly at each step, and from somewhere overhead another bird sang *Pic-ture! Pic-ture!* as if it, too, saw the beauty of the scene. There was the softest of rustles as a slim black snake passed from one tuft of grass to another. Threads of spiderwebs hung golden in the soft liquid light and beneath them on the ground the perfect crescents of gum-leaves were arranged in an elegant display.

As I sat, the river caught the last light, its surface alive with flickering patterns of gold and shining spots where bubbles rose. On the far bank the tangled black trunks of the mangroves stood up to their many knees in the shadowed water. There was the lap of small waves, the gentle whistling music of the she-oaks when a breeze ran through them, the twitterings and chirpings as invisible birds arranged themselves for the night. A cloud of midges hovered in a last shaft of sunlight, each speck gilded by the low sun. As light shifted into shadow, each moment was a kind of soft shock, a wondering astonishment at the beauty of all these simple things around me. The world had created this loveliness, but it had also created some matching thing in me that recognised it as lovely.

Looking back up the slope, between the trees I could make out the darkness that I knew to be the house. As I watched, a point of light sprang out there, failed, grew bright and steady. That would be Mrs Brown lighting the parlour lamp. Then another joined it. The lamp in the dining room.

Soon I would walk up the hill and into that golden light. The children would be there, those beings who had blossomed out of this place. I knew every crease in their bodies, every impulse of their small souls. I knew every corner of those rooms, every pattern of the grain of every floorboard. I knew every tree and rock in my *petit coin*, every shape the water took around the bed of the river at every height of the tide. This land—this dirt and stones and trees—was connected to me now by a thousand days and nights of breathing its air, a thousand filaments of memory. In my seat by the river, it had never occurred to me to calculate which direction England lay in, so I could point my longing beak towards it. This spot did not make me think of somewhere else. I only thought of what was here about me. This sky. This dirt. This water and these stones.

It was not flesh of my flesh, bone of my bones. Devon was the land that held the bodies of every man and woman whose couplings had ended in me, the place where my forebears had lain in the churchyard at Bridgerule for so many years that the words on their gravestones had blurred. Yet I belonged here now, better than I belonged to any other sliver of the globe's mighty bulk.

I let myself enter the story of being in this place for the rest of my life. Of putting my feet down and letting them grow roots. Of walking every afternoon down to this river with its mysterious shadows. Of watching my children—perhaps my grandchildren—grow sturdy on the sunlight and dry sweet air. Of the place growing around me, a second skin. Of growing old and dying here, gladly becoming part of its dust.

Like the hand of a compass swinging and hesitating, wavering and finally pointing, my thoughts showed me what I must have known for a long time without recognising: this was home.

The water was sombre now, the mangroves eerie. Sitting beside this river, seeing the forest gathering shadows on the opposite bank, I could not see how a future here could come to pass. Sooner or later Mr Macarthur would say, *Now we are going home*, and what would I do? I might know this place to be my home, but Mrs John Macarthur was obliged to find her home wherever her husband decreed. Staying here was a dream, a longing without form.

But the idea was stronger than the impossibility of it. Even to recognise that longing and give voice to it was a kind of power.

It was extraordinary that more than two years had passed without a new governor sailing into Sydney Cove. Rumours arrived on various ships. It would be this man; it would be that. He had not yet been appointed; he was on his way. With every ship there was a different story, told with the same breathless certainty as the last.

In the meantime, poor Major Grose became less and less able to go through the motions of his duties. The wounds he had received on His Majesty's service in America had a debilitating effect that no amount of rest seemed to improve. When, on my rare and brief visits to Sydney, I glimpsed him, he was a bad colour, and corpulent in a way that suggested illness rather than high living. It came as no great surprise when he announced that he must return to England to regain his health.

He handed the reins to his deputy. Power did not corrupt pleasant Colonel Paterson: he remained as agreeable as ever. He was happy, as he put it, to do no more than *keep the seat warm*, and did not object to any suggestions made by the Inspector of Public Works. On the basis of our expanded flock, and some buttering-up by Mr Macarthur, the colonel was happy to award him a hundred acres beyond the settlement at a place called Toongabbie, then a further hundred. Mr Macarthur was not the only one to benefit from the colonel's largesse: land was being granted away on all sides, farms springing up near every watercourse.

As more and more land was granted away, the raids by Pemulwuy and the others became more frequent and inflicted more damage. Mr Macarthur might refuse to call what was going on a war, but whatever name you gave it, there was not much doubt who was winning. Soldiers who had been sent to New South Wales to keep order among prisoners were instead standing guard over fields of corn. They could not be everywhere, though, so field after field of precious corn continued to go up in smoke. Settlers in the isolated parts, living in daily fear of a spear sailing out of the forest, spoke of abandoning their farms. From time to time the situation was so grave that there were whispers—hushed as soon as voiced, but persistent—that in the end the colony would have to be given up altogether.

It was true that natives were sometimes shot. But there was never a decisive victory, because the battle was always fought on their terms: the surprise raid, the quick retreat. There seemed no way to tempt them out into open battle, where guns could do their work. They were too clever for that.

I could feel that the matter was becoming personal for my husband, chasing after an enemy as elusive as smoke. Pemulwuy was making Captain Macarthur look a little foolish.

We got word from the *Iconic* that the *Admiral Barrington*, with the new governor on board, was not far behind. Mr Macarthur called for his horse and set off for Sydney before the breakfast things were cleared, determined to be the first on board to welcome him. Had himself rowed out to the ship, he boasted, almost before the anchor was let go. Enjoyed a lengthy private conversation in which he was able to lay before the new man an outline of the various personages and dilemmas he would be dealing with, and Mr Macarthur's own view as to the best way to deal with them.

The new governor, like the first, was an officer of the navy and was immediately christened Old Hornpipe by Mr Macarthur. For a time he was as credulous as Mr Macarthur could wish. But he had been in Sydney Cove with the original fleet and he was no fool. He saw how the colony was faring, as a kingdom run by the Corps and powered by liquor. It was clear from the first month that he planned to get authority back from the officers by putting an end to those profitable rivers of rum.

As far as my husband was concerned, Old Hornpipe's attitude was nothing but malice. It was a wish to destroy him, Captain John Macarthur, personally. It was an outrage. The man was a blackguard and a fool. The Inspector of Public Works threatened to withdraw his services, wrote long scathing letters to Whitehall about the governor, poisoned as many minds against him as he could.

Old Hornpipe put up a good fight. He called Mr Macarthur's bluff on his threat to resign as Inspector and appointed a new one forthwith. Was known to be matching Mr Macarthur's letters to Whitehall with his own, and never let anyone forget that he was, in his person and in his office, the representative on this continent of His Majesty King George the Third.

Colonel Paterson, now deputy to the governor and commander of the Corps, was still useful, and still warmly cultivated by my husband. But he no longer held those godlike powers that he had enjoyed as acting governor. There could be no doubt about it: the officers' glory days were numbered.

More than once I surprised Mr Macarthur in closed dark brooding, a man who had tasted triumphs and now felt them in danger of being taken away. On every side his ambitions were blocked: for the moment there was no more land to be had, his profitable speculations were under threat, and the thing that he would not call a war smouldered on.

I knew the look of that closed dark brooding. It was my husband with something up his sleeve.

One night a messenger from the barracks came to the door with a note for Mr Macarthur.

— Yes, Mr Macarthur said. Trouble at the northern farms. Yes, I see.

He was untroubled, unsurprised, as if he had expected this very note to arrive, if not on this night then on another, and he knew what to do when it was delivered.

— Pemulwuy again? I said.

Mr Macarthur gave me a bland smile I could not read.

— Ah, I had best look into it, my dear.

There was nothing but good cheer in his tone, which surprised me, as his military obligations were usually a source of irritation. He was already out of the room calling for his horse, and he did not return that night.

I slept uneasily. I could not put out of my mind the way Mr Macarthur had been as he read the note. *What are you up to, Mr Macarthur? What do you know, that you are not saying?*

When I rose in the morning all was calm. I went out on to the verandah and Mrs Brown brought me my breakfast cup of tea. Hannaford came around the corner of the house and was about to speak when there was the silly thin pop of a far-off gun, then another. A confusion of shouting came from the direction of the township, whistles blew, a drum started up a jerky banging, there was a flurry of shots.

— What is it? I said, with a sour feeling, because something was wrong, and it had to do with the note that had come for Mr Macarthur, that he had been expecting.

But now the shepherd lad was running up the hill towards us.

– The natives, he panted. The natives are come in! Come in over the river! Two hundred at least!

His eyes were shining with the pleasure of being part of something so grand, but safe to tell the tale.

– Mr Macarthur says to tell you there is no danger whatever, he said. But to stay here, madam. Not to move out of the house on any account.

– The natives, Mrs Brown said. Oh, the Lord help them, they will not get far against the guns.

Even as we were speaking, silence fell. There had been a few dozen shots, a few minutes of shouting.

Whatever had happened, it was over.

By the time my husband returned that night we had heard an account—actually, several different accounts—of what had taken place. The central fact, common to all the versions, was that, an hour after dawn, a large body of natives, some number between ten and a hundred, with Pemulwuy at their head, had attacked the township of Parramatta. There had been an affray. Natives had been killed. Perhaps six, perhaps fifty. In some versions Pemulwuy was dead.

I was impatient for Mr Macarthur to return, because to my ear there were many things about these accounts that did not make sense, in particular the central question: why would Pemulwuy, that clever general, make a direct attack, in daylight, on the most heavily armed part of the colony? A thing he had never done before, that he must have known was doomed to failure?

My husband cantered back up the hill in the evening and swung off his horse with the air of a man who had done a good day's work.

– Is it true what we have heard? I said. An attack by the natives?

Thinking that the story must have taken on a distorted shape as it travelled from mouth to mouth.

— Broadly yes, he said. But wife, let me catch my breath!

Called for supper, sat down and gave it his full attention. I poured his wine and a glass for myself, like any patient wife awaiting her husband's pleasure. But it seemed he would go on buttering his bread for the rest of the evening rather than say more.

— Well, sir, will you keep me in suspense all night? I said, smiling to soften a sharpish tone.

He leaned back in his chair, watching me as if to compare my smile with my words.

— So, he said. This is how it was. More than a hundred natives attacked the northern farms in the night.

It was as if he were giving evidence, or dictating a letter, each phrase clipped out and pasted onto the air.

— The settlers armed themselves and pursued them through the night, and in the morning came up with them on the outskirts of the town.

— Through the night, I said. Through the brush. And the natives were going towards the town? Not away into the forest?

I was not doubting. Only trying to see it.

— Yes, my dear, that is what I have told you, Mr Macarthur said. The settlers came up with the natives on the outskirts of the town. Then, fatigued from their march, they—the settlers, you understand—entered the town. An hour after, they were followed by a large body of natives, headed by our friend Pemulwuy.

The words were so very simple. But those stern and knowing men whose acquaintance I had made with Mr Dawes: could I picture men like them doing what Mr Macarthur had just told me?

— Followed! I exclaimed. Why on earth would the natives follow them, after being chased by them all night?

Mr Macarthur said nothing. He was watching the candle on the table spilling a grey trickle of wax. He bent forward, stopped the wax with a finger, was attentive in peeling it off where it had stuck to his skin. Something was odd in the feel of the room. A mood like a cold draught had come in and sat down with us.

I puzzled away, trying to make a picture out of his words. *The settlers were followed by a large body of natives.* I could only think of one way to make sense of it.

– Oh I see! I cried. They must have been promised something!

– Promised something! Mr Macarthur said. What would they be promised, pray, and why?

He looked at me narrowly, but my question had not come out of suspicion. It was only that *fatigued from their march* had an air of working too hard to explain, while *followed* did not explain enough.

But I had trodden somewhere Mr Macarthur did not want me treading.

– Forgive me, Mr Macarthur.

If I were to find out more, I would have to dispel that draught.

– Only, as you will understand, we heard gunfire close by and naturally I wish to know all.

Know all. I spoke lightly, as if it were no more important to *know all* about the gunshots than it would be to *know all* about the price of a pound of pork at the commissary.

– Indeed, he said. And you shall know all.

He looked up sideways, as if addressing the corner of the ceiling.

– Pemulwuy was in a great rage, he said. He threatened to spear the first man that dared to approach him. And actually did throw a spear at one of the soldiers.

Mr Macarthur's tone was flattening out a *great rage* and *threw a spear* and making these vivid images colourless, of no more interest than *a brief shower of rain* or *a fine day.*

Threw a spear at one of the soldiers. If Pemulwuy had wished to injure or kill the soldier, he would have done so, but Mr Macarthur said nothing of that. I felt I was trying to see the event through a fog. He *threw a spear at a soldier*, that was a plain enough picture, and so was his *great rage*, but what was the motive behind the arm that threw, and the rage that propelled it?

– And if I may enquire, sir, I said, why was Pemulwuy in a great rage? Was something done, or said? Some deceit uncovered or promise broken?

I was trying to match his colourless tone, to lull him into saying more.

– Oh for heaven's sake, woman, he cried. How should I be expected to enter the mind of a savage? Do not press me like a damned lawyer!

Reached for the decanter, poured a precise amount into his glass, took a sip.

– Really, my dear, he said, and laughed in a forced way. How do you expect a man to get a word in edgeways to answer you?

– But Mr Macarthur, I said. This is beyond strange, surely you see that.

– My dear, he said, very silky. You lead a sheltered life here and so you should. But those of us whose daily task it is to deal with the natives are familiar with the fact that they are not creatures of reason.

I waited, though by now I was pretty sure I was watching theatre. He took his time savouring another sip of wine and put the glass down carefully.

– So, he said, Pemulwuy having initiated the conflict by his action, it was then necessary to show the natives the superiority of our firearms.

At last I could picture it. The soldiers, assembled in formation with their guns loaded, waiting for the command to fire. When

Pemulwuy raised his spear and threw it, the command came. From the man in command.

My husband was a soldier. His profession, at least in theory, involved the administering of death. But until we had moved to Parramatta, being a soldier had never meant much more than the uniform, the protocols of rank, the ladder of promotion. Until now, hearing him say *the superiority of our firearms*, I had never felt the flesh-and-blood fact of his profession.

He may not have had a gun in his own hand. He may not, personally, have pressed his finger against the obedient metal tongue and caused a ball of lead to shred the flesh and shatter the bones of another person. But his would have been the voice that gave the command. *Fire!* His would have been the choice. To call the word, or to refrain.

There was a thickness in my throat at the picture of my husband, who entered my body every night, uttering that ugly word.

– How many dead?

The word came out strangely.

– Dead? How many dead? Oh, five or six. And a number wounded.

– And Pemulwuy, I asked. Dead also?

He raised his glass and drained it.

– Pemulwuy was taken alive, he said. With seven pieces of buckshot lodged in his body. He was conveyed to the hospital, where he remains a prisoner.

He wiped his mouth, threw the napkin down beside his plate, sat back with his arms folded.

– I am confident, my dear, that with the sable generalissimo in our hands, we will have no more trouble from the savages.

A GREAT COLDNESS

I walked down the next morning to where it—whatever *it* was—had happened. Guards were stationed at the door of the hospital, but that was the only thing out of the ordinary. The grass, the stones, the dust, showed no imprint of what had happened.

There was only one certain fact. Shots had been fired. I had heard those myself.

Not a fact, but probable, was that Pemulwuy was now a prisoner. *Seven pieces of buckshot.* If true, that was another strangeness in this whole strange tale. It meant that the muskets used against the men Mr Macarthur had told me were dead had been loaded with ball, while the one levelled at Pemulwuy had been loaded with buckshot. One reason for that degree of discrimination came strongly to my mind: there had been a plan, and it had involved the wish not to kill Pemulwuy, but to make a prisoner of him.

All His Majesty's officers had learned their history. They knew that to kill a leader on the field of battle was to run the risk of awarding him the dangerous status of martyr. But to make him a prisoner was to destroy him. He could be paraded and humiliated, he could be executed, he could be sent away into exile. Perhaps he could even be persuaded to make his people surrender. Whatever you might choose to do with him, once he was your prisoner, victory was assured.

I stood with a great coldness around my heart, looking at the emptiness that hid so much. The river dimpled and twinkled in the morning sun, a flock of red parrots darted across the river twittering, a magpie too young to be cautious hopped along the path in front of me. Nothing was changed here. If there had been bodies, someone had removed them and shovelled dirt over the blood. There was nothing to show what had happened. Only the words of that story, snipped out and pasted onto the air.

There was nowhere for me to go, other than back into the house owned by my husband, where the children who belonged to him would be waking up, and where the men and women whose master he was would be attending to his needs. I could go back there and press Mr Macarthur for more details, but what would be the point? He had arrived at his story, and would have no reason to change it.

I stood for so long that I drew the attention of the soldiers on duty outside the barracks. I saw them talking together and looking towards me, and before they could come and ask *What is the matter, Mrs Macarthur,* I turned and set my face towards the house and that man who was, till death us do part, my husband.

Days would pass, weeks, months. The rest of my life. But always, behind every day, would be the ghost of this: the snuffing-out of lives, and a story that did not convince.

FECUNDITY

The place of eels turned out to be a place of great fecundity, and not for the sheep alone. Elizabeth was not yet two when James was born. Oh, he was a bonny flourishing babe, placid and sweet-tempered, and I loved to see his strong grasp on life, so unlike Edward's weak beginning and Elizabeth's continuing fragility. He was the first babe I could love without fear of losing, and my days with him were unalloyed pleasure. It was with a sinking of the heart that I knew, around the time of his first birthday, that I was again with child.

Then James died. Such a bonny babe, but dead in two days from a sudden fever, lying white and limp, his eyes dulling as I watched, and no remedy of any use. Mrs Brown came to me, into the stuffy dim room where his slip of a body lay among the compresses and potions that had been forced on him. She held me, and her stillness made a space in her arms for me to feel the terrible blank. She said nothing, but stayed beside me while I met the fact that had to be met.

We buried him up on the Fairview, a small hole with a small coffin and a small stone with his name chiselled into it. It made the place more precious, a part of this land that was myself, a part of myself gone into its soil.

Grief at his death had to be bundled away, because the new one, John, had to be made welcome. I loved John, but grief clouded the love I felt for him. He lived to be a man, although he died before his time. Perhaps he always knew in his marrow that his mother was not quite ready for him in the cloud of grief around the death of his brother.

In his turn, John was not long past his first birthday when I bore a second daughter, so John and Mary were more like twins than brother and sister. Mary was two when a third son was born—at Mr Macarthur's insistence, he was another James—two years later, William, and later again, the afterthought Emmeline.

I SHOULD NOT HAVE DONE

Like every other gentleman in the colony, Mr Macarthur believed that his children must have a proper English schooling. I had no argument against the idea, for it was true that there was no school worth the name in the colony. I had already shed a few private tears at what must happen to each of the children as they grew. From the age they were old enough to say *England*, Mr Macarthur had taught them that it was the source of all good things, and they spoke of it with rapture.

Soon after Edward's seventh birthday, a Mr Skinner was found, who would take him to England and settle him in a school. Mr Macarthur announced this to me, read off the date of sailing from Mr Skinner's note as if it were a matter of no great consequence. But as he spoke I watched his fingers folding a corner of the paper, folding and smoothing, folding and smoothing.

I had always known this time would come, but always hoped it would be later. Always later. Never the brutal fact of *now*.

– He is too young, I said. Could we not wait?

He flapped the letter against the side of his leg as if slapping himself.

– Nonsense, the mouth above that agitated hand said. There is nothing to be gained by waiting. Nothing to be gained. Whatsoever.

And now to my surprise he came to my side and put his arm around my shoulders.

– My dear, he said, and for once the endearment was gentle. My dear, I understand this is a trial for you. For any mother.

– And not for a father?

He took his arm away, folded the paper, thrust it into his pocket.

– He will have a grand time, he said.

There was a silence as we both listened to the hollowness of this.

– It has to be done, he said, and for a moment we could share that sadness.

Mr Macarthur had instructed me not to say goodbye to Edward. Otherwise, he said, the parting would be too difficult.

– But he must be prepared, I said. He must be told.

– Nonsense, Mr Macarthur said. Let him come on board with cheerfulness. If he thinks it means separation, he will make difficulties.

– But he will make difficulties once the ship sails and he realises what has happened!

– Oh, he will soon get over it, he said, children forget so quickly.

Mr Macarthur and Mr Skinner and I took Edward down to the cabin, and Mr Skinner showed him all the ingenious devices there for stowing and securing everything. While Edward was intent on discovering how the latch of the cupboard worked, Mr Macarthur signalled me to go. I hesitated. He signalled again.

I stooped to kiss the boy. One last embrace. But just then the latch was more interesting than his mother—the latch was new, the mother as familiar and dependable as air. Mr Macarthur urged me out, herded me to the doorway, but as I turned to go I snatched the handkerchief out of my bodice and pushed it in among Edward's bundle.

I did not have to be on board to know that at last he tired of all the novelties of the ship, looked around for Mama, could not see her, and on asking was told she was not there. That he would not see her again for years. Such a span of time would not have much meaning for him, but he would understand the fundamental fact: his Mama had abandoned him. He would look up at Mr Skinner so far above him and know that this was all he could hope for in a seemingly endless future.

It was betrayal that would fuel the wailing. Betrayal, that he had been allowed to run so eagerly, so thoughtlessly, onto that ship.

I should not have been persuaded. I should have sat the boy down in advance of boarding, explained, weathered his protests, been beside him as he came to accept it. Even as late as the last minute, I could have said, Edward, forget the latch, I am leaving you now.

I was a coward, I was flustered, I was unconvinced of myself. Only knew, as I stumbled off the ship, that I had allowed a terrible wrong to be done.

I was weak, and I wish to God I had not been.

HOME

Mr Macarthur had done his best to undermine Old Hornpipe and seemed for the moment to be the victor in that feud. But under his bluster about insults and outrage, I could see that he felt the mood in the colony was changing. He had his finger to the wind, and from what he told me, certain individuals appeared to be avoiding him. In some cases, it seemed, they could be observed sliding quietly behind the protective shape of the governor. Even a wife living in the isolation of a farm at Parramatta could sense it: every man was looking to protect his own suddenly naked neck.

He came to me one night as I sat in the parlour.

— My dearest and best beloved wife, he began.

I felt every nerve tighten.

— You have been a queen among wives, he said. But your patience is rewarded at last. I have formed the determination to sell all that we have here, so that we may return to the land of our forebears.

I was like a person on the edge of the cliffs at Bude, a person who had been walking along trustingly, whose foot had slipped on the grass. There would be an instant before gravity seized her, when she would still think she could step back. There would be no terror, just a picture of a net catching her, or an angel whisking her up. She would still be smiling as she fell.

But no net or angel would appear. There would be a desperate clutching. At a blade of grass, at the air.

— What a delight, I said. My voice shook, and he smiled in sympathy at what he took to be my gladness.

— Oh, what a delight to see home again, what a happy piece of news, I said, as if throwing more words at the idea would stop it happening.

Put a look on my face that I thought was right for someone hankering for home, while I waited for inspiration. This had always been inevitable, but I had let myself think it would not be till tomorrow, till next month, till next year. Now I was appalled at the delusion I had let myself live in. All those evenings in my *petit coin*, all those afternoons up on the Fairview, all the children born and died, and I had gone on as if it would be forever.

— I will offer it to His Excellency, Mr Macarthur said.

There was always a mocking edge to those words.

— No one but the Crown has the resources to buy such a valuable estate. I will ask two thousand pounds. The house alone is worth that. He will not refuse the price.

It was the words *refuse the price* that invited some genius to visit me for long enough to show me what I might do.

— Two thousand pounds! I said. That is a generous act indeed, Mr Macarthur. A splendid gift. His Excellency will be touched.

— A gift! he exclaimed. A gift to His Excellency!

I was all enthusiastic innocence.

— It is of a piece with all your generosity in the service of this place, I said. Working far beyond the call of duty, wearing out your horse going back and forth to Sydney, being instrumental in making the place flourish! And now to make such a noble gift of the best farm in New South Wales, cleared and under crops, with a fine house, not to mention the livestock, the horses and of course the sheep. After all, a dozen of your sheep are pure Spanish, hardly to be found outside Spain!

I made myself stop, the words had started to take on a life of their own and my voice was a pitch too high.

— Of course, two thousand is for the land and house, he said. Naturally there will be another sum for the crops and livestock.

I will suggest to Old Hornpipe that I would not consider less than three thousand.

I nodded, but allowed myself a little frown.

– We have been able to make ourselves comfortable here, I said. I suppose we will not have to live in a very much smaller way at home. Your dear brother would be able to look out a modest house for us. And there may be some of your comrades in arms who could advise how best to manage on your stipend.

There was a promising silence from Mr Macarthur.

– The horses, he said. I was forgetting the horses. The finest bloodstock in the country. Perhaps four thousand would be best.

He did not sound sure, and in truth this was a colossal sum.

– If he desired you to sell for any less, after your years of service, it would be an insult, I said.

He got up as if stung, poked at the fire, and sat down very foursquare on the chair. My trump card, that word *insult*, had done the trick. It occurred to me that perhaps the devious Mr Macarthur and myself were, after all, not so very different from each other.

In that blaze of inspired invention I had done what I was able to. But I could not be sure of the outcome. Yes, it was possible that the Crown would jib at paying four thousand pounds for something it had given away in the first place, and we would stay. On the other hand, he might be so delighted at the chance to get Mr Macarthur out of his life that he would pay whatever was necessary, and we would go.

The governor wrote immediately to Whitehall, he told Mr Macarthur, recommending the purchase in the warmest terms. But Whitehall was not convinced. In fact it seemed that officials there had expressed something stronger than surprise that an officer paid by the Crown to do government service had found opportunity to amass such an estate so quickly. Suddenly it seemed that Whitehall was rather interested in Captain John Macarthur and his doings, especially in relation to the rivers of rum whose importation he had overseen.

There was no more talk of selling up. But I did not allow myself to celebrate. This could be no more than a reprieve. I knew my husband. Once he had decided, he would get his way. Every evening I went down to my *petit coin* as I always had, but now it was in the melancholy of preparing for farewell.

I will confess to other fancies. Arsenic. Deadly nightshade. Might I have taken the thought and turned it into the deed? In a book, perhaps. But my life was at once simpler and more complicated than any made-up story, and I knew I was no murderer.

One evening, a year after the night of *four thousand pounds*, Mr Macarthur unveiled another grand scheme.

– My dearest, he said as we sat down by the fire after dinner, it has been evident to me for some time that we have had the best of what speculation can offer. I have deliberated on our future here, and see that the way forward is in the production of fine wool.

– Of fine wool! I said, and only someone who knew me better than Mr Macarthur would have heard my astonished amusement.

– A thinking man has always been able to see that this colony needs a product fit for export, he said. Wool fits the bill. We have proved how well sheep can do in this country.

I held up my fan as if to shield my cheeks from the fire.

– My Spanish purchases have shown what is possible, he said. The scheme of putting the Spanish to inferior crosses has exceeded all my hopes.

From behind the fan I watched him. He betrayed not the slightest awareness that the scheme, as he called it, was nothing he had ever intended. He was not pretending, not lying. I saw that his greatest strength was to enter so fully into his constructions that he authentically forgot they were not true.

He strode about the room talking with such passion that white spittle gathered at the corners of his mouth. Not only had he put the sheep together in such a way as to produce the finest wool the world had ever seen. He would go further, and take into his own hands every aspect of bringing it to market.

You could not simply put casks of John Macarthur wool on a ship and send them to London and expect the wool merchants to flock down to the wharf demanding it! A knowledgeable fellow would have to be there, someone with a nose for a deal who could be trusted to see the business through. There was only one man who was fit for the task: himself. As soon as he could, he would find a pretext to get leave of absence from the Corps and take a passage to London with a shipment of wool. He apologised that I would be obliged to stay in New South Wales. Laid the flattery on thick.

– I am perfectly aware, my dear wife, of the difficulties you will encounter in looking after our interests here, he said. I am fully convinced that not one in a thousand would have the resolution and perseverance to contend with them. But I have confidence in you, my dearest wife, to surmount them in a way that will make me grateful and delighted.

I had to pretend to doubt my ability. It would not do to look eager. But it was not difficult to strike the right note, because he was hardly listening. His horizon was filled with the picture of himself striding the stage of London, a new-world Jason dazzling all before him with his golden fleece. The more difficult feat was not allowing him to glimpse my relief.

Six months to sail to England. Six months back again. A year in between to get his nose into those deals. Two years, then. And if Hannaford and I could continue to send one shipment after the other, Mr Macarthur might feel obliged to stay in London to sell those too. The challenge—my mind, like his, was flying over the future—would be to make sure that the flow of wool was good, but never so good that it would furnish enough capital for us to return to England. I let myself imagine it: two years, four years. Eight years.

But told myself not to hope. He was not gone yet.

There was a beautiful logic to it all. Mr Macarthur wanted to trade wool. I was content to be left behind to produce it. It gave me wry satisfaction to understand that in this business, if in no other, Mr Macarthur and I fitted together as sweetly as a dovetail joint.

TWO CHANCES OUT OF FIVE

Before Mr Macarthur had organised a passage, some kind of rebellion began to rumble among the officers. It was about the governor. My husband did not tell me the ins and outs of it, and I did not want to hear them. But there had been a trial, run, as all trials were, by the officers of the Corps, and the governor had been foolish enough to disagree with the judgment of that court.

Something about Mr Macarthur had the effect of sending people into a frenzy in which they acted contrary to their own interests. His greatest art may have been that of provocation: to incite others to folly by cold precision, icy scorn, lofty contempt. *Sir, I could have told the governor, on no account stir the hornet's nest of my husband. You may think you will win, and for a time you might, but in the end you will be destroyed.*

With Mr Macarthur's encouragement the business spiralled into rage. The officers made a pact to refuse any communication with the governor, going so far as to ignore him in the street. All but Colonel Paterson. Peaceable by nature, he had other motives as well. He was an old friend of the governor, and both men were protégés of the all-powerful Sir Joseph back in England. The colonel could make an enemy of the governor and Sir Joseph, or he could make an enemy of Mr Macarthur. He was exactly where Mr Macarthur liked to see his enemies: between the jaws of a trap.

When the affair came to a crisis, I knew only that there was a hurricane in the house, of Mr Macarthur rushing in from Sydney and clattering around in his library, fetching down the case containing his duelling pistols. I stood in the doorway as he checked them, his hands trembling, not with fear but excitement. The spring inside him was wound tight.

– Paterson has challenged me, the fool. The Lord have mercy on him, for none will he obtain from me!

– Mr Macarthur, I said, and put out a hand, but no words would have made him listen. He was smiling, his eyes crinkled up in pleasure, as if looking forward to a treat.

– He is my game, he said. I charge you, my dear wife, not to attempt to interrupt me in the chase!

– Mr Macarthur, I said again, unable to work out whether I should try to stop him or encourage him. Consequences radiated out from each choice, but I could not compute them.

– Never mind any of that, he said, though I had found nothing to say. I am now so deeply in that the game begins to be amusing.

– Amusing, I repeated. The game.

Outwit, outwait. That motto had served me well, but I had run out of wit, run out of time to wait.

After he left, the house was very quiet, as if it were holding its breath. I stood looking out the front door at the garden, the sound of his horse spurred to a gallop fading slowly into the distance.

The duel would happen behind the Parramatta barracks, in a private space among trees where I knew several bloodless duels had already been fought. I imagined everyone assembling there: the principals, the seconds, the surgeon. The pistols would be loaded— by Mr Macarthur, of course. Then there would be the ceremonial pacing-out of the distance. Then the shots. If I stepped outside the front door, I might hear them. One, two.

And then? Some cool part of me laid out the possibilities. Both men might miss their mark. Mr Macarthur might wound the colonel. The colonel might wound Mr Macarthur. The colonel might kill Mr Macarthur. Mr Macarthur might kill the colonel.

The arithmetic told me that there was one chance in five that in an hour my husband would be brought back a corpse. One chance in five that he would be arrested as a murderer. Two chances out of five, then.

I did not quite put the thought into words: *Two chances out of five that I will be free of him.* But let me be frank, I did that calculation with hope, not dismay. There is no point pretending in these private pages.

It was very late when Mr Macarthur came home, but he was neither dead nor a murderer. The colonel's ball had missed its mark entirely, but Mr Macarthur's trick pistol had sent his ball through the colonel's shoulder.

Even in tumultuous New South Wales, sending a ball through one's commanding officer could not be overlooked. The governor was obliged to act. Until it was established whether Colonel Paterson would live or die, the governor put Mr Macarthur under restriction: he was not to leave our house. Whereupon of course the prisoner wrote to the governor to ask whether he was permitted to walk from room to room within his house? What about the verandah? And the outhouse?

Once it was clear that the colonel would survive, Mr Macarthur began to agitate for a court martial to clear his name. The governor wanted none of that, and showed himself willing to release him, on surety that he would keep the peace. That was a poor move: it was easy for Mr Macarthur to refuse the governor's offer. He had only to stand on his honour, that corrupted bit of tinsel.

It was then that I understood. If he refused the governor's offer, the governor would be obliged to send him for trial to England.

Mr Macarthur left Parramatta on the packet boat to Sydney on a fine November afternoon. The following day, he would board His Majesty's ship the *Hunter* and sail out of Sydney Cove, past the bays and headlands of the harbour, between the cliffs that the *Scarborough* had brought us through twelve years before, and onto the ocean that would take him to England.

I watched the little boat head off with the tide down the river, take the wide bend where the mangroves spread out into the stream, and disappear. First it was there, then it disappeared as if smoothly swallowed by the mangroves: bow, body, stern, the last flap of the flag hanging behind. I stood watching as if it might appear again, grow larger, return to the dock, as if the whole idea of Mr Macarthur leaving was a delicious fantasy.

I watched for some unmeasured stretch of time, of the new time that belonged to me. Then there were only the dancing points of light on the river, the busy lap of water against the stones of the jetty, a gull sweeping past with one hard sharp cry, and myself, a woman breathing the sweet air of solitude.

FORTY YEARS HAVE passed between then and now, as I sit in the sunny little room in the house at Parramatta where for so long I attended to business. Mr Macarthur called this place Elizabeth Farm, but at the top of my letters it is simply *Parramatta*, and I never write the word without thinking of the people whose language it is, for whom Parramatta has always been, and always will be, the Place of Eels.

Now, after so many years here, I know better than ever what has been done to the Gadigal, the Wangal, the Cameraygal, the Burramattagal and all the others. Not just the turning-off from their lands and the damage to their old ways. Not just the cruelties inflicted. Not just the deaths. Behind all that is another, fundamental violence: the replacement of the true history by a false one.

Closest to home—literally, as I sit here looking down towards the river where the event is supposed to have taken place—is what happened an hour after dawn on that summer morning when Pemulwuy threw a spear at a soldier.

He escaped from the hospital, the fetter still around his leg. He led another few years of *depredations* till at last a reward was offered for him to be caught, dead or alive. A settler shot him, and to prove the fact cut off his head, which was sent to England for the scientific gentlemen.

The death of one man did not mean the end of attacks: they continue to this day in the distant parts. How could it be otherwise? *Depredations and outrages* are our words. Another way to describe what is going on is to call it *defending a homeland*.

But after that morning the settlers felt a new confidence. They called the affray The Battle of Parramatta, as if those few minutes of hubbub could take their place beside the battles of Thermopylae or Agincourt, a victory that signalled God's approval.

The Battle of Parramatta confirms the story the settlers tell themselves about the people they displaced: that they are irrational and lack good sense. Heavens, they thought they could take on one of His Majesty's fortified garrisons! The story, and all the others like it, convinces the settlers that, in dispossessing the first inhabitants, they are simply part of the natural order, in which the strong and clever replace the weak and foolish. It might be sad, but they assure each other that it is as inevitable as night following day.

Mr Macarthur wrote an account of the affray, which must have been sent to the governor, who must have relayed it to Captain Collins, who was at that time in England. Collins used it in his account of the colony, and as far as I know it has never been questioned.

Perhaps it was my lessons in astronomy that make me doubt what seems beyond doubt. That, and my knowledge that Pemulwuy's people are neither weak nor foolish. The story relayed by Captain Collins is really only credible if you believe they are.

I cannot tell you just what happened on that far-off morning. I only know that it could not have been as Mr Macarthur told it to me, and as Captain Collins has told the world. Knowing my husband as I do, I have no doubt that it was some tale of trickery:

a trap or an ambush or a promise betrayed. Whatever it is, the truth has been silenced, and this other story put in its place.

I am a newcomer here, ignorant of the inner grain of the place. The lifetime of one woman cannot be put beside the uncountable generations of the people who were here before me. Still, newcomer though I am, this is home to me now. Any other place would be exile.

I understand, though, that *mon petit coin*, that room made of leaves down by the river, is not really *à moi*. Like most of the other newcomers, in the past I never gave a proper name to what I was doing. Now I am prepared to be more honest. As Mrs Brown did, I have to face the fact that I am a thief. More a thief than Mrs Brown, who was a thief only once. I have been a thief for every one of those forty years.

Yes, I make sure the people who live within our boundaries are treated well. I supply them with various items that they seem to value, although they lived without them until recently and, after all, it is because of our coming that they need them now. We greet each other by name, and we converse a little—in English, since their English is so much better than my Burramattagal—about this and that, like any other neighbours.

But underneath that goodwill, we all know an undigestible fact: I am not prepared to give them back what has always been theirs. Not prepared to gather up my children and get on a ship and return to the place of our forebears.

I can see no way to put right all the wrongs done, no more than I could all those years ago when I picked up the stick belonging to a Burramattagal woman and heard what it was saying. The difference is that now I do not turn away. I am prepared to look in the eye what we have done.

That repairs no part of the sorrow of it, I know. But it is the first thing, the first hard truth, without which no repair can ever be hoped for.

Outside the window the last glow of the day lies softly on the garden, and beyond are the big calm trees that have been growing for so many years, long before Elizabeth Veale took up space in the world. What comfort there is in knowing that trees, sunlight, birds go on, indifferent to the life in this house, or in the heart of the woman at its heart.

What I see now is that destiny, Providence—whatever name you might give to bald luck—gave me two glorious stretches of time without Mr Macarthur. His first absence was four years, the second closer to a decade. When he returned the second time, the alternating bouts of mania and black gloom had taken over his life. He was like a machine that runs too fast and smokes and creaks till it tears itself to pieces. What a glorious irony that his madness in the end took the form of a conviction that his wife was being unfaithful to him. Many years after his wife had revelled in the embraces of Mr Dawes, Mr Macarthur spoke the truth, but by then he had been too mad for too long, had made too many accusations, and no one listened.

The years of his absence presented me with chances offered to few women. Managing the flocks without him, I was not wife, not widow, not old maid. None of those, yet all of them at once. In the ambiguity of my situation I could be nothing more or less than myself, and to be what we all are, especially at the end: alone.

What an unsung pleasure it is to be alone, when we are supposed to fear it. Dull it might seem, but as a woman who has survived an interesting marriage, I am happy to be dull.

Now, in what I suppose a poet might call *the evening of my life*, it is the evenings I love best. At the end of the day it is like a prayer to walk down to the river when the shadows are lying long over the grass. Every evening there is lovely, but today a storm had recently passed, and in the orange glow of sunset a tremendous sky laid itself out like a vast noble text. There was every kind of cloud: crisp white flecks stippled in loose lines, white wisps like an old man's hair, dramatic piles laid thick as carpet, pink puffs catching an edge of sunset, and, as if wandered in from another sky altogether, two small bright clouds exactly the shape of Mr Dawes' lenses.

I sat on the log watching the light fade, the river holding the soft glow of the sky. There were five Burramattagal children picking their way along a slip of sand, each child's long thin legs straightening and jointing, straightening and jointing, legs made for walking great distances, never tiring, and every jointing, every straightening, reflected with absolute fidelity in the water at their feet so it seemed there were ten children, five upside down and five the right way up. Each seemed as real as the other, so you could wonder which was child, which reflection. Which the eternal past of this place, and which the eternal future, those feet part of the land through all time.

I write this—why? What does it matter that those children made a thing of such beauty that I felt compelled to record it? What does it matter that there was a person the future will remember as Elizabeth Macarthur, who wanted to be known for who she was?

I will give this private account no title. I see it as a river like the one I grew up beside, always curling on, dimpling and surging in its bed, never fixed and measurable but only ever a moment—There! That!—giving way to another moment—That! There!

Mr Dawes would say: Write nothing. Leave nothing. What do you care if people in the future believe the insipid fiction of your letters? He would be right. In the unimaginable future when these papers are found, no one will remember Mrs Macarthur, and her glorious husband will be nothing more than a dim name in a dull book about the past.

Mr Dawes would be right, but he would be wrong, too. I am no poet, but like them I am greedy to be remembered, even by some stranger of the future, as one true person, speaking straight into the face of time. Others want to find God. I have always had a more modest aim. I am happy enough to find myself coming to meet myself in what I have written here, and stand up in greeting.

There is a bush down by the river that in this season is hung with a thousand seed pods, each one twisted like a question mark. They dance silvery pale among the dark leaves, the whole bush laughing, it seems, trembling in the breeze, the fine leaves and the tiny curved pods asking their question. I stop as I pass, and smile as if at an old friend.

And in a way it is an old friend, because when I see it I think of Mr Dawes. He would have enjoyed the question-mark bush. I can imagine him saying, *If we wait long enough, Mrs Macarthur, the entire sentence may be revealed to us.*

Well, Mr Dawes, I would like to hear that sentence. And I am ready to wait.

AUTHOR'S NOTE

No, there was no box of secrets found in the roof of Elizabeth Farm. I didn't transcribe and edit what you've just read. I wrote it.

But this story follows the events and people who emerge from the letters, journals, and official documents of the early years of the colony of New South Wales. The extracts from her letters that 'Elizabeth Macarthur' quotes are from the letters of the real Elizabeth Macarthur.

I've taken some liberties in order to shape this work of fiction. The passage of time and the order of some real events have become a little slithery in my hands, for example, and two governors have become one. This book isn't history.

At the same time it's not pure invention. Those old documents were my inspiration and my guide. I arrived at this story by thinking about them in the way 'Elizabeth Macarthur' recommends: by not believing too quickly.

Kate Grenville

Readers' notes and further information about this book can be found on my website: kategrenville.com.au

ACKNOWLEDGMENTS

I'm very grateful to the Darug Custodian Aboriginal Corporation (in particular Leanne Watson and Erin Wilkins) and the Metropolitan Local Aboriginal Land Council (in particular Nathan Moran). Both groups welcomed me warmly and were generous with their time and knowledge. I thank them, and the others in their organisations, for being so willing to engage with this attempt to explore aspects of our shared history. As a non-indigenous writer I'm conscious of how easy it is, in telling stories about the past, to be blind to our own cultural blindness. Please accept my warmest appreciation of the generosity you showed me.

I'd like to thank the many people who went out of their way to advise on the indigenous aspects of this story: Trish Adjei, Andrew Bovell, Wenona Byrne, Heather Goodall, Ashley Hay, Anita Heiss, Kim Mahood, Bruce Pascoe, and Chris Wallace.

My warmest thanks also to Lynette Russell and Ramona Koval. Both these kind friends read the manuscript and encouraged me in my many moments of doubt.

For expert and generous consultation about the so-called Battle of Parramatta, I'm deeply indebted to Stephen Gapps and Henry Reynolds (though they shouldn't be held responsible for Mrs Macarthur's speculations). On matters of botany, Patrick Matthew shared his expertise with his usual insight and humour—thank you, Patrick. For saving me from many ignorant errors about sheep, I'm indebted to Suzanne, Sal and George

Falkiner, and to Barbara Holloway. As one writer to another, Susan Hampton selflessly made over to me some vivid sheep-lore she'd been saving for writing of her own—thanks, Susan, for your generosity. On matters of early colonial houses I'm grateful to Robert Griffin for sharing his knowledge with me. Any mistakes on any of these matters are mine alone.

Eve Salinas will recognise an important line that came out of her kindness towards me. Judith Upton, of Cornwall Online Parish Clerks, went out of her way to help me with detailed information relating to the parish records for Bridgerule. Thank you, Judith, for your guidance and for the work you and your fellow volunteers do.

Dr Helena Berenson gave informed advice about the possible nature of John Macarthur's ailments, as well as unfailing support and friendship.

Michelle Scott Tucker was generous in encouraging another admirer of Elizabeth Macarthur. Her excellent book *Elizabeth Macarthur: A Life at the Edge of the World* will remain the standard biography of that remarkable woman for a long time to come.

The extracts and image from Elizabeth Macarthur's letters are from the Macarthur Papers in the collections of the Mitchell Library, State Library of NSW, and are used with the kind permission of the library.

My first readers, as always, were Tom and Alice Petty. Their encouragement means more than I can say. I'm undeservedly blessed to have them in my life.